Out of Character

VANESSA
CRAFT

Out
of
Character

A NOVEL

KEY PORTER BOOKS

Library and Archives Canada Cataloguing in Publication

Craft, Vanessa
  Out of character / Vanessa Craft.

ISBN-13 978-1-55470-049-3; ISBN-10 1-55470-049-3

1. Title.
PR6103.R33O98 2007   823'.92   C2006-905961-6

 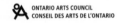

The publisher gratefully acknowledges the support of the Canada Council for the Arts and the Ontario Arts Council for its publishing program. We acknowledge the support of the Government of Ontario through the Ontario Media Development Corporation's Ontario Book Initiative.

We acknowledge the financial support of the Government of Canada through the Book Publishing Industry Development Program (BPIDP) for our publishing activities.

Key Porter Books Limited
Six Adelaide Street East, Tenth Floor
Toronto, Ontario
Canada M5C 1H6

www.keyporter.com

Text design: Martin Gould
Electronic formatting: Jean Lightfoot Peters

Printed and bound in Canada

08 09 10 11 12 5 4 3 2 1

To SG, for believing in my true character.

Conventionality is not morality.

CHARLOTTE BRONTË

I wonder if I've been changed in the night?

Alice's Adventures In Wonderland

meet
jack

Chapter 1

It wasn't hard to give Jack Gordon the hump. Many people did, and on a daily basis. Take his job—yes, it was a great job, yes, he got paid ridiculous sums of money and, yes, he had lots of young totty hanging off him at private members' clubs looking for a sugar daddy or a mentor or, hell, just to get laid and party all night. But even with all the perks (and he worked damn hard for them), Jack's survival hinged on the people he worked with—men who talked a good game but had no opinions of their own and no clue what it meant to be a real power player. In his business, depending on people like that can be the kiss of fucking death, mate.

Sometimes Jack hated his job. He hated the part of him that hated his job. But what he detested more than anything in the world—seriously, more than anything—was a guy with no balls. Someone that wanted to do something, or say something, and they just didn't have the balls. Jack was surrounded by men cowering in their cubicles and surfing the Net. Guys that went home talking about how important they were and how they handled this deal or that deal, so their wives could fuss and fawn with the hope that one day they could get another facelift or send little Timmy to the college that the Windsors go to.

Mergers and acquisitions was a serious business with serious competition. Jack had to be ten steps ahead of everyone else. He had to trust people with his vision, let analysts do the dirty work and hope they didn't screw up the numbers and leave him sitting in a meeting room in Germany for a week, trying to explain to the Sauerkraut why the profit forecasts are way off.

Rule number one: Don't fuck with Jack's money.

Rule number two: Don't. Fuck. With. Jack's. Money.

Jack was not in the mood for entertaining clients. He got back from Frankfurt at seven that morning, and came straight in to sign off on paperwork. He should have stayed home and had it faxed to him, but it's the trust thing again. Better to be there, considering this deal was going to pay for the place he wanted in Dubai.

The intercom flashed. "Jack, your taxi will be downstairs in five minutes."

"Cheers, Annie. You can get out of here if you want, thanks for staying." He clicked off before he could hear her say, "Cheerio, then!" like she did every night, like she was an extra in *Mary* bloody *Poppins*.

Jack picked up his phone, hovered over the speed dial. Where the hell was she?

His daughter was the sort of person who would apologize if you bumped into her on the street and stomped on her foot. That's exactly how she was—a one-step-behind-the-rest-of-the-world kind of girl. Jack couldn't understand it. He'd tried so hard with her, but kept coming up with nought. No idea about men, no sense of style. Good-looking if she could get it together, but no, she always had her nose shoved in books about butter-churning women in petticoats.

He changed his mind and put the phone down. Right. Entertainment mode. Time to hit dinner, drinks and God knows what.

"Hey handsome."

A very blonde, very sexy girl extended her hand. Long Ferrari-red nails pointed in Jack's face.

"I'm Chanel. It's nice to meet you."

Why did they bother to shake your hand? He gave an obviously forced smile.

"I love a man in a nice suit. You look very dapper."

Jack didn't answer.

"You don't seem very happy this evening," she said, undeterred.

"I'm fine. Really. Look, we've only just got here, can you give us a minute or two?"

Chanel pouted, then leaned forward and whispered something in Jack's ear that made the blood flow away from his brain. Against his will he grinned, but with a firm hand stopped the Ferrari driving up his thigh. He explained he was there to entertain clients.

His clients were doing their best impression of cavemen in need of attention, waving wildly at every woman walking by, wedding rings shining like beacons. Jesus, what idiots.

"Fergus," Jack said, leaning around Chanel, "let me get the drinks in, and then we'll take care of the entertainment, alright?"

Fergus gave him the thumbs-up. "How many do you reckon are in here tonight?"

In such a cavernous place, it was impossible to tell. A kingdom built with gold-gilded ceilings, Roman pillars and blood-red squishy carpet. Around the room, winding glass staircases led to round podiums with tall brass poles—damn, there were several of them Jack could see from there alone. At one end of the room, a massive Baccarat crystal chandelier sparkled over a long centre stage. Impressive. The music was banging sexy and heavy bass lines, songs made for getting into trouble. Everywhere Jack turned he could see men in suits. And women: laughing and drinking champagne, dancing, taking their clothes off.

Men in suits, and women absolutely everywhere.

Jack fought the urge to relax on the comfy animal-print sofa. The darkness of the club was enough disguise to feel a little nameless, a little undercover. Even his two companions looked better, which said a lot. Andrew's greased slick of hair looked less greased, and Fergus looked almost presentable.

Chanel was still waiting, clearly not going anywhere. Jack gave her some attention. Her body was poured into one of those tight little stripper dresses. She looked like a Vegas showgirl in shimmering silver and blue. And she was very, very good looking.

"Okay," he said, "you can join us, but you need to get some dancers for my friends here. The more the merrier."

"Sure. What kind of girls do you like? Blondes? Brunettes?"

Jack turned to his clients.

Feigning indifference, Fergus shrugged. "No matter. But no cellulite. And no Eastern European slags either."

"You've obviously done this before," gibed Jack.

"Hey, I jest want a lass that can speak English, is all," Fergus answered, adjusting his large carcass back into his chair and loosening the tie that had been threatening to cut off his big head all evening.

"*You* don't even speak English," Andrew said, his raspy insect voice barely heard above the music. He told Chanel, "Get us a waitress, we're dyin' of thirst here, luv." Then he turned his focus back to the redhead on the round podium behind them.

Tonight was going to be a long night, and Jack wished he had some blow. So hard to get into it all without anything, but he promised her he'd only party on weekends. God, she was twenty-five going on sixty, that girl. If he had her free and easy life when he was her age...well, he probably would be a permanent resident at The Priory, detoxing with a bunch of celebrity rich kids and their mates, but still, at least he would be living, making memories, stories to tell the grandkids. What went on in her head? Jack hadn't a clue how she felt about anything. What kind of father did that make him? He pushed that out of his mind. This was not the time to be reflective—he needed to win over these clients.

Chanel returned with two girls. One of them, Destiny, a petite beauty covered in jewellery, sat on Fergus's lap, seemingly undaunted by his overgrown caterpillar eyebrows. The other, an extremely buxom redhead, perched on the arm of the sofa and introduced herself as Bailey with a husky hello.

"I never got your name, did I?" Chanel smelled of strawberries and cigarette smoke.

"I'm Jack."

"Has anyone ever told you how much you look like that movie star...what's his name?"

He looked nothing like any movie star in the history of motion pictures. "I don't know."

"The sexy one from *Pretty Woman*."

Jack puffed up a bit at this. "Don't know who you mean," he said casually.

"That's my favourite movie of all time."

Of course it was. Hooker with a heart of gold finds a sugar daddy that's actually attractive. She agrees to kiss him on the mouth and he sends her to Rodeo Drive. Roll corny music and a happy ending.

"Have you been to the club before?" Chanel asked.

"Yes, a long time ago. I've been to clubs like this many times…"

"Dirty boy!" She slapped his thigh.

"…with clients," he finished.

"Well, this is the best club in London. And you've got the best girl! I'm gonna take good care of you. We're gonna have fun tonight." She ran her hand across his chest, her nails tickling his tie.

On the main stage, a girl in a turquoise sequined bra and G-string, announced as "Bambi" hung theatrically upside down with one foot hooked around the pole that ran up to the ceiling. Slow as honey, she slid to the floor and stretched out, hair in her face, her whole body arched. If you wanted to see more, the DJ said, it was only twenty quid for a private dance. He didn't mention that a song lasted just two-and-a-half minutes. No one cared. She was sexy as hell.

Jack turned and saw the waitress opening two magnums of Dom Perignon. The girls applauded this, giggling. Two magnums? That's taking the piss. You can always tell what kind of clients you're dealing with by watching what they order when they know someone else is footing the bill. No discretion, no class at all.

"That one's a real peach," Andrew hissed as the waitress left.

"She is, but don't waste your time, my friend," Fergus said. "The waitresses here are uptight."

"That's 'cos you never leave a tip, you cheap bastard."

Fergus raised his eyebrows and for a moment looked like he was going to say something intelligent. "I'll give 'em a tip...a wee tip o' this 'ere Scotsman!" He guffawed into his glass.

Jack laughed too, didn't show his irritation. How could either of them think they could ever pick up the girls that worked here? These women probably made more in one week than Fergus did in a month. More importantly, why were these cretins handling this merger? Their boss obviously thought Jack was a fool, or worse, placed little importance in this deal. Things just weren't the same anymore.

The club reminded Jack of California, a place built for good times with beautiful women. If he hadn't been sent to L.A., how different would his life be now? He wasn't one for regrets, but what if? What if he had gone to New York instead of out west in the sunshine, sucker-punched by the promises of a silly girl with purple toenail polish?

He should have known.

"You're not paying attention!" Chanel pouted, looking over her shoulder at Jack.

Jack apologized and tried to concentrate on the pert bottom wiggling in his line of vision. The tag on her G-string, a pale pink stitched "xs," was showing. For some reason this had a sort of poignancy to it, and Jack felt uncomfortable. What was wrong with him? Usually he would be up for this. He gestured to a waitress for a refill and emptied his glass quickly.

Oh shit.

"Gordon, you dirty dog!"

Well, at least Jack's night couldn't get any worse. "Carl Bosworth, how are you?" he said, standing to shake hands with the vice-chairman while Chanel put her dress back on.

"Just married and I find you in a room full of tarts. Knock me over with a feather."

"Well, I know your mother works here, and I wanted to help pay for her next operation."

Carl laughed and put his oversized cigar back into his mouth. He clapped Jack on the shoulder. "Good to see you too, mate. With clients?"

Why else would I be here?

"I'd introduce you," Jack said, "but as you can see, they're too busy having their wandering hands restrained by security."

Most men Jack knew—himself included—considered going to strip clubs "legal." Window shopping, so to speak, and therefore harmless. Carl, however, who had been married for twenty-five years with several grandkids, treated clubs like Platinum like a pub. He preferred the down-market places in Soho—knocking shops fronting as "gentlemen's clubs"—where you could get your evening prolonged for a fee. In an hour, he'd be popping a Viagra and heading to Wardour Street to find more hands-on activities.

"Is it his first time in here?" asked Carl, nodding at Andrew, who was thrusting his midsection without a modicum of rhythm toward Bailey as she gyrated above his lap.

"What do you think?" asked Jack, pulling a chair out for Carl. "I'm done now," he told Chanel, handing her some money.

"Oh? But we were only getting started," she said, looking disappointed. "Why don't I give your friend a dance while you cool off?"

Carl let Chanel sit on the arm of his chair and began stroking her leg. "You're a lovely girl," he said. "I'd love to see what you've got underneath that sexy dress of yours. But business comes first—you know how that goes—and we have a few things we need to discuss privately. So why don't you take this..." He handed her three times the amount Jack had. "...and come find me. Soon."

"I can't wait." Chanel gave Carl a slow, wet kiss on the cheek. "See ya!" she said to Jack.

"That's the only way to get rid of them," Carl said. "You can't throw a twenty at a girl like that and expect her to do what you want. Good thing I'm here, or you'd get slaughtered."

"I know how to handle the women in here. Buy them drinks and get dances all night, they'll have you until the wallet's empty. Then suddenly you're not that interesting anymore. I'm not in here to be taken advantage of."

Carl popped a few smoke rings out of his mouth and set his cigar down in the glass ashtray. "Susanna know you're here?"

"I'm working."

"No need to get defensive, Jack. You want to get defensive about something, let's talk about what happened with Project Greenbelt."

"Let's not and say we did."

"I come back from vacation to a voice mail full of apologetic, brown-nosing bullshit from your vps."

"I know you're looking for someone to blame, but it's not me. I'm as pissed off about it as you are. Take it up with Research, they're the bad guys."

"Research does what your team tells them to. You're the head of the department, it's on you."

Jack adjusted his tie. It wasn't good to argue with Carl, especially when they both knew Jack had fucked up. It also wasn't good to argue with Carl when Jack recently took an unprecedented three weeks off work for his honeymoon in the Far East. Regardless, Jack wasn't going to discuss confidential business matters sitting in a strip club surrounded by cash-grabbing women and the idiots that loved them.

"See you at the Greenbelt meeting," Carl said. "Still can't believe Jack Gordon took a walk down the aisle. You better have an air-tight pre-nup, my friend."

"Enjoy your evening," said Jack, turning to watch the stage show. He gave Carl less than ten feet before he would be set upon by Chanel and led off by his teeny, tiny balls for some non-contact mind games.

The energy in the club shifted. Everyone's attention was drawn back to centre stage, where a well-dressed man appeared to be tipping a dancer hundreds—wait—maybe *thousands* of pounds.

Fergus whistled and nudged Jack.

"Unbelievable," he said. "What on earth d'you call that?"

"Insanity," Jack answered. "Pure and simple."

He leaned back in his chair in an overly nonchalant pose: the music playing had caused a physical reaction inside his chest. A song he hadn't heard for years and years, lyrics that caused his skin to prickle.

Jack fumbled in his jacket pocket for his cigarettes and cast a quick glance at Fergus, still riveted by the scene in front of them. The woman dancing was wearing a black bra and matching black lace knickers with small red bows tied on the sides.

She had on sky-high, glass-bottomed stilettos and her thick, dark blonde hair tumbled down the middle of her toned, bronzed back. Fifty-pound notes flew around her like confetti in a wind machine and twenties thickly layered the floor of the stage. Her makeup was flawless, eyes drawn dark as midnight, syrupy pink lip gloss, her face like a doll. She was elegant, regal, truly a stunner. And as she leaned forward to collect a handful of money in the black lace garter riding high on her thigh, Jack realized the woman he was watching was his daughter.

...Reason having come forward and told, in her own quiet way, a plain unvarnished tale, showing how I had rejected the real, and rapidly devoured the ideal...

JANE EYRE

meet
emma

Chapter 2

Of course, she was late.

Charging out of the tube station, an expensive bottle of wine precariously tucked under her arm, Emma decided to risk the dangers of running in the rain across wet leaves and cobblestones instead of the hideousness of being the last one to arrive at the party.

With a reputation both affluent and fashionable, Holland Park cast itself as the more tranquil, elite sibling to trendy Notting Hill (in fact, Emma's father frequently referred to it as "Notting Hill without the riff raff"). Many houses dated back to the 1860s and were enormous four-storeyed single homes, with large canted bay windows and decorative cast iron and glass entrance canopies. Many were well set back from the road with sweeping loose stone driveways and high front walls for privacy. Wide, tree-lined streets with Victorian street lamps and towering white stucco facades provided a backdrop for a variety of inhabitants—you were as likely to run into a toy poodle on a velvet leash as you were a towering Great Dane with a thick hemp-based collar. Old money met new, traditionally wealthy lived alongside cosmopolitan money-makers. All enjoyed the area's quaint French patisseries, organic butchers, one-off designer boutiques and beloved open woodlands of the park.

Susanna Philips opened the door. "Why did you ring the bell?" she asked, drawing Emma inside with a nippy hug.

Susanna's sinewy body felt tight like a guitar string stretched to its limit and her feather-light blonde hair tickled Emma's cheek. "Couldn't find my keys," Emma said, pulling away. She peeked over Susanna's shoulder to see how many coats were hanging in the corridor.

"Everyone is already here," Susanna chirped, her eyes flicking over Emma's lopsided striped shirt and mismatched long wool skirt. "You look...lovely."

"Sorry I'm late." She took off her glasses and wiped them on her sleeve.

Susanna took Emma's jacket and waved her toward the dining room. "It's fine, don't worry."

The house was living proof that you could buy good taste. The cavernous foyer had been expertly designed with two majestic curving staircases forming a mahogany-fronted, lamb-skin and imported silk trimmed orifice. Emma was sure her father had really wanted to say "Playboy Mansion" to the interior decorators, rather than deferring the entire project to the expert eye of Susanna's chosen designer. It was gorgeous, but delicately conventional. It lacked the self-absorption and testosterone-fired energy of a man still clinging to bachelor-hood. If she knew her father, there was a grotto hidden somewhere in the basement.

Emma slipped discretely into her seat at the table. "Everyone" turned out to be two people: Lottie Philips, Susanna's older sister, and George Weeks, her father's lawyer and best mate since university days. An overwrought centrepiece of lilies partially blocked Emma's view of her father, sitting opposite. He leaned to one side of the flowers and winked at her. Emma knew this wink. It meant, *here we go!* A cajole to trick her into thinking this was fun, to get her involved in the verbal repartee, *please, for me?*

Emma didn't understand her father's love for Susanna. She was beautiful, but in an obvious, unmistakably groomed way that Emma viewed with disdain. Susanna's features were refined, but suspiciously symmetrical, her long hair impossibly glossy and glamorous courtesy of twice-weekly visits to a stylist in Kensington. Susanna was fickle, constantly changing her mind on politics, careers and dietary choices; preoccupied with what was going on in other people's lives to the point of obsession; and she cried the minute a news piece came on the telly about lost children or oil-covered sea animals. Her character was a weak one, meant for subplots and back stories. Since announcing her engagement, Susanna's work organizing charity functions and fundraisers had begun to taper off; Emma seemed to be the only one who noticed this.

When Emma asked her father why he'd proposed to Susanna, he said, "She's put in the time, I guess."

"That's your reason?"

"Don't squawk at me, Emma," he said. "She's from good stock, and she's great looking. Not to mention she thinks I'm the dog's bollocks. You don't let a woman like that go. Come on, I know you want your old dad to get married again."

She didn't actually, and he knew it. Emma had seen so many of her father's girlfriends come and go—it always came back to the two of them. Or just him, really. She wanted him to be happy; but none of the women he brought home were ever anything like her mother. She wasn't sure what that meant. When her father broke up with his last mid-life-crisis-masquerading-as-a-relationship, she suggested he hire an escort for important functions instead. He was livid, and wouldn't speak to her for ages.

Emma knew Susanna was different than the others, and it made her nervous. Always photographed in the society pages, her future stepmother was well-connected and intelligent, with a master's from INSEAD. Unlike her father's other girlfriends, Susanna had her own money, inherited from a family of prosperous landowners and investors.

When they met (a year ago, during the Christmas party season), Susanna was dating an executive from a rival bank. Although Emma was sure her father had met Susanna before, when she was a very high-profile single on the scene, he waited until that evening to make his move. The other man didn't stand a chance, not against his well-honed blend of roguish charm and confident persistence.

On the way home in the cab, he kept recounting their dialogue.

"I know. I was there," Emma said.

"I was on top form tonight," he said, basking in his conquest. "Didn't hurt that the *Financial Times* just published that profile piece calling me the King of Commodities."

"I *know*. I read it."

"I know that old toff she's dating definitely saw it," he said, laughing to himself.

Three weeks later, on New Year's Day, 1999, he took Susanna to St. Tropez to celebrate her twenty-ninth birthday.

"Why on earth am I sitting at the head of the table, Jack old boy?" asked George loudly. Emma looked at her father.

"You know I don't believe in all that head of the table stuff," Jack said, drowning his bread in olive oil. "You do, that's why you're sitting there."

George smirked, his thin lips curving down instead of up. "Quite so. But you don't have to make everyone else aware of it." The table laughed.

"An empty glass is an unhappy glass!" said Lottie, waving at no one in particular for a refill of her wine. Physically, Lottie was the opposite of her younger sister Susanna. She reminded Emma of the big tree in her father's back garden: imposing, with a wide trunk and rotting inside. "And she did look ab-so-lutely stunning," Lottie said, continuing a conversation Emma didn't remember starting. "Honestly. I've never thought she was beautiful, but you know how she's so tall and slim? She looked gorgeous. I was still in my suit from work, and considering she had been out until half past three in the morning the night before...I just wanted to go home. Fabulous figure. Porcelain skin. You know how you don't want to stand next to someone?"

"*Exactly*," said Susanna. They both looked at Emma.

After a moment's pause, George said, "They mean you, Emma."

Emma swallowed her bread without giving it enough of a chew. "What do you mean?" she choked out. George must be very drunk.

"See Jack, that's what makes your daughter even more gorgeous," George said. "She hasn't half a clue."

"What were you saying, Lottie?" asked Jack, pointedly ignoring George.

"Yes, do carry on, Lotts," said Susanna.

"Well, I mean, that's it. Martin showed up with this girl, she was incredibly beautiful. Looked like she was fifteen. I mean, honestly, she was twenty-four. Tiny little hips. Absolutely incredible girl. Really. Got him on the dance floor, all eyes in the room. You can imagine."

Susanna nodded gravely.

Emma asked, "Who's Martin?"

"The new chairman of the charity trust," Lottie said, attacking the butter.

"You've met him darling," said Susanna, resting a weight-less hand on Emma's arm. "At the spring formal last month. Short, with a rather delicate-looking hair attachment."

Normally Emma would have been more conversational. In fact, she consistently annoyed people with her enquiries about seemingly unimportant details, like what song Martin and his date had been dancing to at the party, for example, but she was preoccupied. Susanna had sent out the wedding invitations and Emma received hers this morning.

It was really happening. Jack wasn't just toying with the idea, or entertaining it on Susanna's behalf. How could he be sure? How could he be ready to declare to the world that Jack Gordon, free, single and irresponsible, was now off the market?

Susanna and Lottie were looking expectantly at Emma for an answer.

"Oh, *Martin*," Emma said. "Yes. I remember him because of his lisp—" she caught herself and adjusted her napkin for the third time.

"That's rather inappropriate. He speaks like that because of a terrible riding accident."

Susanna shook her head. "That's not the reason, Lottie. He just has dreadful teeth and he's too miserly to have them fixed." She laughed. "Emma's spot on."

Lottie conceded. "But the point is, Emma, this girl was absolutely stunning, and that's all that matters."

George stared at Jack across the table, but he wouldn't meet his gaze.

After dessert, Emma made her way downstairs to the kitchen. Susanna followed close behind, carrying a freshly topped up glass of wine and the half-eaten cheese plate.

"I don't know what to do," Susanna said, standing by the fridge. Her organza blouse had slipped and her bra strap was showing. "What do you think?"

Emma was thinking that Susanna didn't need to wear a bra. She hadn't much to organize.

"Hey, honey? What do you think?"

Emma waved her off. This was none of her business.

"Please? It *is* your father."

Emma glanced down at the pointy red shoes pinching her toes into a perfectly painful triangle. She regretted her last-minute decision to wear the overpriced designer shoes Jack had given her; it's not like he would even notice. Now she was Dorothy from the land of Choo, trapped with Susanna, the Good Witch of West London, eager and pretty and waiting for an answer. Emma felt a little drunk and wasn't absolutely sure she hadn't said that out loud.

"I think if he would go and see someone about it—to ease his mind," Susanna continued.

Emma click-clopped over to the fridge, ignoring Susanna's pleading puppy dog eyes staring through the open glass door.

"Jack's nearly fifty," she said, taking out a big bottle of water and pushing it toward Susanna. "A baby? Just isn't him." She said a silent prayer that Susanna would let this go.

Susanna ignored the water and took a drink of her wine. She stared off into space for what seemed a very long time. Then she sighed and took another drink.

"Are you busy tomorrow?" she asked.

If Emma wasn't busy, she would have to spend Saturday as the shopping partner. She coughed and waited for an excuse to form in her brain.

"Have you gone for your dress fitting yet?" asked Susanna.

"No. But I will."

"You're going to love it. It's dramatic but understated—vintage couture," said Susanna. "Silk and tulle. Empire waist. Grosgrain ribbon. The most beautiful dark orchid colour—just like your eyes. No glasses. Wear your contacts. The dress is just the right shade to pull out those gorgeous olive tones in your skin. I've told you to avoid neutral colours before, haven't I? Yes? Makes you look sallow and ill. And I think we'll tidy up your hair, pull it off your face into something chic, like a chignon, to show off those cheekbones. It will be perfection."

Emma coughed again. She hated Susanna's ongoing descriptive fixes of her looks. Once she had called Emma's rare use of makeup "utilitarian understatement" and her face "an exotic cornucopia of youth and intensity." How could her father possibly marry this woman?

"Why don't we make a day of it?" Susanna continued. "We can get you fitted, have lunch? I've got a million errands to run and bits and bobs to pick up."

"I thought you had a wedding planner." Emma couldn't stop herself from behaving like a sullen adolescent when this topic came up. She knew she was supposed to be happy for her father, but what if? Wasn't there still a chance her mother could come back? Jack was already married, and that was the only wedding that counted. She'd seen the photos, taken under the shiny leaves of Malibu palm trees. She'd seen how beautiful her mother looked in a simple lace dress as she held the hand of her relaxed, blissful new husband. Jack smiled with his eyes, posed playfully by a fountain. It gave Emma pause to see how happy her father looked then. "What's Jack doing tomorrow?" she asked.

Susanna set her wine glass down by the edge of the counter. "Conference call with the Paris office all morning, then an early supper with my parents." She leaned back, jumped on the granite counter, and knocked her glass onto the floor.

"Oh!" said Emma. "Where's the broom?"

"Leave it." Susanna said, waving her hand. "Stay the night, and we can have a girly day tomorrow."

Emma crouched down with some paper towel.

"Emma! Leave it, will you? We have people to clean that up. What do you say to a little shopping, some lunch? We can talk about you...and how things are going with your exciting new job."

New? Emma had been working at *Oxygen* for nearly two years. "It's not an exciting job," she said, discreetly kicking the bigger pieces of glass under the counter. Jack would hate the mess.

"Oh yes it is! It's a great job, I don't know why you are so...I don't know the word...about it. I mean, God, look at me, what do I do all day? I run around trying to convince the likes of Bronwyn Davis to join the charity walk for Bosnia.

Eyes glaze over, Emsy. Dead topic." Susanna started to reach for her wine, then remembered it was on the floor. "I read that magazine religiously, you know that don't you? Cover to cover. I do."

Working at *Oxygen* might seem an exciting job—many of the in-house writers for the magazine were readily identified on the London scene, known for their authoritative opinions on culture, politics and style. They were engaging, popular and well-travelled. Outwardly they appeared to be having fun, but they were unfulfilled, Emma was sure of it. She knew these things because that was where her expertise lay: as an informed witness to the world rather than a participant. From her desk at the back of the office, behind the stacks of filing to be done and stationery boxes to be unpacked, Emma's biggest accomplishment so far had been in becoming part of the furniture. She was seen as a reliable, if unassuming, fixture in her colleagues' minds. Oh, and her desk drawer always had the good pens.

Jack came thundering down the kitchen stairs.

"Over my dead body!" he shouted over his shoulder. "Jesus, don't these people have homes to go to?"

He gave Susanna a noisy, damp smack on the cheek and ruffled Emma's hair, grinning at the alarm on her face as she tried to smooth everything right again.

Susanna wiped her cheek, making it look like she was scratching an itch.

"I was inviting Emsy to stay over tonight."

"Emma doesn't want to go shopping with you tomorrow," Jack said. "I'm sure she has something better to do, like kill herself."

"You're hilarious," Susanna said. "And she doesn't have anything better to do. Do you?"

Emma looked at her father.

"See! She's missing the shopping gene, Suzy. I'm going to donate her to science. Anyway, why would you ask her to stay? Does she *ever* leave?"

Emma spent a lot of time at Jack's house, even though she had a place of her own. Since the wedding had been announced, she'd been staying round theirs even more than usual. Her father had spent a fortune getting her a flat in Maida Vale, choosing most of the modernist, high-styled furniture himself, but she could never explain to Jack what she suspected he already knew. His house offered what her flat did not: action. Emma liked entering a house knowing someone else was there, whether she popped in after work, or spent the weekend reading on the sofa, something was always happening. A cleaner silently dusting, an opera aria floating on the breeze from the summer concerts at the park, a delivery man waiting for a signature in the foyer, Susanna and her friends gossiping over coffee in the kitchen. The silence in Emma's flat was all-consuming, and if she tried to read a book, the characters got out of control, loudly echoing and bouncing off the bare walls, making a mockery of her seclusion.

"Let's at least go for breakfast then," Susanna said to Emma.

"Alright, alright," Jack said, patting Susanna's behind. "We know Emma doesn't care much for socializing. Now baby, lover of my life, we've left our guests alone upstairs. They're probably about to start routing through the good wine— or worse, the bad wine."

"Fine," Susanna said amiably. "Let no one say I can't take a hint." Susanna picked up the cheese plate again and went unsteadily upstairs. "Love you both!" she called over her shoulder.

Jack waited until Susanna disappeared from view, then he opened the cupboard and got out the small broom. "Get up and out of the house by nine or she'll get you," he told Emma, sweeping up the crunchy glass with concentration.

Emma held back a sigh. The large family-sized kitchen was wasted on Susanna. Watching her gingerly sip an herbal tea for lunch or carefully pick the avocado out from her salad angered Emma. It was so clichéd. How could Jack not be bothered by it? It was a different kitchen when Emma's mother, Imogene, was in it. Food had been a huge part of their lives, whether cooking, shopping for vegetables or laughing and talking over dessert until way past her bedtime. Her mother was so comfortable with her physical self—taking yoga, dance and dozens of movement classes—that Emma had always seen food and fitness as happy bedfellows under the blanket of good living.

Imogene and Jack would argue passionately about food and flavours while they cooked; it seemed they never agreed on anything, and then, just as suddenly as the argument had started, they would be giggling like teenagers, disappearing in another room and leaving Emma at the dinner table by herself, trying to cover her ears and eat her potatoes at the same time. Emma felt rejuvenated by the memory but she knew better than to mention it to Jack.

"How did you like the party?" Jack asked, casting a disgusted look at the amount of leftovers on the counter. "Bored out of your mind? I thought you were bringing a date." He studied his reflection in the glass door of the refrigerator. "Do you think your old man is getting fat?"

"Dinner was nice. And you knew that I wasn't bringing anyone."

"And...?"

"And, no, you're not getting fat." This was typical Jack conversation after a party; Emma knew how to play along.

Jack began struggling with his shirt, roughly tugging at his cufflinks with his teeth. Emma studied her father, aging, drunk, handsome. She helped him remove his diamond and platinum boy-jewellery and decided she would get up for an early run before Susanna could find her. They knew Emma was going to stay the night anyway. She always did.

Since the renovations, the upstairs of Jack's house was like a fancy private hotel. When guests spent the night, you were privy to the sounds of doors closing, taps being turned on, muffled laughter, hushed arguments. Those were the best things about staying at Jack's house: hearing so many lives around you, and getting to fill in the blanks.

Stretching out between the sheets under her father's roof, Emma struggled to fall asleep. She knew how much Jack getting married would bother her, but had succeeded in avoiding the thought of it by beating a hasty retreat when the topic came up. She couldn't understand it. Jack was no more ready to move on than he ever had been. How could he let go? How dare he?

Those feelings were coming back. The ones that demanded the world be shut into a box, the feelings that made Emma want to climb inside the pages of a book and live in two dimensions forever. The memories came along, too, especially the ones where a monstrous, ogre-like Jack forced Imogene to leave him and her daughter behind.

Emma had it figured out before Jack did, that Imogene was really gone. Jack kept buying her mother's favourite coffee and the imported apple jelly she ate straight from the jar while rehearsing her lines. "It will be here for her when she gets back then," he'd say to Emma when she'd remind him Imogene wasn't there.

If Emma had any hope of her mother's return, it soon faded. Birthdays passed, blurry as road signs on the motorway, her and Jack too numb to notice. Life without Imogene was unsettled and unstructured, ferried between her grandmother, after-school activities and babysitters; she hated it all, couldn't understand why she was being punished for her father's mistakes.

Jack was also the one who said Emma should tell people Imogene had to go back to South America because her mother was very sick.

"But that's a lie!"

"Well, where has she gone then?" Jack demanded, his voice mossy with desperation.

His intensity scared Emma; she had no answer.

Emma rolled over, hugged her pillow. The only thing she'd ever had in common with her father was the void left by her mother. Just because they didn't talk about it didn't mean it wasn't as much a part of the daily routine as brushing your teeth. In six weeks' time, Jack would be married. Then what?

Emma had felt this uneasy stirring in her stomach before. She recognized it as want, but of what she was never sure. She knew this: watching the world continue to move on while she remained stock-still was making it harder and harder to breathe.

Chapter 3

"Morning," Jack said, when Emma appeared at the door of his study. "I'm telling you, there is nothing like working on a Saturday. Try it sometime."

Emma came in and unzipped her windbreaker. "Morning."

"Are you as hungover as I am?" Jack asked. "No, of course, you never are. I had to keep drinking to make our guests seem interesting." He reached in his desk drawer and pulled out a pill bottle. It gave a rattle. "Hallelujah!" He popped several back without water.

"I'm not hungover, but I'm tired," Emma said. She hadn't slept well, dreaming of grosgrain and orchids and Imogene. "I managed to get dressed, but I can't be bothered to go for a run now."

"Too bad you can't read and jog at the same time, huh?" Jack said, commenting on the book in Emma's hand. "Go on then, what are you reading now?"

"*Jane Eyre*," Emma said, sitting on the edge of Jack's desk and yawning.

"Again? Rubbish."

"How do you know *Jane Eyre* is rubbish if you've never read it?"

"How do you know it isn't rubbish if you do?"

Emma made a face.

"Why don't you read a nice condescending book about a thirty-something woman trying to find a husband and balance a career in advertising? What's wrong with books like that?"

"I leave those books for Susanna to read."

Jack grinned. "Good one. Here's another question: why aren't you that quick-witted at dinner parties? If I had a pound for every time I had to bail you out of a dying conversation I'd be having this conversation from my private island in the Indian Ocean."

Emma took a breath and let it out slowly. She thought she had done well yesterday.

"Did you see that halfwit George trying to hit on Lottie last night?" The phone rang and Jack answered it with a flourish, nearly dropping it.

Emma wandered over to the bookshelf by the picture window and began browsing, even though she knew it was full of financial periodicals no one, including Jack, had ever read. Looking at the rows of books made her a little anxious. She considered slipping out and heading to her room, where she could get through a few more chapters before lunch.

Emma didn't simply read books, she set up house inside them and took on the character's lives as her own. Macbeth had absorbed her thoughts for weeks. In the laundrette: "*Out, out damn spot!*"; at the dinner table: "*Is this a dagger I see before me?*"; and daily, when she walked to the tube through the city smog: "*Fair is foul, and foul is fair. Hover through the fog and filthy air.*" She rarely caught herself before she said these things out loud. The drama was too powerful to keep inside, too much meaning to mute in her mind.

Emma was always looking for a magnificent character. Their call to fate, their explicit sense of fatalism—the feeling that once something had been set in motion, there was no turning back. For Jane Eyre, the moment she made a choice to want for more in her life, her call was answered with drama and heartache, a crazy lady in the attic and eventually resolution, but the call was answered. Macbeth's power-mad lunacy was made all the more fascinating by his valiant attempts to fight his destiny, to struggle with his morality.

"What's up?" Jack had the phone to his ear and the other end pointed up at the ceiling so the caller wouldn't hear him.

"Push the mute button, Jack."

"Gotcha." He hit the button with relish. "So what's up?"

"Nothing..."

"How's work?"

"Work's fine," she said, casually.

"Sounds thrilling." Jack made his eyes really wide. "I should have read that pill bottle. I think I've popped some of Susanna's Xanax. I feel weird."

"They weren't yours?" Emma reached for the bottle.

Jack snatched it off the desk first. "Oh, now you want some? There's none for you, little Emmalina. You need more reality in your life, not less."

"What do you mean you feel weird? Are you okay?"

Jack sprawled out in his chair and let his head hang off the back.

"Please, what do you mean? Don't joke around."

"Loop-y," he sang, his Adam's apple jutting out sharply. Suddenly he bounced up and took the phone off mute. "I agree completely. That market has bottomed out." Jack hit mute again. "Nope, not the Xanax, it's this conference call."

"You've got to stop taking that stuff, it's not good for you, Jack."

"I am and I have. Get off my back, it's eight o'clock in the morning."

It was closer to eleven, but Emma didn't correct him.

Jack probably had taken something; he'd never grown out of taking drugs. He acted so idiotic when he was on them, trying to convince Emma they were a necessary evil if he was going to still be seen as one of the boys and get through another eighty-hour week. It bothered her how out of control Jack was. It bothered her even more that she was the only one who felt that way. His world was not that far removed from other people with money and power, like rock stars who kept young girlfriends and old coke habits, carrying on until they were embarrassing, crowd-surfing crotchety pensioners.

Perhaps if Jack had been a rock star they would have been closer. She would have grown up on the road in the back of a tour bus, being passed around by the various groupies while Jack destroyed another hotel room. He could have loved her fiercely, madly—writing songs and dedicating albums to her before collapsing on stage in Berlin and being shipped off to an intensive detox centre in America. His music would never have been the same after that.

"There's an opening on our media team," Jack said. "Why don't you come in on Monday and say hi to everyone."

"I have a job."

"How can I put this... Working for a magazine started by some pot-smoking, limp-wristed fashion victim doesn't count as a career."

"Michael isn't gay." Emma knew that for an unfortunate after-work, mismatched, drunken, fact. "He doesn't run the magazine anymore." Thank God.

"See—even he was smart enough to move on to another job. He's probably running Amazon now."

"I've been getting more involved in things lately…"

"Sure you are. If you hadn't quit the city when you did, you'd be an associate at my office by now." Jack lit a cigarette and took a short drag. "We agreed you could do the creative thing for a year and see what happened."

"Did you read my feature on new movies last month? My boss went out of her way to commend me on it and say she really liked it."

Sylvia didn't say *exactly* that when they met in the lifts. "Saw that sci-fi malarkey you panned," was more like it.

"Oh, right. Great!" Emma said, nodding like a plastic beagle stuck to the rear window of a car.

Sylvia smiled. "I thought the movie was complete tat as well."

What Emma should have said next was: "Tat is in the eye of the beholder" or "I blame the Ewoks." That would have been good. By the time she thought of an answer, Sylvia was already halfway down the corridor.

Jack leaned forward to flick his cigarette in the ashtray. "…At least an associate. You wouldn't have to do the grunt work like the others. Let me help you. I could be putting you up for the best transactions, the best deals. You could travel, you'd be making good money, have some job security instead of this silly freelancing you do—no one gets paid by the hour over the age of thirteen. I don't really know what you do at *Oxygen*. As far as I can see, you research articles for some private school ponce to take credit for."

Emma knew when she quit working at the bank with Jack that what little faith he had in her career would be long gone; there was no point in going back now. "There's more than one way to measure success," she mumbled. "It's not always about money or the corner office."

"It's not like you're a war correspondent or something credible. And let me say right now, hell will freeze over twice before I allow you to be a war correspondent."

Emma glanced down at the photo of Susanna on Jack's desk. It was taken when they first started dating—Susanna's hair was shorter, she was dressed in black. Susanna rarely wore dark clothing now because Jack didn't like it on her, said it made her look like a wannabe artsy type. Emma ran a finger along the edge of the gold and silver frame and said gently, "Jack? Are you and Susanna trying for a baby?"

Jack grunted. "*That* would be a miracle." He paused before taking a drag of his cigarette. "We're not going to have a baby. I repeat, we are not having a baby." He went back to his phone call, waving at Emma to go. "Trust me on this one," he said.

Emma didn't know if he was talking to her or the phone.

London Underground, or the Tube as it is more commonly known, was built in 1863, and anyone travelling on it harboured a suspicion that it hadn't been modernized since. The demands of a billion journeys a year on an antiquated system were heavy, and Londoners were very demanding. They didn't like the delays, they didn't like the dampness in the winter or the stifling heat in the summer (thirty-four Celsius *inside* the trains last July), and they hated having to share their personal space.

This made Emma an atypical London Underground passenger: she loved the tube. The busier, the better. Mice? Just watch the reaction of people on the platform when a tatty grey rodent runs past. Delays? Fantastic—even more "everyday" people getting riled up and antsy, showing their colours shoving past old ladies to get on the train. Delays equal twice as many stories that no one would ever imagine but Emma.

The tube jolted to a stop at Baker Street. "Mind the gap!" barked the intercom.

Emma's head lolled forward. Sleepless nights had become a regular part of her schedule and she was unable to fight her tiredness once the stale, uncirculated air of the carriage hit her. She was not a person who appeared peaceful or relaxed when deep in slumber. Emma's expression was of a person trying to pat their head and rub their stomach at the same time. Her glasses sunk all the way down her nose, her mouth unfastened and lax.

A man with a guitar tripped over Emma's feet and she woke up with a jump. "*I will not do as you ask*!" she cried, pulling her shoes in over the grimy newspapers on the floor, her skirt caught inelegantly between her long legs like big balloon trousers. She pushed her glasses up and tucked her murky brown hair, with its permanent kink from too many ponytails, behind her ear. Feebly, she retrieved her novel, which now rested on the knees of the woman beside her.

Emma squinted under the harsh tube lighting and looked up at the graffiti-branded journey planner. DON'T BE A MUG— BUY A CAR! ONE TRAIN EVERY 20 MINS WOT A FUCKIN JOKE.

Rain had been blowing through London for days, and the train smelled of wet wool and old burgers; Emma's crinkled nose decided to let her mouth do the breathing. Her fingernails went to their familiar, comforting assault between her teeth while she watched the bumbling transition of passengers—those hurrying to get somewhere and those outside the train waiting to get on, hopeful and exhausted.

Directly across from her slouched a middle-aged man, hair cut short to disguise the thinning, in an unzipped khaki-green bomber jacket. The neckline of his shirt failed to cover the masses of dark hair sprouting out toward his throat, and acne scarred his weathered face. He worked as a plumber, a contractor, slaving for his tyrant of a boss. He suffered adversity as a teen, cornered at the school disco in 1975 by the boys in wide trousers, taunting him to ask a girl to dance, knowing what the result would be. He would go home, chest burning, and when his kindly immigrant mother asked how his evening was, he couldn't speak to her, and instead would push past, up the worn carpeted stairs, tears stinging his eyes, to lock himself in his bedroom. Emma decided his name was Archie.

She switched fingernails and resumed her studies.

The woman sitting beside Archie adjusted the toddler sitting on her lap. She had a cherubic face with a mess of curly red hair pulled back by a flowered hair band. There were no other children. The one she did have was a miracle—when she was a child, she suffered from a mysterious illness and the doctors said she would never bear children. This led to years of sexual promiscuity, looking for love she knew she would never find, not like this, not as half a woman. Then she met him, and fell in love, and he was married, and she was pregnant. She knew what he would tell her to do, so she ran away to another place, taking her broken heart and the secret growing inside of her. Her name was definitely Cecilia.

Feeling more herself, Emma opened her book and began reading.

After her childhood as an unloved, misunderstood orphan, Jane Eyre was sent to a charitable institution for girls. Her studious manner and penchant for self-sufficiency led her to go from pupil to a reliable, appreciated teacher, but an internal struggle was raging. A hunger had started to grow that needed more than the same meal of habit served cold every day, every year.

I tired of the routine of eight years in one afternoon. I desired liberty... "Then," I cried, half desperate, "grant me at least a new servitude!"

The anguish, the palaver! Emma almost stood up herself to address the underground passengers. How did Jane decide to make a change? Was she bent over a chipped enamel wash basin, scrubbing her simple garments when she realized her life needed new meaning? Perhaps one of her students, Mary— a sprightly young redhead—asked for help on a math problem and as Jane crouched down next to her desk she caught the scent of Mary's lye soap, saw her ink-stained chubby hands, and was filled with grief.

Jane's longing made Emma ache.

———————————

Sylvia came into the Monday meeting late, balancing a large coffee on top of her notebook.

"OK, everybody shut up," she said.

No one had been talking, but everyone sat up a bit straighter and assembled their work faces. Near the end of the table, Emma sat staring out the window watching the flower stall. The handwritten signs for imported orchids and spring daffodils were twisting and turning in the wind, the letters leaking into each other from the rain pelting down. She watched Eddie, the stall owner, run from one sign to the next trying to keep them from blowing away, like a circus clown spinning plates.

The usual meeting discussions on circulation, deadlines and upcoming issues were taking place. The features editor, James, bounced a few story ideas around. "I think we should do a piece on gentlemen's clubs. You know, *gentlemen's* clubs."

Everyone laughed. "Of course you do, Jimmy," said Sylvia. "Anyone else have anything decent to contribute? Like something to Irish up this coffee?"

"I'm serious." James stood up and ran his hands through his hair. Several of the women in the room cast knowing glances at each other. "Right now strip clubs are cool. Movie stars in the States are going to pole-dancing lessons to keep fit. It's the in thing."

"Fine," said Sylvia. "Where's the story?"

"What I'm thinking is that we do a feature from inside the club—what it's really like."

"Been done before," Sylvia said. "What's the angle? Not more bullshit about empowering women, please."

James shook his head. "No, a real-life behind the scenes, a day in the life of. Or a 'what I learned about men from pole dancers' slant. Tongue-in-cheek, obviously. I reckon we send in one of our girls to do it." He grinned. "I'm looking at you, Geri."

Again, everyone laughed. Geri, their outspoken food critic, was at least fifty with a purposely paunchy way of dressing.

"What's so funny?" Geri asked. "I could make millions!"

"Sit down, Jim," said Sylvia. "Maybe this isn't bad. No one really knows what happens in there. Most coverage plays it like they're all emotionally damaged man-eaters. But there's gotta be more to it than that, a twist to the usual single-mum stripper or student-in-college thing."

"Exposé writing isn't really our style," said Toni, the society page writer, unfolding a paperclip to clean under her fingernails.

"Ironic, coming from you," said James. "I'm not talking aggressive exposure—nor sugar coated—just real. We send someone in to work undercover and befriend the girls."

"You could try and get some dirt on the customers that go in there," Geri suggested.

"There's definitely something there about the lifestyle," James said. "The status—these girls are dating rock stars and footie players—it's not like they're ashamed of it."

"Right?" said Sylvia. "The stigma is changing."

Emma continued to stare out the window, keeping one ear on the meeting. A big crawly bug stuck in a web outside the glass had caught her attention. It was rolling around in the wind like the flower signs, with little chance to escape, but it kept trying, kept struggling, refusing to accept defeat. "*I resisted all the way: a new thing for me…*" Go big bug, go. Jane would approve.

Emma imagined Jane living at the Thornfield estate, looking out the blue chintz-curtained window of her bedroom, discontented and restless, desperately wishing she could interact with the outside world. This was a very poor replica of a nineteenth-century estate, and James's insistent voice was ruining her imagery.

"If we did it in a really upmarket club, a really exclusive one, there would be some great punters and great stories," James said.

"Could be intriguing," Sylvia admitted. "What's the name of that one all the celebs go to in the West End?"

"Platinum. That's the one I was thinking of. One of the biggest clubs in Europe. They have their own private jet."

"You know a hell of a lot about this," said Toni. "Wait—a jet?"

"We need to hammer down an angle," Sylvia said. "It would have to be very real…very authentic. The journo would have to totally commit…"

"Yeah, but who?" asked Toni. "And don't look in this direction, everyone knows me in this town."

"So we've heard," said James and Sylvia at the same time.

"C'mon, I'm serious. We'll have to commission the bloody thing." Toni didn't like it. A debate was about to begin, girls against boys.

A voice came from the twisting belly of the big crawly beetle in the web in the window. It said, "I'll do it."

Everyone shut up.

"Sorry?" said James.

It is in vain to say human beings ought to be satisfied with tranquillity: they must have action; and they will make it if they cannot find it.

Emma put down her pencil and looked at Sylvia. "I said, I will do it."

Chapter 4

PLATINUM CLUB HOUSE RULES

1.   Stage shows: Don't be late for your stage call. You will be fined if you do not perform. You'll be given a two-song warning by the DJ, make sure to pay attention to which stage you are called to. Platinum has one main stage (accessible only through the dressing room), three podiums & a bar stage. The restaurant also has a bar stage.

2.   A good show = good tips. Make the effort and represent the club well.

3.   Music: we do not allow hardcore metal or rap music at the club.

4.   Remember, smile! You're on stage.

5.   Presentation: Your look must be nothing short of perfection. This should include:

    a.   Showgirl-type hair and makeup. Use dramatic and glamorous jewellery, hairpieces, gloves, etc. Remember: style & elegance are what we do best.

    b.   Floor-length gowns and high-heeled shoes that are approved by the Club Management. Your shoes must have at least a 4" heel and must never be taken off when in the public areas of the club.

c.   You may wear a short dress, special themed costumes or lingerie during your stage show. We recommend you make the effort to advertise yourself in an appealing and exciting manner.

d.   No see-through G-strings. Stay sophisticated!

6.   Body lotion is strictly prohibited before your stage show. This makes the pole slippery and dangerous. Do not use it! Any dancer caught putting another at risk will be immediately fined.

7.   Big attitudes make big money!

8.   We recommend all new dancers attend the Platinum Academy courses run on Sunday afternoons. These cover essential information like how to approach customers, sales tips and pole instruction.

9.   Platinum girls don't chew gum.

10.   Dancers can never be in the company of a customer except in an area open to the public within the club.

11.   Private dances: When dancing for a customer there must be no physical contact between you and the customer at any time. Dancers must keep two feet on the floor at all times when giving a private dance.

12.   Before you start dancing you must make sure the customer is seated with hands by their sides and ensure that someone from security is in the private dance area.

13.   This club is topless only. No nudity!

14.   Do not walk around the club in an intoxicated, lecherous manner. After a private dance you must get fully dressed before returning to the main floor. You may smoke cigarettes at tables, with customers only.

15.   At end of your shift you must leave in a club-approved, booked taxi, or a member of security will escort you to your car.

16.   The Platinum Club has zero tolerance for: prostitution, solicitation, unlawful drugs, violence, theft. Be smart. Do not lose an incredible opportunity to work at the best Gentlemen's Club in the world.

Chapter 5

They said to bring a long, elegant dress.

The Platinum Club was located in the centre of London's busy West End, bordered by a flashy car dealership on one side and a short, well-lit alley on the other. The word "Platinum," outlined in a cursive silver font was barely visible above the black granite wall of the building. Two burly men in suits and earpieces stood behind black velvet ropes leading to the discreet entrance. The subtlety of the entrance belied the grandness of the lobby. A wide black and white marble floor reflected hundreds of tiny fairy lights twinkling from the ceiling like a night sky in the country. Several bouquets of white lilies were arranged on tall plinths, and a flickering fireplace cast soft shadows over the walls, which were draped with peacock-blue velvet curtains.

A striking woman sat behind a tall counter, her hair parted deeply on the side and pulled tightly in a bun. She had two tasteful pearl drop earrings dancing on her earlobes. Were they real or fake? Emma wanted to ask, but felt shunted in this womb of hushed voices and fabric-draped ceilings.

"I called earlier," she whispered to the lady. "About getting a job...?"

The woman nodded, made a note of something. "Go back outside and around to the entrance on the left. I'll let the manager know you're here."

Trey, a weedy middle-aged man in a well-cut dark suit, led Emma down the stairs through the back of the club.

"Wait—" Emma said, "I need to see the club, where the customers are."

"You will," he said. "But not looking like that."

"Looking like what?"

"No street clothing," he explained, swiping a card through a reader and pulling open a wide fire door. "Dancers aren't allowed in the front door. Use the side door."

"Why can't they—we—use the front door?" Emma asked.

"Why do you think?" Trey asked, more than a hint of annoyance in his voice. "Spoils the impression. You ladies are supposed to be untouchable dream girls. If they see you in your baseball hat and jeans, it's over before it's begun."

Emma scanned the unpainted concrete hallway for clues of what the club might be like, but there was little worth reporting on. A dank smell of pipes and a heavy vibrating bass sound coming from above was all she had to work with. "When can I see the inside of the club?" she asked.

"Fill in the application forms and talk to Eileen, our house mother."

"What's a house mother?" Emma asked the back of Trey's spiky, gelled head. "Also, can you tell me how many girls work here?"

Trey gestured toward an unmarked frosted glass door. "Anyone ever tell you that you ask a lot of questions?" he said. "We've got one-fifty on tonight. That's about average." He flicked open his mobile phone and continued down the hall.

Emma stepped inside a very crowded and very warm dressing room. Her hands shook as she tried to fill out the application form, and the pen she had didn't work very well. It didn't seem to matter. Eileen, introduced as the house mother, didn't give it a glance.

"The lady who does our auditions is off sick," she said. "But what else is new? Go get dressed and I'll have to take a look at you. What did you bring to wear, luv?"

Eileen was in her late thirties, with bright red, cropped hair, a nose stud and several earrings in each long, stretched lobe. She wore a tight black T-shirt that spelled out "Goddess" in sparkling purple letters. She took out a Polaroid camera and pointed it at Emma.

"Say greed!"

"I don't think I have the right dress." Emma said as the camera spit out her image. "I'm fairly certain I'm not properly prepared."

She dug around in her gym bag and pulled out the dress she'd worn to *Oxygen*'s Christmas party last year.

"You'll be fine," said Eileen. "Write your name down on that, please." She looked up at Emma's dress, a loose-fitting, gypsy-style smock. "No. You can't wear that. That's shocking. Take a look around—you need something like the girls here are wearing."

Emma gave an apprehensive peek at the women in the dressing room, who, if they had any clothes on at all, were in beads and sequins and dramatic glittering gowns slit to the waist.

"Also," Eileen was saying, "that dress is not going to be very easy to get in and out of all night. Go see the dressmaker at the back and buy one. If you don't have the money you can pay it out of your earnings tonight."

Emma didn't move. The "getting in and out of all night" bit had set a fire in her armpits.

"You need to be dressed and on the floor by nine. I'll get one of the other girls to buddy you tonight, so you can see how it works. I'm too busy to sit with you, I've three waitresses gone walkies. This freakin' place is killing me."

"But, what about the audition? I'm starting tonight?" Emma had something lodged in her throat. It felt like a big beetle.

"What's your name?"

"Emma."

"Emma. Luv. I'm giving you a bly tonight, so take it, yeah? Now, you need to put more makeup on. A lot more. There's a makeup artist in Wednesday to Saturday and it's a tenner. Get her to do your face a few times and learn. We cater to an exclusive crowd. It's about untouchable glamour, okay?"

Emma thought it was fairly obvious she was not a glamorous person. Eileen must have thought so too, because then she said, "The girl-next-door types do really well, too."

Some girls came through the door and were pushing up behind Emma.

"Eileen, about my house fee, yeah? Can I pay you the rest later?" asked one, thrusting a fifty over Emma's shoulder. Emma noticed the girl said "later" like this: "lay-ahh," like they did on *East Enders*.

What was a house fee? How was she going to claim this as an expense? Emma doubted they would give a receipt. This was no way to start a job. She didn't know what she was supposed to be doing. Did everyone have their own space? What if she took someone's seat by mistake?

She had never been anywhere like this before, had never seen anywhere like this before. She was fascinated and terrified at the same time. She should be taking notes, but surely it wouldn't be possible to keep up with what her assaulted senses were experiencing. The air was visible: cigarette smoke weaving a hazy web through a dozen perfumes, deodorants and hairsprays. At the front of the changing room sat stacks of multicoloured hair dryers and hair straighteners, an ironing board, a mound of grey towels and some well-thumbed gossip magazines. Trails of toilet roll stretched out across the floor, and boxes of garters, stockings, mints, hair gel and brushes were piled on the desk where Eileen sat scribbling and shoving money into a cash box. Along the left side, mirrors decorated with fingerprints were positioned above a cracked Formica countertop, with studio bulbs blazing bold, unforgiving wattage. Lockers with scratched beige paint were packed in anywhere there was space, including the centre of the room, and thrown on top of them, rows of gym bags sat overflowing with clothes. Stuck to one of the mirrors was a photocopied ad for flatmates looking to share a loft apartment in Battersea.

Emma tried to get past some girls doing their makeup, but they didn't move. Some of them were naked, standing there having conversations with each other. Emma squeezed up tight against the lockers to get past and whispered, "Excuse me... sorry." Searching for a spare seat, she felt like a backpacker at airport arrivals, looking for a friendly face. A spot at the back of the room next to a large rail of clothing caught her eye and she headed in that direction.

A lady holding a needle and thread sitting at the clothes rail watched Emma come through the hive of goings-on. She looked like she could have been Eileen's mother. The dress lady smiled a mouthful of missing and/or gold teeth. Make that Eileen's grandmother.

Two girls rummaged through the clothes while they passed a glass of wine between them.

"I'm telling you, it's not worth coming in early," said the girl in the black satin robe tied at the chest, cleavage heavily rounded over her bra. She tucked a strand of her blue-black bobbed hair behind her ear and sulked.

"That's not true, Rox," said her friend, wearing a fluffy bathrobe and brightly coloured rollers in her hair. "I always make my money early. By the end of the night it's just tossers."

"Fine. But no one that spends any money is here at eight o'clock," Roxy replied.

"What about this?" asked the girl in the bathrobe, holding out a pink bikini. She had something in her belly button. It was a sparkly red jewel of a Playboy bunny.

Emma tried to make eye contact as she unpacked her bag. Perhaps they could help her.

"Pink does look nice with dark hair," she offered.

It seemed neither of the girls heard her.

"Can I try this on?" Roxy asked the dress lady.

Perhaps it was a little premature to start making friends. Emma pushed her bag as far under the counter as she could, tucking the chair in tightly so no one could steal it. The clothing on offer was outrageous—American flag short-shorts, race-car driver catsuits, bejewelled bras and dresses that wouldn't be out of place at a ballroom dance competition. Some of the underwear was so small Emma couldn't tell which was the back and which was the front. Twenty-five quid for a pair of knickers? Emma could get a dozen from her catalogue for that much money.

She was being watched by a girl on the other side of the rail. "First night?"

Emma nodded.

"First night here, or first night *ever*?"

"Ever."

"We've all been there. Never mind. Give it a week or so to get situated and you'll be good to go." She was gorgeous, this girl with huge cocoa eyes and skin like a long vacation in the sun. "What's your name?"

"Emma."

"No—your stage name?"

"My what?"

"You have to pick a name for when you work here. No one uses their real one."

"Oh, right."

"I'm Bambi."

Emma snorted. "Bambi?" She probably shouldn't have snorted.

Bambi stopped flipping through dresses and studied Emma over the top of a fluffy marabou negligee.

"You need a stage name." She walked over to the mirror and lifted up her dress. "I hate these ones," she said, adjusting the silver zipper on her vivid pink underwear, "but they look wicked in the black lights." She looked at Emma in the mirror. "You need a name that has nothing to do with real life. Something like a fast car or an animal. Or an American soap opera name."

"I quite like my name," Emma told her. "It's in fact a literary sort of name, Emma. You know, like the book by Jane Austen. I think I'll stick with my own name."

Bambi turned around and bent over.

"Can you see that spot on my bum?" she said, looking over her shoulder. "You could be an Anastasia. Or a Carmen. No, I think there's a Carmen here already. Or Nikki. That's a sexy name."

She reached in her purse and got out some makeup, which she dabbed on the pimple. Satisfied with the results, she flipped her head upside down, and shook out her hair.

"See you around," she said.

Chapter 6

As soon as Emma got to her desk, Geri and Toni pounced, primed for details.

"Hello!" said Geri in an unnaturally high voice.

Toni smiled. "I like your scarf, is that new?"

"Uh, yes, thanks…" Emma said. She pulled her scarf away from her neck a little and logged onto her computer.

"Well?" Toni said, "How's it going? Your little foray into the world of seedy strip clubs?"

"Fine. It's fine, I guess," Emma said carefully.

"We want to know everything," said Geri. "Ev-ery-thing."

"It is rather extraordinary." Emma could tell by Geri's face that wasn't the right thing to have said.

James joined the group. "Back off ladies, I want the gory details first. Don't talk to them, Emma. They'll use it against you later."

"Shut up, Jim," said Toni. "You only want to know about the naked ladies."

"Oh so do you," James said. "And I already know all about naked ladies, don't you worry."

Toni turned back to Emma. "How is it—really?"

"It certainly isn't Moulin Rouge," Emma said.

Geri and James exchanged looks.

"What the hell does that mean?" said Toni.

Emma checked her computer was working; it was taking ages to bring up the welcome screen.

"What did you wear? Did you have on those appalling plastic shoes?"—this was Toni.

"Did you have to take your clothes off straight away?"—then Geri.

"Were girls making out in the dressing room?"—followed by James.

"No, nothing like that. I'm still getting to know my way around." Emma wished they would leave her alone. She had a pile of post to open.

"You're going to have to really go for it, if it's to be a good story. You *know* that right?" said James.

"I think Jim is having a hard time picturing you doing this." Toni said, nudging James. "He doesn't seem to think you're G-string diva material."

"I really have to get to work."

"Well…good luck," said Geri.

"*Disastré*," Emma heard James say as they walked off.

She took off her scarf and shoved it in the back of the desk drawer next to the vitamins. It really wound her up the way people thought she was some kind of peculiarity. This might not be one of her best decisions—volunteering to cover Ascot or some new literary festival might have been easier, but they probably wouldn't have assigned it to her.

What's the big deal, anyway? You put on a pair of shoes, you sashay around a club, you write a story about it. She was good at blending into the background, she was a great observer, she knew the story Sylvia wanted—this could be her big break. Easy breezy.

Emma lowered her head slowly onto the desk. She was a dead woman.

That goddamn Jane Eyre.

"Emma, you're a lovely girl, but you have got to go on stage this evening." Eileen adjusted the buckle on her Marilyn Monroe screen-printed jeans and continued. "I let you off on your first night, but now you're taking the mick. Everyone else has to do it, and no one gets special treatment around here."

Emma tried to protest but couldn't, because the makeup artist, Tanya, was carefully painting her bottom lip to look like a sticky candy apple.

"If you can't hack it, you'll have to go," Eileen said. "You look gorgeous, by the way. Look at yourself."

Emma focussed instead on the reflection of a girl behind her kicking a stuck locker door to try and distract herself from the horror of having to take her clothes off and dance in front of a room of men. More terrifying than that was the prospect of all the other dancers watching and judging her.

"Look!" chided Eileen.

Emma took a glance at the face reflected in the mirror. Her skin was perfectly even, dewy, soft. Her cheekbones subtly contoured to dramatically lift her face and emphasize her eyes, which were outlined in liquid black eyeliner—feline, intensely seductive. Pale shimmering shadow covered her eyelids making her look both child-like and wickedly devilish. Her mouth, glossy and clearly defined, had been accessorized with a round dark chocolate beauty spot drawn just above her top lip. Tanya had set Emma's hair in hot rollers and told her to tip her head upside down while she combed through a multitude of hair products. Tanya clipped in a hair attachment underneath several layers of Emma's hair and the result was thick, glossy waves spilling over her shoulders and down her back.

Emma's first purchase from the Platinum Club dressmaker, a black satin halter neck dress with a low-cut, keyhole front, wrapped around her body like a second skin. Lace panel inserts on the side helped to nip in her waist and curve out her usually boyish hips. She was red-carpet glamour, girlishly innocent and purely sexual all at the same time.

She was completely unrecognizable.

"You're on the stage roster," Eileen told Emma. "You'll hear your name over the speakers. Tell Mike what music you want."

"Be confident." Tanya said, shaking a can of hairspray to lock in her efforts with Emma's hair.

Fresh from the stage, Bambi arranged her cleavage inside a tangerine orange bra. "Don't overdo it," she said. "Just go slow. Listen to the music and relax. Pretend you're doing it for your boyfriend."

"Bambi!" called a girl from the other end of the room, "Chanel's looking for you, she's in the restaurant."

"Thanks, sexy!" Bambi yelled back. "Yay! I gotta go. Here, take my wine." She gave Emma a quick peck on the cheek. "Remember, suck it in and stick it out!"

Emma watched Bambi leave. She looked back in the mirror and picked up the glass of wine, watching this strangely foreign person drink it all down.

Many of Emma's memories of her mother were reflections in the mirror—Imogene painstakingly applying her makeup, rehearsing her lines, doling out advice to Emma through her two-dimensional counterpart. For a time, Emma was convinced the mirror existed only for Imogene. "Getting into character," she would say, if Emma walked in to find her bent forward over the mirror, delicately adding a pair of false eyelashes to her own with a pair of tweezers.

Imogene was very comfortable with disguise and dressing up. Emma remembered a rainy Sunday when her mother emptied out the big cupboard in the basement and found some old costumes from her first theatre group. She dressed Emma up, head to toe, complete with cigarette holder and face paint. When she had to go to the shops, Emma didn't want to get changed, so Imogene brought her along as she was. Emma remembered how it felt to walk down the street and around the supermarket aisles when camouflaged.

Imogene loved it, she thought Emma's show of dancing around and singing to strangers was because she was a true entertainer at heart. She enrolled her in the children's theatre group and encouraged her to be an actress. Emma considered acting as a career, until Jack had prohibited it.

She was behind a mask here, and Emma's unusually clear memory of her mother and the mirror helped. She felt hopeful. She stood up, as determined as she could manage, and took a long look at the stage door which stood directly across from the door for the DJ booth. "*Curiouser and curiouser*," Emma muttered. "*Which door to choose…?*"

The door to the booth flung open.

"Are you Emma?"

"Yes."

"I'm Mike." He glanced down at the clipboard in his hand. "You're on next. I've been calling you to get your music." Mike looked like a pizza delivery man in his uniform of black trousers and white shirt. He had a gold chain with a crucifix swinging against his pasty mayonnaise-coloured chest.

"Right. What does that mean, exactly?"

"What music do you want for your set?"

"Oh, of course. I don't really know. You pick!"

Mike looked unimpressed. He wasn't very friendly considering it was his job to play music for people like her. How long had he been working here? Emma was sure it must have been some time. He probably had dreams of being a musician, and pounded drums in a band about to break the big time. But he fell in love with a dancer from Platinum that he met on a boy's night out with the record company and to the shock (and disgust) of everyone he knew, quit the band to become a DJ because he was so jealous—his love for her was consuming, rampant—and he wanted, no needed, to be around her when she worked, even if it meant he had to throw away his dreams.

"What kind of music do you like?" Mike asked, Emma realized, for the second time. He really did seem like someone who had endured hardship in his life.

"Sorry. I've not gone on stage before—I don't really know."

"Most girls bring their own music. Nothing too heavy and none of that shite dance music, I won't play it. Do you like rock? Soul?"

"Sure…" Emma said. She couldn't think of any song she had ever listened to, ever.

"Strip down to your knickers but DON'T take them off, whatever you do. Just topless. Okay? Go through the stage door, down the stairs, and wait until the other girl comes off and I introduce you."

Emma went down the stairs to wait her turn. She put a hand on her chest, feeling her heart knocking at her ribs ("*against the use of nature*!" As Macbeth would surely agree). A girl dashed past, clutching her dress up to her chest, her high heels muffled on the carpeted steps.

Platinum's main floor was a titanic space so large Emma was barely able to make out the faces of the girls dancing at the other end of the club. The room was an oblong shape with towering ceilings and on busy nights like tonight, the near capacity crowd of five hundred barely caused a ripple in the openness of the space. Along the left wall, four private dance areas were guarded by doorman with earpieces and beefy folded arms. Scattered randomly through the crowd were a handful of wait staff that couldn't possibly keep up with the amount of customers on the floor. Seating, in low-backed lounge-style chairs with small round tables was focussed around the main stage and the circular podium stages on either side of the private dance areas. The bar (the only place in the club where standing was allowed), was staffed with half a dozen bartenders and was buzzing with dancers and clientele four people deep.

The club's décor was inconspicuous and theatrical at the same time. Warm, cherry wood tables and wall trimmings with fine Italian alabaster uplighter lamps met with animal print loveseats and over a dozen different chandeliers. The rounded ceiling was gilded and cast a beautiful light around the room and its inhabitants.

Tucked away on the second level of the club, the restaurant overlooked the main stage. In contrast to the lofty feel of the main part of the club, the restaurant's ceilings were lower and the music quieter. Tables were well-dressed with crystal glassware, candlelight and white Egyptian cotton tablecloths. The VIP area was also located at restaurant level, away from the action of the main floor. Used by celebrity guests, sports stars and wealthy groups of businessmen, the curtained-off booths were hosted by concierge services and private butlers. They sat a maximum of eight people in high-level luxury: vintage champagne, imported cigars, a professional masseuse available for head-and-shoulder massages, a separate exit to the rest of the club for those who didn't want to be seen by anyone and a limo service to get them home. The privilege of going VIP wasn't without cost: a thousand pounds per hour, and guests were required to buy several bottles of champagne during that time.

The main stage stretched out onto the middle of the club, a shiny brass pole at its centre. Chairs curved around the edges of the stage, and there was a low divider that had several ashtrays and space for drinks. The tip rail, Emma thought. The polished black marble floor was slippery underneath her feet; she could see her reflection, distorted and headless, around her ankles. The light show kicked in and the strobes ganged up on her, making her lose direction and feel dizzy. She tried to remember everything she had been told, but of course it was too much.

Emma saw the pole, shining like a symbol of all that was safe and unmoving, a stable focal point that would at least be something to bloody well hold on to. She arrived without incident, and grabbed it with both hands. The brass was cold but Emma's damp hands skidded south, her ankle tipping outwards painfully. She hoped her grimace wasn't seen by the men sitting near the stage, but she knew it would have been seen by the hungry eyes of all those girls lurking, watching, waiting for her to die on that marble desert, alone and friendless, with "The Thong Song" playing during her last rites.

Two men sitting at the tip rail were watching with interest. Another dancer would note that their suits weren't expensive, and they were only drinking beer, but they were up for a bit of fun and there was still money to be made. Another dancer would play up to them, give them some attention, smile to see which one liked her better, so that when she came off stage she could go straight over, that was easy money.

Emma didn't notice any of those things, nor did she notice the man on the right with the navy striped tie waving a ten-pound note in her direction.

This was the longest song she had ever heard.

She had lost track of time and couldn't remember what she was supposed to do. A Rolodex of men, and the way they looked at her began to flash before her eyes. Michael, former magazine editor and internet porn lover: at his apartment, staring at her naked back thinking she was still asleep. James, features editor and general hack: at the office, reflectively sordid, over his coffee cup. Max, childhood bully and first kiss: across the schoolyard, wiping his nose while scrutinizing her tree-climbing skills. Jack, father: in his study, self-consciously, at her sweat-wet transparent T-shirt after a long run in the park.

Emma decided it was time to get undressed. This was a relief, as it gave her something to concentrate on other than the concern that she was on stage at a strip club thinking of her father. She hurried to take her dress off, forgetting she was supposed to take it slow and tease. In her haste, she ended up with a foot stuck in her sleeve, her heel piercing through the sheer fabric like a knife through mosquito netting.

This violent assault on her new dress confused Emma. She didn't know why or how it had happened, and she decided to stop everything to investigate and solve the problem. Alas, her twisted bra strap had trapped most of her hair around it and Emma had to first free her bent neck before tending to the dress.

The man in the striped tie with the ten-pound note leaned forward in his chair. He was interested. Before she knew what she was doing, she smiled at him. He grinned, and placed the money in his teeth. Gratitude washed over Emma, her newly shorn dress, and her hair-eating undergarments. This stranger was offering her a tip, some recognition for her determination. Maybe she didn't look so bad up here in her bra and twenty-five-pound knickers.

Abruptly, Emma realized she was being examined in a different way than before; it was her choice, to be watched. There were men in front of her, beneath her, in their chairs, who wanted to look at her. She was fulfilling something for them by being on that stage. Emma's skin began to prickle, her hair stood at attention. She approached the man with the money and reached to take it but he pulled his head back and frowned.

The man beside him said, "Use your mouth."

"Oh, okay. Thanks for that," Emma said, and then thought how stupid that must have sounded. She tried to manoeuvre herself closer but her knee suddenly rolled underneath her and she slipped. She couldn't grab onto the side of the stage in time and she pitched forward, hitting her chin on the rail and then falling headfirst into the lap of the man in front of her.

Chapter 7

There is a moment—usually in childhood—when you discover the world is not as it has been painted, that you may have been misled in believing life will always be as it should be: right winning against wrong, good winning against bad. There's also a time when you begin to understand the power of people to disappoint you, of life simply being unfair. Funny enough, it didn't happen when Emma lost her mother. It was a few years later, when she met Cheryl Mercedes.

It started with romance. A man and a woman on a remote desert island, the crust of their broken boat left for driftwood against the chalky white sand. Miss Mills (ship nurse) lay in a torn cotton bodice, her bosom bursting through the delicate lace edging, slender, elegant arms outstretched toward Boon (deck hand), shirtless, muscles glistening in the burning tropical heat. Boon searched for palm leaves to build a shelter. They were *Lost in Paradise*.

Summers at Nana's house took their time, meandering through the weeks and eventually coming to a standstill as Emma's boredom found no borders. Jack promised this would be Emma's last summer in Dulwich, but he'd pledged that for years and she'd given up hope.

Until Cherylin Mercedes arrived, all the way from Houston, Texas, with her big white piano and piles of romance novels.

The day after Cheryl moved in, Emma wandered over and soon had an invitation to make herself useful unpacking the many boxes stacked in the dining room. Cheryl had racks of brightly coloured clothing rustling in plastic cocoons, a tall white dressing table with an ornate decorated mirror to match, claret red velvet baskets overflowing with antique dolls, makeup and magazines.

Cheryl told Emma she was going to put a pool in the over-grown back garden as soon as she could. "I've got the cutest little bikinis, but I never get to wear them!" she said. "Do you like swimming?"

"I prefer sports that are drier," Emma said.

Cheryl laughed. "You're right, who wants to mess up their hair?"

"England isn't as warm as Texas," Emma told her. "You might be better off putting in a solarium."

"That's a big word for a small person. You must be smart. Thanks for the advice, but I think I'm going to stick with my plan for a pool."

Emma blushed and focussed on a stubborn bit of tape on a container full of crystal. Even though she knew she would be careful enough to unpack them, she still made sure not to touch, just in case, and gingerly left them on the dining room table. She focussed on the next box, which was full of books—

nothing like the ones she had seen at her grandmother's, with Winston Churchill or Princess Diana's wedding—these all had pictures of pretty women with long, flowing hair, and handsome men that looked like soldiers or adventurers. There were boxes and boxes of them, with titles like *Mississippi Sunrise Over Heartache*. She was mesmerized.

One morning, as Emma and her grandmother washed the leftover dishes from breakfast, they peeked at Cheryl relaxing in her garden. Barely wearing a pair of skimpy denim shorts and a cropped Wham! concert T-shirt, she stretched out and took a sip of her drink through a spiral purple straw.

"Oh, it's a hard life," Nana said, rinsing off a glass and passing it to Emma. "Swans around with her expensive suitcases and flouncy hair. England isn't that kind of country. We don't flaunt ourselves like that." She sniffed and wiped her papery hands on her spotless apron. "Americans like to show off what they have, but that doesn't mean you have class. I wish I could spend all afternoon lolling in the garden while my hired help unloaded trunks of fancy underwear into the house."

Emma finished drying off the chipped coffee mug from Brighton Pier 1962 (the year the world started to go downhill, Nana said) and unhooked her big toe from the foamy split in the chair she was standing on. She climbed down nicely and folded the dishcloth over the handle of the cooker. She liked Cheryl's hair *because* it was so flouncy. And though Cheryl had lived in America, it was her husband that was American. Nana spent a lot of time in the garden, too. She might not have a moving man to carry boxes, but she did have Edward the bully with his bad teeth, who helped her with groceries and things around the house. Emma didn't say anything, otherwise she might be forced to stay inside today.

"She needs something to do with her time. It isn't good to be idle. Do you see me wasting away doing nothing?"

"No, Nana," Emma said. She didn't say that she thought Cheryl Mercedes was as beautiful as her name, as glamorous as the covers of her colourful books, in her swooshy yellow blouses and high heels, with hair the colour of burnt golden syrup.

Later that day, Emma saw Mr. Mercedes' majestic silver car parked at the house and ran straight across the lawn to ring the bell. The man that opened the door had thin, grey hair and a big stomach half tucked into beltless trousers. He was nothing like the men on the covers of Cheryl's books. He didn't even have a dimple on his chin.

"Well, hello there!" he said. "You must be Emma. Have you come to see my wife?"

People never were how Emma imagined them to be. "She was going to teach me about wraps."

"Wraps?" There was a cracking sound as Mr. Mercedes knelt down to Emma's level. "What are they?"

Emma hated it when adults spoke to her like they didn't know what she meant. Her father had started to do this. "For your head," she said. "It looks like you're a movie star. When you go out to the shops, or in the car with the top down."

He smiled. His teeth looked funny—too shiny, and the colour of the bathroom sink. "Oh yes, I know what you mean. Very glamorous. Cherylin is taking a nap. Why don't you come back later and learn about wraps?" He tweaked her nose.

"I will." Emma waited until he shut the door before crinkling her face up and sticking her tongue out at the mailbox. She didn't understand why Cheryl would be married to a man like Mr. Mercedes instead of Boon from *Lost in Paradise*. It didn't seem fair that Cheryl should have a husband like him, any more than Emma should have to stay at Nana's waiting for the summer to end. She would tell Cheryl how she felt—explain to her that she had made the wrong choice. She needed a man that would compliment her—a man that would come home from work early, a big bouquet of tulips in his hands, and walk into the garden where Cheryl was lounging, drinking a glass of juice. He would surprise her with a big romantic kiss. Cheryl would laugh and toss her hair, and he would pick her up and spin her around and around. Then they would see Emma, standing shyly in the background, perhaps holding an earring that Cheryl thought had been lost in the move, and she would be embraced too, with Cheryl declaring, "My little angel, you are wonderful!" They would adopt her as their own child. They would take her with them on their holidays around the world, on a big boat across the ocean. Emma and Cheryl would wear matching polka-dot bikinis.

Emma groaned and opened her eyes. She wasn't wearing a polka-dot bikini. There was no doting, smiling Cheryl Mercedes. There was, however, the bright lights of the Platinum dressing room, and several of the other dancers flitting around, taking a peek at Emma's bloody face, whispering and giggling to each other as they preened in the mirror. She was a new girl that nobody knew, but within minutes the dressing room was filled with people coming to check her out. Dazed, left half in the memory of Cheryl Mercedes, Emma struggled to focus.

Every time Emma thought about what had happened, she would start to float up above the dressing room, over the ripped and worn grey carpet with the chewing gum marks and the abandoned glitter shimmering from its edges, to watch the scene from above. Every time Emma saw herself falling into that man's lap, she became suspended next to a locker that no one used because the bent door didn't close properly—the one that held knickers, bras and stockings that had been left behind in a hurry to get home early, for once.

And Emma was really trying very hard to go home early, to tiptoe up the wide, curving staircase of her father's house, to fall onto the high bed with the soaring oak headboard and fanciful toile bedspread, with her limited edition Classics set in hardback on the night stand, where she would sleep peacefully until the next morning. A young woman languishing in bed, waking slowly to the pleasures of a fresh spring breeze and the hum of Holland Park. Slow-moving cars easing past the window, dogs barking with the glee of being walked by one of the children instead of a leash-tugging adult, and sunlight fighting the clouds to anxiously peek in at her before succumbing to the London grey. That sounded good. Oh, and her hair would have come loose from its elastic tethering, having revelled in a good nights' sleep, all knotted and untidy. She could picture it perfectly.

Well, she would be able to picture it perfectly if only the music piping in from the speakers overhead and the DJ's voice, calling, "Destiny, this is your FINAL call to main stage!" would stop bringing her back to the dressing room.

Since Cheryl, Emma had learned how to deal with people not living up to her expectations, but it was harder to deal with others' dissatisfaction in her. Even these girls, who she had never met before, were irritated by her presence. Her usual technique of heading off into the distance, separating herself from a bad thing, should have worked. But tonight, pulling out wasn't working. There was something going on inside, but what?

"Are you alright, luv?" Eileen was holding a big two-way radio to her ear, and it kept barking for someone to pickup door three. "It's only a scratch, heads bleed a lot." She held out a tissue. "Some of our best girls have had nightmares on stage—wigs flying off, tampon strings hanging out—everybody trips over. I'm sure nobody saw you."

"Change your outfit," said Bambi, standing nearby with a mouthful of hair pins. "No one will know." She began attaching a clip-on ponytail high on her head.

Emma knew everyone had seen it. Not just the girls, but the waiters and waitresses and bartenders and floor managers, not to mention customers. Absolutely every single living breathing thing had seen her fall, half-naked, off the stage. This image started to send Emma back to floating above the locker with the broken door.

Emma wanted to explain why she Could Not Go Back Out There. She wanted to say, "*I am afraid to think what I have done; Look on't again I dare not!*" but Eileen was unlikely to understand the amazement Emma felt from truly identifying with Macbeth's words. Oh, no one *ever* understood.

"Eileen!" The two-way radio wanted attention. Eileen gave Emma's shoulder a squeeze and left her to the blood-stained tissue.

Roxy put out a cigarette under the tap and called over, "Go home, sweetheart. You've no chance here."

Emma looked up too late to meet Roxy's eye, but she caught the gaze of several women, who wore bemused, unsympathetic expressions.

"Newbies..." one of them said. "Fucking hate 'em."

A brunette fiddling with an eyelash curler nodded in accord. "Who's the poor sod who's been buddied up with you?" she asked Emma.

Emma's "buddy," a girl named Bailey, had spent ten minutes walking her around the club pointing out which security men were "arseholes" and which were "gems." She finished Emma's induction by showing her how to get free cigarettes out of the machine in the toilets.

"I can't remember her name," Emma lied. "But she's not in tonight."

"Wait," said the brunette. "Tonight isn't your first night?"

Cue unrestrained laughter.

Emma's eyes burned with the start of tears, and she began rummaging through her handbag for something, anything. Her humiliation was turning into a palpable fear that these women might harm her for actually being inexperienced. Who was she kidding? She had no place being here.

A girl with the longest legs Emma had ever seen was sitting on the floor, touching up a chip in her toenail polish.

"Put away your claws, ladies," she said, twisting the cap back on the bottle and admiring her handiwork. "Girlfriend probably has a concussion."

The girls chuckled, softened, and went back to preening.

Except for Roxy.

"Who are you, Jade? The stripper police?" she asked. "Give me a break."

Jade stood up and flicked her waist-length, pencil-thin braids over her shoulder.

"*You* give me a break, Rox. I can't take the bitching." She turned to Emma and said, quieter, "It's 'cos you're new and you're cute. Don't worry about it."

"I fell off the stage," Emma said.

"Mmm, that sucks for you."

"Here's some free advice," said Roxy. "Put that fucking notebook away, you little swot. There's no quiz at the end of the night to see if you've been paying attention."

Chapter 8

Emma's weekday lunch breaks from *Oxygen* followed a standard routine: she picked up a sandwich from Marks & Spencer's on the corner, said a quick hello to Eddie at the flower stall and arrived at Anderson's Books in less than five minutes.

Over a hundred years old, with a grand, vaulted doorway and a rickety jazz shop in the back, Anderson's had fought the invasion of chain bookshops on Tottenham Court Road by maintaining a family-run charm. Staff were knowledgeable, if not a little grouchy. Flickering light bulbs hung from the paint-chipped ceiling. All five floors of stairs creaked. Anderson's was Emma's kindred spirit, her sanctuary. It wore its defiant quirks well, and she took inspiration from that.

Up on the fourth floor, around the corner from the (rarely visited) Military History section, were several tall bookshelves of second-hand fiction. Between these shelves was a small wooden stool that nobody knew about except Emma, and this was where she had her lunch everyday.

Except today. The stool was gone, replaced with a stack of boxes that didn't even look like they contained books, and two very unliterary looking builders standing nearby discussing a hole in the ceiling.

Emma didn't know what to do. She knew every nook and cranny of the shop and there was nowhere else she could go. She fought the urge to think about how Jane would handle this situation. She was starving.

"Hungry?" asked Ben, tucking his laminated work pass into his apron pocket. "That's some pretty aggressive tummy-rumbling."

Emma blushed, but she was relieved to see Ben, one of the floor managers at the shop. He knew the value of Emma's secret hideout; he never interrupted her when she was reading, and only said hello when she was on her way back to work.

Thinking of Ben (which she did far too often), Emma imagined he came from a large family—a boisterous, everyone-talks-at-the-same-time family. Raised to be studious and well spoken, Ben and his siblings of humble origins began working at a young age: folding clothes at the local laundrette or washing dishes at the Greek restaurant on the corner. Sensitive and unassuming, Ben had little escape from the craziness of the household—the numerous stray dogs his youngest sister kept bringing home, the pile of newspapers by the door his packrat older brother wouldn't throw away, not a moment's peace in the bathroom—so he worked tirelessly, at several jobs, in order to afford his first apartment, a tiny bed-sit to be filled full of books and car manuals in Islington, or Finsbury Park. Definitely North London, she would have thought.

Emma interpreted Ben's decision to work at Anderson's—instead of some dismal neon-fronted chain store—as a sign of his artistic-principled, anti-herd mentality. Ben's relaxed amble through the aisles, his untied shoelaces among the corporate suits clattering past to buy over-hyped bestsellers gave surprising comfort to Emma; he didn't care what people thought of him.

"So, how are you?" Ben asked.

"Oh fine," Emma said. "You know, same servitude, different day." Servitude? Jane Eyre was still swirling in her mind. Ben must think she was an idiot.

"I hear you. It's all servitude these days."

Emma smiled. Perhaps "servitude" was making a comeback. "Do you know—"

"The builders?" Ben shrugged. "Some sort of leak. Think you'll have to make do with a different lunch location for a few days. You're not stressed out are you? You look a little hot and bothered."

"No! Goodness no," Emma said, forcing a laugh that sounded more like the squawk of a maniacal bird than the soft rebuff she was aiming for. "Why would I be stressed?"

For as long as she had worked at *Oxygen*, she had followed her lunchtime schedule, sitting in her lunchtime location. Being forced to come up with an alternative never crossed her mind. That most people wouldn't consider a situation like this to be much of a dilemma didn't cross her mind either.

Ben yawned and rubbed his eyes.

"I need a nap," he said. "Early staff meeting."

Emma nodded and fished around in her jacket pocket to avoid watching Ben stretch his long sinewy arms over his head.

"We have ours after lunch," she said. "It's...um, better than the morning..."

Ben nodded, took a cigarette from behind his ear and rolled it under his nose.

"So, I finally quit," he said. "I just smell them now. Mmm...want one?"

"No. Thanks."

The way Ben looked at her as he coaxed the cigarette back behind his ear made Emma feel twitchy.

Ben leaned up against a bookshelf and crossed his arms.

A pretty girl carrying a box of books cut in between them.

"Hiya," she said. Emma was sure she winked at Ben.

"I better go," Emma said, tucking her book under her arm.

"Sure, see you later," Ben said, still looking in the direction the girl with the box had gone. "But hey, I can find you a seat in the café upstairs—you don't have to leave."

Emma shook her head. The café was noisy and smelled of burnt cheese sandwiches.

"I'll tell you what," Ben said. "I'm due a break now—why don't you have lunch with a real person instead of a two-dimensional one?"

Emma was back at her desk, hungry and frazzled, when she realized Ben must have meant himself.

———————————

"Gordon!"

Emma jumped. Sylvia stood at the door of her office looking hassled, her hair frizzy around her oblong face. "Let's talk."

Emma picked up her notebook, and then changed her mind and put it down. She saw the delicate flower pattern of her scarf squashed at the back of the drawer, and pulled it out and hastily tied it back around her neck. A timely, stylish knot would help in this meeting.

"Fill me in on everything," Sylvia said when Emma eventually came into her office stuffing the scarf into her skirt pocket. "How many nights have you worked at the club so far?"

"Well, let's see...a few. Four or five, I suppose," Emma said. The answer was two, definitely two.

"And you're out there—working, dancing, talking to the guys that come in the club, getting to know the girls that work there?"

"Yes." Emma sat on her hands.

"You don't sound very convincing. Jim went down to the club all week, and said you weren't there."

Emma tried to stay involved, but there was an interesting looking letter on Sylvia's desk that was challenging to read upside down. That would help to stop the waver in her throat. What would Jim have thought? She felt ashamed of what other people saw in her.

"I'm kidding!" said Sylvia. "But by the look on your face..."

"I've been clearing up some of my other work first," Emma said by way of explanation.

Sylvia sighed and opened a packaged sandwich, carefully removing the slices of cucumbers. "I've been in this business for a long time, and I know what we need for this feature. I want grit in a cute package. I want drama, I want truth and a non-corny ending that sums up the experience. Tell me what you have to do to earn money; tell me the other girls are being bitches to you. Make friends, enemies, whatever. That means you need to get your arse in the club and act like a bloody stripper. Do you hear what I am saying to you?"

"Yes. I think so."

"Really? Do you know what you want out of this feature?" Sylvia's sandwich gestured around at the office walls, crumbs drizzling down onto her desk. "This here. It's what you want. Do you know what that is?"

Emma admitted she didn't.

"Sure you do. It's what everyone wants."

"Their own office?"

"For some." Sylvia pointed at her prominently displayed Marcus Morris award. "Or, one of the highest accolades in publishing, maybe. Perhaps it's about being in a position where you decide what is worthy of publication, or it could be as simple as writing something that really gets people talking, challenges you and your audience, makes you learn something about yourself to write it. I am giving you that shot. Not to be in my position, mind you—forget about that—but to get your foot on the ladder. I assume that's what you want."

Emma nodded.

"Tell me if I'm wrong, but you've got to have a desire for something in this business. I'm not one to give pep talks—personally I think they're condescending—but I feel you have a real chance here." Sylvia smirked. "I think you're afraid to do this. That is what I think."

"I'm not afraid to do it." Emma said, and started chewing on a thumbnail. She considered putting on her scarf.

"Obviously you are. You're having difficulty talking to me about it here."

Emma decided to be honest. "Sylvia, I feel like a complete outsider with these girls. I don't really know how to bond with them. They're these incredible creatures—well not *creatures*—but they're so foreign. They are the most beautiful women I've ever seen, and they're this bizarre combination of hardness and overt feminine authority. They're so mysterious...and so frightening." She frowned. "I don't know how

I'll ever convince anyone I'm one of them. The first night I went into the club, which I am at a loss for words on how to describe, and—"

"Give me the end of the story Emma, not the beginning."

Emma paused and tucked a non-existent piece of hair behind her ear. "It may be that I'm not the right person for this story."

"No shit. What is it; you don't want to get naked?" Sylvia spoke like she could never imagine Emma had breasts or a sexual nature any more than the cucumber slices limp and gasping on her desk. "Why did you volunteer for this then, if you didn't think you could do it?"

That was a good question. "I don't really know," Emma said. "I'm not entirely sure, really."

Sylvia took a deep breath. "That damn James and his ideas," she said, throwing her half-eaten lunch at the bin and missing. "I nearly vetoed the idea after I'd thought about it properly—seemed a bit sensationalist to me, not to mention your inexperience in doing this type of feature. Plus, you do have this bizarre lack of social dexterity."

Emma shifted her attention to Sylvia's bread crusts left on the floor.

"If you're finding it hard, I can understand that, anyone would. But remember, you're not one of *them*, you're a journalist. Think of it like what's-her-face studying the gorillas in the mist. This is the type of story that can open up a lot for a writer."

"I hear you," said Emma.

"So, give me the gossip. What was the audition like?"

"I didn't have to audition, they took me on straightaway."

Sylvia frowned. "Well, that's shit."

"They seem to hire in huge numbers," Emma said. "There are over two hundred girls on their books."

"You're kidding?"

"It's a very large club."

"Do the girls have to pay a percentage of their earnings to the club?"

"No. Well, yes. You pay eighty pounds as a house fee when you arrive, then you keep everything else you make."

"Can't wait to see your expenses."

Emma wondered if Sylvia planned on picking up her bread crusts. She suspected her boss was a secret slob—she looked the part of a professional, together person, but she really wasn't. She imagined Sylvia's apartment—everything minimalist, nothing on the bookshelves or tables, but if you opened a cupboard door you'd be buried in old newspapers or hat boxes and a heavy pink bowling ball would narrowly miss your toes and roll past you down the hall.

"They have a training program called the Platinum Academy," Emma said. "I'm going to try that."

"What on earth are they going to teach you?"

"How to use the pole, how to talk to customers…"

"Fine. But don't let it run on into the story—I don't want a piece about how to become a stripper," Sylvia said. "Oh, and it might be best to keep what you're doing to yourself. Other than your closest friends, I'd let everyone read about it long afterward, rather than put their oar in when you're trying to bond with the underworld."

Emma stifled a laugh. Who would she tell? She certainly had no intention of talking to Jack about this. If he hated her university education going to waste while she wrote about a new celebrity vacation spot, she couldn't really see him flushing with pride and joy over this assignment. She imagined her opening line: "They've brought in a mandatory G-string dress code at my office." Oh yeah, that would go down a treat.

She had tried to tell her father things before. When she was nearly expelled from Holby Primary (for rather brutally hitting Kelly Johnston with a wooden ruler and leaving her crying in a puddle), Emma tried to state her case to Jack. She tried to explain what Kelly said about Emma having no mum. Everyone in the schoolyard had heard—they were all reminded that Emma had no mum. As if they didn't know already.

If she had a chance to explain, maybe Jack wouldn't have been so angry for being interrupted from his busy office to come down to the school and apologize to Kelly's parents and pay the doctor bill, which he said had been greatly exaggerated.

Jack yanked Emma all the way to the car, halting any of her protests by telling her NOT TO TALK RIGHT NOW, followed by a tirade about how she couldn't keep hitting other children or he was going to send her away somewhere. That shut her up. She didn't want to spend another summer away.

Sylvia gave Emma a long look. "I'm sure that somewhere behind those glasses of yours that should only be worn by women no longer of childbearing age, there is a young woman with some form of ambition, and bravery who can do this piece. I believe in you, Emma."

"Thank you."

Sylvia began laughing. "I'm being completely sarcastic. I don't believe in you anymore than you believe in you. But, I don't *not* believe in you either. I want the feature. And in a sick sort of way I like imagining you suffering to give it to me because that's what true journalism is about. Well, as true as it can be when that bastard MD of ours wants to turn us into a gossipy rag mag. If you knew half of the nonsense I had to do when I first started out...reporting on textile fairs in Swansea, covering the birth of a new elephant at the Bristol zoo—you've got it made, let me tell you." She looked at her watch and stood up. "Enough. The summer interns will be piling in next week, I'll give you one to pass over some of your work to. Let's talk in a few weeks. Don't screw this up or I'll fire you. Kidding. I'm kidding!"

Chapter 9

Eleven o'clock and the Platinum restaurant was buzzing. A large table of silver-haired men in tuxedos stood having a raucous toast as waiters wheeled out their chateaubriand. In the back corner, an American supermodel famous for her risqué European photo shoots animatedly whispered to her date, a well-known British architect. The girls were flocking to a table of International rugby players who were ordering champagne, cigars and lobster for everyone.

Emma spotted a man sitting alone at Platinum's main bar and approached, walking carefully in her newly purchased Perspex-heeled stilettos. The central bar of the club had been designed for maximum impact; this was no ordinary, run-of-the-mill locale. A staircase with tiger-print carpeting led dancers up to a tall, narrow stage that ran across the front and side of the L-shaped bar. Velvety red lights spilled down onto three shiny poles running up to the ceiling. Closer to thrones than stools, the plush bar seating was designed for two things: placing customers directly in front of a vast display of expensive liquor, and an unparalleled view of beautiful women taking their clothes off. Bailey had told Emma that dancers liked the bar stage because of the view it afforded into several private rooms, to see what girls were making money from which customers and to see who was at the coat check to spot a potential high roller before the rest of the girls did. The bartenders loved being eye-level to hundreds of pairs of legs, and always left free drinks at the feet of their favourite girls.

"What's your name?" The man Emma had approached finished signing a credit card slip and looked her up and down.

"Emma. Nice to meet you."

"What's your *real* name baby?" He put his hand on her back and pulled Emma closer until she was wedged in between his legs with a bar stool trapping her from behind. "I know how these places work. That's your stage name."

"That's really my name."

"I'm Paul."

"Hi Paul. So, tell me, have you ever been to Platinum before?" Emma was sure this sounded forced, but she overheard Bambi say it to a man at the bar last night, and he spent the whole night with her at a champagne table.

"You're new aren't you? I know all the girls in here and I've not seen you before. I'm going to let you know right now that I won't be going to have a dance with you, so don't bother asking. I don't have dances. I'm not that kind of guy." He waved toward the stage. "That's nice and all that, but it's too impersonal here, I prefer a more private dance."

"You don't have to have a dance on the main floor," Emma said, reciting what Elaine told her last week during a Sunday training session. "We have rooms that are more private," she added, forgetting to say that it was a better place for them to "get to know each other better," or that "she could relax more and let go" in a private room, with just the two of them, away from the crowded main floor.

Emma was supposed to make the man think he was getting special treatment, but it was a complete con. The private rooms were far from it; they had space for over a dozen people, small windows that people walking past could see into and a hefty security man standing in the middle of the room watching everything that was going on.

"Emma, baby, don't try to hustle me," Paul said. "All the girls know me here, you can ask. They know I don't have dances."

Emma nodded, unsure what to do next. Paul's hand began to weave a message on her back. She cringed.

"How long have you been working here?" he asked, his voice wet with booze. "Look, why don't we meet up sometime, forget this club environment, it's so fake."

"I really couldn't..."

"Why not?"

"It's against the rules of the club. It's not allowed."

"Yes, yes, very good, but I'm not from the council, so you can save that speech."

"I don't know you. And really, it's not allowed."

"How would anyone ever find out if you see me outside the club? It makes much more sense for me to spend my money on taking you out for the night instead of blowing it in here."

"Well...it's just that...I really shouldn't."

Paul took his hand off her back and signalled to the bartender for another drink. "Your loss," he said, turning away.

Emma wasn't sure what she'd done wrong, and was relieved when a girl named Destiny (whom Emma recognized from the dress rack on her first night) stomped over and climbed up on a bar stool in a huff. Her tiny, toned abdomen sprung to life as she exhaled, contracting into six little squares. "I am so wound up!" she said to no one in particular, crossing her legs and hitching the bottom of her slinky Lycra dress over to one side.

"What happened?" asked Emma.

Destiny paused, seeming to consider Emma's status, then turned and began speaking to the bartenders. "I swear, I hate you men sometimes," she said. The bartenders rolled their eyes and continued to make drinks.

Destiny reconsidered Emma. She pointed at her drink. "Can I?" she asked.

"Sure," Emma said, pushing her glass of wine in Destiny's direction.

"I forgot to tip Mike last weekend," Destiny said, between gulps. "So when I go onstage tonight, he plays *The Birdie Song*, like he's a flippin' comedian. *And*, just now I spent the longest time working this guy in the restaurant and all he did was buy me dinner. He didn't give me any money."

"Oh…"

"I should have arranged it with him, but I never do the restaurant. He had plenty of cash, trust me. He sent me to do a dance for his friend and paid me with a fifty—he had a great wedge of 'em, he's loaded. So I thought he was a player, and knew the score. When he asked me to have dinner I figured I was paid." She exhaled angrily, making her fringe fly. "An hour and a half I sat there when I could have been dancing."

"I've done that too," Emma said. "It's hard because some guys seem like such high rollers you don't want to offend them by talking about money so blatantly." She didn't know what on earth she was talking about.

Destiny finished Emma's drink and thumped it back down on the bar. "You know what the worst is? When you sit and talk to a guy for I dunno, ten minutes, because you know he needs a bit of time, one of those that you can't rush, and then when you ask if he wants to go have a dance he says he can't because he's 'gotten to know you' and feels weird about it. He didn't know me ten minutes ago, but now he knows me too well to see me naked. What the hell is that about?"

"You know what I hate?" Emma said. "One time, I was talking to this guy and the entire time we spoke he kept his Maserati keys on the table." Emma had seen this happen at a table last night.

"Wanker. Like that's gonna turn you on to see the car he drives." Destiny's skin glistened under the lights—her intimidating perfection softened. "Well, actually…please tell me you got money from him."

"A little, but he was more interested in talking about himself and his exciting life," Emma said. "What should I have said to get more money? I never know."

"Just that you really want to get to know him better, spend more time with him, but it'll cost money."

She made it sound so easy.

An attractive man in a blazer walked up to the bar and ordered a Bloody Mary.

"Hey there…" said Destiny. "What's your name?"

Smiling, the man introduced himself as Jackson.

Destiny's body language had completely changed. She was leaning forward, wrapping a strand of hair around her finger with her head tilted to one side. "Jackson...I love that name. I'm Destiny, nice to meet you."

Emma asked the bartender for a refill of her wine, and when she turned back to Destiny, she was hopping off the stool, hand in hand with Jackson on their way to a private dance.

Damn it. Emma stood up and rubbed her hands across her goose-pimpled skin and tapped each heel on the floor to stop her toes from hanging over the ends of her shoes.

"Your feet aren't hurting already?" asked Terri, a pretty waitress in the Platinum uniform of a long, body-hugging tuxedo jacket, boy shorts and fishnets. "Still a good four hours to go before closing time."

"I'm not used to the shoes," Emma said. "I don't understand how you stand in them without toe overhang."

Terri said, "I saw you talking to Paul at the bar. Don't bother with him, babe. He's pathetic."

"He seemed a very insincere person."

Terri raised an eyebrow. "Yeah, that's one way to put it. Arrogant twat is another. It may be busy tonight, but the punters that are here are complete tossers. I've not gotten a single tip yet—guys are scraping their change off my tray before I can blink. Have you done any dances yet?"

Emma shook her head.

Terri pointed out a man across the floor. "What about that one over there. By himself. The blue shirt."

"I don't know..."

Terri tapped Emma's bottom with her drinks tray. "Go on, do it. You could be his dream girl—you never know."

Emma went over to the table and said hello. Marcus seemed friendly, but soon she was struggling to steer the conversation in a private-dance direction.

A private dance, Emma had been relieved to discover, was much easier than getting up on stage in front of everyone and using the pole. A private dance meant a lot of eye contact, slow moving, and running your hands over your body like you were really enjoying the music and the company. *Really* enjoying it. It was posing more than dancing; it was swaying, wiggling and flicking your hair a lot. It went really quickly and it seemed very false, but Bambi assured her it worked.

"If you feel nervous, think about the money and remember you are completely in control," she had said. "This bloke thinks you're good enough to spend money on just to be able to look at you, remember that too. And focus on being sexy—it's like acting. 'Kay? You're acting like you're this little sex pest. Always ask if they want another dance. You'll see how easy it is. Unless they're cute—then you're in trouble."

Shadows kissed the fabric-draped walls of the private room where Bambi demonstrated for Emma the most seductive ways to move. The polished pewter wall lamps cast a soft glow onto Bambi's smooth, toned skin. The music seeped in, muffled by the thick carpet. The air rested heavier on the soft, woven fabrics of the sofas and mahogany end tables. The private rooms felt less intimidating to Emma than the vast exposure of the other club areas.

Bambi let the straps of her dress fall off her shoulders and made her eyes really wide. She leaned in toward Emma. "See how I make it like I want to kiss you? I look at your lips, then I smile or I play with my hair—you get it? You gotta make him think he is the only person in the entire world you're interested in."

"I'm embarrassed," said Emma, looking up at the ceiling as Bambi's nipple nearly took her eye out.

"Don't. Look at me," said Bambi flipping her hair over her shoulder and leaning in so it tickled Emma's face. "Don't I look like I'm totally into you?" She moved forward and exhaled slowly in Emma's ear.

"Yes, but..."

"No buts. He is paying you to act into him. You say you're embarrassed now, but once you see how ga-ga the guy is when you get 'em out, you'll be loving it."

So Emma got 'em out for Bambi, who said she needed to slow down and take her time, but was very complimentary. "You have a great bod, but you take your dress off way too quickly. And your bra comes off much slower—not until the absolute last second of the song, so the guy wants to see more, and he has to pay more."

"I don't really know how I'm going to get anyone in here in the first place," Emma said.

"You need to be more hands-on before you take them for a dance," said Bambi. "You're not flirty enough."

"I thought we weren't allowed to touch?"

"Only when you're giving a dance. You can practically sit in their lap if you've got your dress on. You're definitely not touchy enough." She took Emma's hand. "You need to sit a hell of a lot closer to them. He's the most interesting person you've ever met. Touch their arm when you talk, you know, stroke their arm. You have to massage the money out of them. Hold his hand, rub it—you're a little genie."

Emma resolved to memorize this. She wanted to look at least a tiny bit like she was supposed to be there. She wanted to come swaying out of the private booth pulling her dress down, or stuffing her little satin purse with handfuls of money like the other girls. It was an uncommon feeling for her to want to fit in so badly, but her desire to belong outweighed any inertia she had about taking off her clothes.

"So what's your job like?" Emma asked Marcus. She leaned closer to him.

"It's stressful. I work in finance. I enjoy it," he answered, making eyes at a girl doing a handstand off the pole. "Today was crazy, so I've come in to unwind before I head home."

Their conversation was anything but sexy. More like the dialogue you'd have with someone on a train. At a champagne table on the other side of the stage, two girls sitting with a man in a suit were giggling and laughing like old friends. One of them toyed with his shirt buttons while gazing into his face, hanging on his every word. The other girl had her arm around him, playing with the back of his hair. She had his tie around her neck. Maybe they did know him from somewhere.

"I don't mean to sound rude," Marcus said, "but you really don't seem like a stripper."

"Sorry?"

"It's your manner. The way you are, you're obviously smart if you're referencing Shakespeare...but you don't seem like the other girls here."

"I'm sure there are girls in here that know Shakespeare."

"Don't think so. But it's not just that, you're too smart for this, really, you shouldn't be in this place. We've been sitting here for what, ten minutes, and you've not asked me for any money or if I want to have a dance. Trust me, that isn't like the other girls."

"Do you want to have a dance, Marcus?"

"No. Thanks. Really. You're very nice—and very pretty. Maybe later," he patted Emma's leg like it was the top of a cab driving off with his wallet inside. "Thanks."

Emma passed Terri on her way back to the dressing room. "If he's in the club, he can buy a dance." Terri nodded toward Marcus, who was being dragged off to a booth by a tall redhead. "Never let them say no."

Emma wanted to ask Terri if she was such an expert on stripping why wasn't she working as a dancer instead of a waitress, but she didn't. Instead she smiled and headed through the double doors marked Private.

Chapter 10

Much as she wanted to (and she *desperately* wanted to), Emma wasn't going to quit the assignment. Not yet, anyway. She wanted to believe this was because of her desire to impress Sylvia, to make her mark at the magazine with some intensive background research and ballsy reportage. But the truth was that Emma couldn't bring herself to quit because of good old-fashioned nosiness.

The women at the club were layered in contradictions, unbreakable yet exquisite, closed off but so sexual. When she added these women to their club habitat with its surreal glamour of a million-dollar music video set and its sober reality of chewing-gum-sticky backstairs, the battered cigarette machine that stole your money, the round podium stages by the restaurant with onyx floors that showed deep shoe scratches when under the unsympathetic house lights at the end of the night, Emma was left with such curiosity for this alternate world she could taste it.

Although Bambi seemed surprised by Emma's invitation for lunch, she agreed to meet her at a sushi bar in Knightsbridge, and arrived laden with shopping bags in a whirl of designer sunglasses, skin-tight jeans and lip gloss. She sat down in front of the conveyor belt full of sushi plates chugging by and threw her fur-trimmed handbag on the counter. "I'm starving!" she announced, grabbing the first plate that took her fancy and popping a roll in her mouth without soy sauce or wasabi. Or chopsticks, Emma noticed.

"It's nice to see you," said Emma, arranging her napkin on her lap and looking for a waitress. "How are things?"

"Good," Bambi said with a dramatic swallow. "I've spent a week's wages on Sloane Street though. Oh, well." She gave Emma the once-over. "The contact lenses are good. When are you going to get your hair done?"

Bambi and Eileen had both told Emma she had to get hair extensions. "Do I really need to?"

"Do you want to make money? Everybody has them," Bambi said pointing at her dark, shiny hair. "It was such a good look when Tanya did your makeup and put that hair-piece on you."

Once (and only once), Emma got roped into having a makeover with Susanna. She had been surprised by the face looking back at her in the mirror and she kept finding excuses to see her reflection—borrowing Susanna's compact, saying she had something in her eye and ducking into the bathroom when no one was looking so she could marvel at the transformation. Then Jack saw her. He stared until Susanna nudged him in the ribs, to which he shook his head and grumbled, "You look just like Imogene." Emma was astonished; Jack never mentioned her mother.

The wedding was only three weeks' away and showed no sign of being cancelled. A sharp, sticky pain in her stomach called out to her at this thought. And still, Jack never mentioned Imogene. That hurt nearly as much as not knowing where her mother was.

"How long does it take to be good at it?" Emma asked Bambi, remembering her decision to never think about the wedding. "Not just using the pole, but to go up and talk to people?"

Emma's time at the Platinum Academy had taught her one thing: she needed a lot of professional help. The pole would come—that was a matter of stamina-building and technique. She needed to work on her flexibility and strength, and was surprised at how physically demanding it was, but the dancing was just a series of elongated poses and flowing movements. She couldn't get her head around the sales pitches or making conversation with strangers who were in the club just to see her take her clothes off. There was nothing natural about it, and she couldn't imagine ever being able to do it.

Bambi took another three plates of sushi off the revolving rack. "Not long," she said. "Like they tell you in training, practice makes perfect. No one is profesh when they start. Five, six months and you'll be amazed at the difference."

"I don't have six months."

"I know, I know, you need the cash, everyone does. You'll work your ass off and you'll make money. Don't worry, even stupid, ugly girls make money. And I'm not saying you're ugly—you'd be cute if you fixed up a few things. The contact lenses are definitely working for you."

Emma felt drowned in her duty to *Oxygen*. She didn't feel like bombarding Bambi with queries; she didn't feel like herself. Maybe that was for the best, if she was going to get this article done. She pictured Sylvia and her tortoiseshell fountain pen's disapproval. She imagined not being able to carelessly leave a copy of her groundbreaking, most-talked-about, edgy cover story on Jack's desk and instead, having to endure the same conversations about her lack of ambition for the rest of eternity. What bothered her the most was knowing there would always be that trout-sized flip-flop in her tummy that she had let down every character she had ever read about, every character that had let Emma share their adventure, but she wasn't prepared to take one on herself.

Bambi stuck a neatly manicured peach-coloured fingernail between her front teeth and pulled out a bit of seaweed. "It's not rocket science," she said. "You shake your ass in their face, they fork over the cash."

"I still can't get my head around how everything works," Emma admitted. If the Platinum Academy held exams, she would be the first to fail.

"You walk around the club and find guys to talk to. Easy peasy, lemon squeezy."

"I need more information than that," Emma said.

Bambi sighed. "Okay, most girls try to get money from doing dances, which is fine, but that means you have to go to, like, twenty people to make money you could make off one or two. It's all about regulars and sit-downs."

"Sorry," Emma said. "What is a sit-down? Sounds painful."

Bambi didn't laugh. "It's like a VIP thing. You *have* heard of that, right? If they want to go to a VIP room and have you spend time with them, they have to pay. You charge for the time you sit with them. Therefore, it's a sit-down."

"What *exactly* am I charging for by the hour?"

"Your time." Bambi looked affronted that Emma wouldn't know this.

"I'm charging someone to sit and talk to me?"

"Yup. You negotiate an amount for an hour. You decide how much—but never less than 250 quid. You have to think about how many dances you could get during that time. Or just how much you think you can rob them for."

Sylvia would never believe this; Emma would need a signed affidavit to prove this happened. "What are you telling them they're going to get for their money?" she asked. "Are you promising sex?"

"The dumb ones do. Honestly? It's how you sell it," Bambi said. "You say: 'I'd love to spend more time with you but I have to work. But if you can pay me for my time, I'll stay here with you for as long as you want—I'll be *all* yours.' You put on a sweet voice and talk about how much fun it will be getting to know each other better, and how you can't wait to dance for him—all that jazzerati." She took a gulp of her drink. "They buy it."

Emma tried to think back to what it was like starting other jobs. It had never seemed so confusing or scary to be shown how to use the research library or call a press office. "What about the dancing?" she asked.

"You really ask a lot of questions."

"Sorry."

Bambi's face hardened as she paused to let off a melodic belch. "Last bit of advice, and I'm out. If you're gonna survive a minute at Platinum you seriously need to sort yourself out. First of all, don't let the other girls see you're bricking it; they'll use that against you. No one's at Platinum to make friends. This is business—everyone wants the big money, everyone wants to be the queen bee."

Emma silently picked at her napkin.

"I'm not trying to bring you down, but this isn't your typical office job," Bambi said. She laughed. "Thank fuck for that. Does your local secretary get the cover of FHM or get to be a Page 3 girl three times already this year? Don't think so. Does your friendly neighbourhood recruitment consultant get flown to Milan to go shopping with footie players?"

"That actually happens?"

Bambi cocked an eyebrow, looked smug. "Last year Destiny's regular bought her a Merc."

Emma nearly gagged on her tuna roll.

"Straight up," said Bambi. "And she's a fucking pheasant farmer or something in the daytime! Driving around the stables in her convertible! This is the best job you'll ever have, sweetheart. I'm best mates with Chanel. You've heard of her, right? She's the queen bee, she runs Platinum. Stick with me and you'll be handling some serious business. You're working tonight, right?"

"I guess…"

"You *are* working. Thursday's a big money night. Hey, you'll be fine. You should have seen me when I first started! I really had no idea. I was so timid and shy." She rolled her eyes. "God, I used to be such a loser! I'm like a totally different person now."

"Er, no," said Sylvia, crunching Emma's notes into a ball and pitching it toward the bin. "Really. I don't like the angle. 'The psyche of the stiletto?' What the hell is that about?"

"It's about the power of the shoes." Saying it out loud didn't improve it. "Let me explain—I've noticed that there is this sort of transformation that occurs as soon as the girls put their high heels on. They're like a sort of armour, I think."

"No, no, no," said Sylvia. "You're focussing on the wrong things. Talk me through this. Did you try out the day shift this week? What was it like?"

With less than thirty girls working, and customers rare until late in the afternoon, the day shift at Platinum was an entirely different animal—the women were older, not as attractive and, frankly, they looked like strippers instead of the untouchable stars of the evenings. Emma was intrigued by this, and was sure they would have stories Sylvia would warm to, but she knew not to mention it. Sylvia wanted the glamour of the nights. And so did Emma.

Regardless of the extra pressure and competition, it seemed much too strange to leave the club and walk out into daylight into a world she couldn't escape. The difficulties Emma had inside the club (approaching customers, mastering the pole) were a breeze next to dealing with Jack's impending wedding, her solitary flat and doubting *Oxygen* colleagues. Out the window of her afternoon taxi, the working world continued without her. Everyone wore their identity like a flag—the secretary in her low-heeled court shoes and respectable skirt; the art student in his second-hand army jacket, black leather portfolio under his paint-stained sleeve; but Emma's trade was squashed down inside a gym bag, weathered and sweat-stained.

"The story isn't in the day shift," Emma said. "But it's given me a view into the hierarchy of the shifts—the day girls are on a much lower rung than the worst night-shift girl. I'm looking into the chain of command on the evenings between the girls. Not much on the men at the club yet. I'm working on that."

"How's the stage?"

"I'm getting better on the pole," Emma said. "I've even learned a few tricks." She pulled up her sleeve and proudly showed Sylvia a purple bruise forming above her elbow.

"I'm a bloody genius commissioning this," Sylvia said, staring off into the distance with a faraway look in her eyes. "Now, I appreciate you wanting to show me your work in progress on this, but I'd prefer to wait until you've truly got something going on in there to talk about. First rule of journalism, don't tell the story until you have something to say. Undercover work takes time. Getting into the mindset, unearthing the dirt, getting the girls to trust you…three weeks isn't enough time for that. You'll find your angle—and it won't be about a pair of stilettos."

"The girls at the club are the story," Emma said. She filled Sylvia in on her lunch meeting with Bambi.

"Why is she helping *you*?" Sylvia asked, looking genuinely interested in Emma for the first time. "Does she help all the new girls? It's interesting that she's giving you advice and taking you under her wing. I thought it would be more competitive."

"So did I," Emma said. "She's been really nice to me."

"What could you have that she could possibly want?"

That was food for thought. "I'll find out," Emma said. "Perhaps she likes to be in the all-knowing role. If Bambi wants to take the credit for moulding my career, fine with me."

"What's the pecking order? Maybe she wants to add you to her cluster of girls. Is she the top of the food chain?"

"Don't think so. Bambi seems popular and she's so gorgeous it's mind-boggling, but no."

"Who is?"

"Chanel."

Chanel's air-brushed photo adorned many of the posters and advertisements for the club. According to Bambi, she used to date a Formula 1 driver—Bambi couldn't remember which one, but he was "well minted." That was all Emma knew.

"I love these dancer names," said Sylvia. "Brilliant. What's yours?"

"I've just been using my real name."

Sylvia was visibly astonished but didn't push it. "Okay, so Chanel is number one. Why?"

"I haven't met her yet," Emma said. "But I've been told she's the queen bee—she must be making the most money."

"Sure. It will be more than money, though," said Sylvia, looking thoughtful. "Find out who's trying to take her crown. *You* should be trying to take her crown, by the way. Are you going home to get some sleep now?"

"No, I'm going to the club," Emma said.

"You look tired."

"I'm fine."

"You're okay with this, right?"

"Yes, Sylvia, I'm fine."

Sylvia nodded decisively, spinning her chair around to look at a multicoloured wall chart. "Miss Gordon, you're officially on the editorial calendar."

Chapter 11

"How did you get started?" Emma asked a girl named Carmen, as they wolfed down their midnight meal of stodgy baked potatoes and mayonnaise-blanketed tuna in the dressing room.

"Usual way, really," Carmen answered. "Needed money. I wanted to buy a car, hated my job, wanted a change. Here I am."

Under the bright fluorescent lights, Carmen had terrible acne-scarred skin invisible out on the main floor. "How long have you been dancing?" Emma asked.

"Started on the sly when I was seventeen."

"How old are you now?"

"Twenty-two. I'm so old! I'm gonna quit next year, you know. Honest. I'm gonna open my own salon. I've started saving all my money now."

"Does your family know you're working here?"

"Uh uh. No way. They think I'm a podium dancer in a nightclub—like, legit. I don't hardly speak to them."

Emma nodded, poked at an odd-coloured bit of potato. "No one knows I'm doing this."

"No point in getting everyone excited for nothing, 'cos I ain't stopping."

"Me neither," Emma said. "I am not stopping." She liked the way that sounded. "You know what? My mum would probably support this." She glanced at Carmen in the mirror.

"No shit," Carmen pushed her plate to one side and prodded around in her purse.

"Really. She's the liberated type. Women's empowerment, stuff like that."

"Empowerment? Fuck off."

"I'm saying she probably would get a kick out of it."

"So tell her."

Emma could picture the scene. It wouldn't be any different than how it had been, Jack disapproving and Imogene flying around without a bra on, but she had a feeling it would have been fine. Her mother would have been happy to discuss the politics of women's rights until the sun came up. Imogene was cut from a different fabric than the rest.

Nana Gordon certainly thought so. Not a summer would go by without her telling Emma the same stories about Imogene over and over—she wanted home schooling for Emma and Nana had to step in to veto it because Jack would have agreed to anything. Then there was the one about Imogene wanting to take Emma to Portugal for her fourth birthday. As if Emma could possibly remember anything of the trip later—how wasteful. And the most frequently brought-out tale of how Imogene let a very young Emma cut her hair with dangerously sharp scissors.

Emma thought she might want to be a hairdresser as well as a famous actress, so Imogene said Emma would be her first customer. She said she was tired of her hair and wanted a change, but Emma made a mess of it and Imogene had to get it all cut off in the end. Emma cried because her mother's beautiful hair (that Jack loved so much) was all gone, but Imogene was happy. She kept looking in the mirror, stroking the nape of her neck, faraway in thought. She said it was how she used to wear it back in America.

Emma couldn't understand it. One day Imogene was there, sitting on the sofa in her homemade sundress with Jack's head in her lap, and the next day she was gone. And all she took was a handbag.

What Emma should have been worrying about: Jack. His wedding was a less than a week away.

What Emma was worrying about: how Roxy did such powerful spins on the pole using only one hand.

Jade strutted across the back of the main floor under the appreciative scrutiny of several men. She saw Emma, smiled, sat down beside her and asked how she was doing.

"I'm fine," Emma lied. She wished Jade hadn't sat down so close to her. She should be watching her from a purely objective point of view, but she was quite simply awestruck by Jade. This was hard enough, Emma didn't need to be so close to something she would never be.

To drive this point home further, Jade leaned forward on the table and rested her head on one hand, giving Emma a posed three-quarter profile of dark almond-shaped eyes, sculpted cheekbones and mahogany cleavage bursting through her neon pink tube dress. Emma liked Jade (not least for defending her early on in the dressing room), especially after seeing that the inside of her messy locker was covered with photos of her two baby boys. She was always late because her husband never got home from work on time to babysit, and Emma would find her in the dressing room, painting only the toenails that would show through her open-fronted shoes.

"Can I ask you a question?" Emma said. "What's been your worst night here? I'm having a nightmare out there tonight. Again."

"Worst night? Don't get me started," said Jade. "Once I had a three hour sit-down with a guy and he left without paying."

"I've not even earned my house fee," Emma said. "It's nearly midnight."

"Oh, don't worry about that. Lot's of girls make their money late, when the guys are paralytic from the booze."

"Really? How?"

"You can do twenty dances in a row because the guy's in love and can't remember how much he's spent already."

Emma smiled. "I'll remember that. If I ever get a dance."

"Some have been known to lift a wallet or two from an intoxicated punter," Jade said, leaning in. "But you didn't hear that from me."

Emma was shocked. "Who? Which girls?"

"Mostly the Russian contingent," Jade answered, examining the end of one of her braids and starting to re-plait it. "I hate those bitches—they're making all the money now. Oh! I remember a bad night...Okay, picture the scene: I had the worst migraine. When I was at the bar, the strap on my dress snapped and I had to stick it together with Kat's nail glue because I didn't bring a backup. My hustle wasn't working, and then when I finally did get a dance, the guy tried to steal my purse. My empty purse."

Emma clucked with delight. "That's fantastic."

"Cheers. I'm not finished, though. So I start talking to this guy and he spills his beer all over me and then he fucking fell over. I step over his ass and move on to the next guy and he's a spitter—every word he says is this fountain of saliva on my cleavage. And he tells me that he has a dick that looks like an acorn and would I like to see it?"

"That's awful," Emma said. "Are the men frequently vulgar?"

"Frequently vulgar?" said Jade. "You've got some vocab there, girl."

"I'm working the thinking-man's sophisto-crumpet angle," Emma said, reminding herself to stop acting like a journalist.

Jade burst out laughing. "That is the perfect persona for you! Men love the innocent librarian type who's buck-wild underneath."

"Thanks...I guess all the girls have personas, then?"

"The ones that are smart do. Gotta protect your mental health, you know?"

Emma considered the sexy librarian angle. Could she really pull it off? What would she wear? How would she act? "Can you tell me how most girls choose their alter egos?" she asked. "Is it something discussed—"

"You know what I hate the most?" Jade said, leaning her head back onto the back of the sofa. "When guys ask me how much money I make. I'm like, 'How much money do *you* make jerkoff?'"

Emma thought about this. "That is really rude," she said. "It's as if the normal social boundaries aren't at play anymore."

Jade gave her a funny look.

"I mean," Emma thought quickly, "that shit is messed up."

"For real. One night, I asked this man for a dance and he said he was looking for a very specific type of girl, and I was *definitely* not it. Then I hear him saying to his friend that he wouldn't have sex with a single one of the girls in the club." Jade recoiled at the memory. "Like we're offering!"

Emma smiled at Bambi, who was strutting past with a customer.

"Bambi still helping you out?" Jade asked.

Emma nodded. "She's been great. Really nice about everything."

"Do-gooders in strip clubs are either really, really stupid, or really, really smart. Guess which one Bambi is?"

"What do you mean?" Emma asked.

Jade raised her eyebrows, clearly not about to elaborate. Emma knew a warning when she heard one, but what was Jade trying to tell her? Wasn't she friends with Bambi? Mapping out the girls at the club in her mind, Emma wondered if she'd missed something—the divisions in the club seemed arbitrary. She filed this away for later.

Roxy finished dancing on restaurant bar and joined them while she put her dress back on. "Fabulous," she said. "You seen who's in the restaurant tonight?" Tugging on her shoulder straps, Roxy pointed out a well-dressed older man chatting with one of the waiters.

"Oh, snap," said Jade. "I didn't even see him."

"You know who that is, newbie?" asked Roxy.

Emma shook her head.

"I thought Chanel was still in Spain." Jade sighed. "Emma, honey, prepare yourself."

"For what?" asked Emma.

"The Phillip and Chanel show, that's what," said Roxy, acridly.

Jade gave Emma the background:

A regular customer of Chanel's, Phillip had been coming to Platinum for over a year, and the club rolled out the red carpet as soon as he arrived outside in his chauffeur-driven Bentley. He was a high-level executive in banking or a property mogul or something, and he came to see Chanel (and Chanel only) on the last Thursday of every month. He was in a class all his own. He would buy every dancer any drink she wanted and frequently order a dozen bottles of Cristal when he arrived, just in case he wanted them (and he never did). The waitresses or the doormen ended up taking them home.

Phillip was happy to speak to other girls at the club, Jade explained, but he only spent money on Chanel. Trying to change this was a futile, dangerous mission that would only end in embarrassment and Chanel at your throat.

Mike's deep baritone rumbled over the loudspeaker as he announced Chanel's stage show. Emma straightened up and let her anticipation drown out Jade and Roxy talking. She had been waiting to see Chanel for nearly a month; she was eager to see what the fuss was about.

The lights went out. As Emma's eyes adjusted to the darkness, an electric guitar rang out. Atmospheric, ominous chords began playing over a subtle, moody rhythm.

I can feel it coming in the air tonight, oh lord...

The skin on Emma's arms rose into goose flesh. The song was nothing like the other music played at the club—it was so slow, so wrought with drama and tension. The lights around them began to rise back to their normal, low candlelight levels, but the stage remained dark.

A red spotlight shot onto the stage, focussed at the bottom of the pole. It softened and widened to reveal the silhouette of a woman hanging upside down, halfway to the ceiling.

Chanel's right leg was wrapped around the pole, her head thrown back, and her back arched. Her left leg hung loosely toward the floor, continuing the "C" shape created by her back, so fully arched that her head was just inches from her hanging left foot. The only areas of her body making contact with the pole were the outside of her ankle, the inside of her thigh just above the knee and an inch of her left hip. Her arms extended gracefully back—she created a shape Emma would expect to see a gymnast or a trapeze artist make, like a gazelle: fluid, athletic and powerful.

A spinning mirrored light began to bounce jewel-sized splashes of colour off the stage floor, picking up on the sparkling cinnamon-red fabric of the outfit Chanel was barely wearing: a halter bandeau top that tied around her neck leaving her back completely bare. Second-skin-tight high-cut short-shorts with cutout sides. Both were woven with red sequins in the front and stretch glitter fabric at the back. Six-inch stilettos with a cerise ribbon tied at the ankle. Her body was as much as part of the outfit as the fabric she wore. Lines of softly defined muscles in her stomach and thighs, smooth, taut skin over her back and shoulders.

Chanel brought her hanging leg up and pivoted her body to face the pole. Using her legs as control, she slid slowly down, head first, her chest lifted up and away from the pole, arms back. Just before she reached the stage, she put her hands onto the floor and released her legs from the pole, into jack-knife splits as she held herself in a handstand.

"Wow..." Emma said.

Jade nodded. "She's the queen."

Chanel was, as Emma had expected, larger than life—a sugary, full-haired blonde with anatomically impossible proportions, a small, turned up nose, full pouting lips, dark chocolate eyes.

She was every stereotype of what men wanted.

And as far as stereotypes go, she was a magnificent one; Emma felt like she was watching a movie star performing as a stripper, not the other way around. Chanel was fire and ice: sexual, strong, delicately girlish, intimidating and inspiring, inclusive and completely untouchable.

Phillip had moved to sit in one of the chairs at the tip rail by the front of the stage, holding what looked like a very thick roll of money in his hand. The only people she had ever seen with a roll of money were on television; even her father didn't carry cash like that.

After a moment of watching Chanel dance, he stood up and leaned across the front of the stage to tip her by throwing a handful of several fifty-pound notes in the air over her head. Poppy red Queen's heads fluttered down around Chanel on their seesawing, leafy descent to her feet. Red. Red. Red.

Chanel took a dizzying spin around the pole, her head thrown back, her hair flowing behind her. She winked at Phillip as he continued to throw more and more money on the stage, as if he was casually tossing a losing hand of cards across the blackjack table.

Strobe lights. The music building. Emma felt she was witnessing something rare, something she would never be able to describe to anyone. She was unable to override the rational part of her brain telling her to remain unbiased.

She forced herself to look around the club, which had come to a standstill. All eyes were on the stage. The bar patrons had turned into cardboard cutouts. Not even a bartender dared to pour a drink.

"Where does the money come from?" Emma asked.

"Don't know," said Jade. "He's a big gambler. Casino money, probably."

After a slow hip roll, Chanel confidently wiggle-walked toward Phillip and waited patiently as he tucked a solid wedge of cash under the side of the thong, which she was lifting up out of her shorts. He alternated between throwing money in the air and tucking it into the waistband and sides of her shorts.

"The money skirt," Jade and Roxy said in disgusted unison.

"Wow," Emma said again.

"What gets to me," Roxy said, kissing her teeth, "is no matter how much money you make tonight, it's ruined for you. Doesn't matter if you're on the roll of your life, you're shit, you know? You're nothing compared to Chanel."

"Notice she still hasn't taken off her top yet?" Jade said. "She's the master of stretching that out to the absolute last second of the song. Make them wait for it..."

Phillip said something to Chanel, and she threw her head back to laugh wickedly, riotously. The aura of intensity was broken by this private moment; she became sexier than before. Though her eyes never left Phillip's, Chanel didn't forget this was a show for everyone. She broke away to dance toward the pole, effortlessly gliding into a tight corkscrew spin.

Emma turned to Jade. "How did she get to be the queen? I need to know."

"She worked her ass off."

Roxy shook her head. "She's a prozzie, innit. No question."

"So she's having sex with him?"

Roxy hesitated. "She must be! Him, and Tony, all the customers. I know she's flashing guys in the private room, too."

"Flashing?"

Roxy wiped at her button nose and sniffed. "Yeah. That minger's lettin' em see inside her knicks—"

Jade held up her hand to stop Roxy. "Chanel is a hustler, pure and simple. You see how Destiny is constantly working, never letting a single guy sit for a minute without getting onto him? Chanel's a different kind of hustler. She looks for guys that are after her type. Guys that want the girl they could never have."

"The fantasy," Emma said.

"Hell, yeah. You're selling something that *doesn't* exist," Jade said, with a smirk. "This is total fantasyland. They get their perfect woman, and you get rich."

Roxy laughed. "That's the best part."

Chanel began coaxing the straps around her neck off, millimetre by millimetre. She turned her back to the audience and pushed her halter top over her stomach and down past her hips. In a seamless move, she had flicked it onto one foot and kicked it toward the stage exit. She cast a teasing look over her shoulder, and gently lowered herself to the stage floor. Like a cat with the thickest, richest, fine bone-china saucer of cream, Chanel crawled across the stage and purred at Phillip. She dropped her head forward, paused for the music to build and then flicked her tousled, bouncy mane of platinum blonde hair over to one shoulder. She dipped her chin and smiled coyly at Phillip, her eyes electric, before laying down and stretching out on the stage as if she was waking up from a deliciously long and naughty dream. She rolled over, giggled, and sat up on her knees, covered in money that clung to her glistening bare skin.

"I want to be like that," Emma whispered.

Jade took a cigarette out of her purse. "Leave yourself at the door," she said, "and you're halfway there."

"But...how exactly do you manage to do that?"

Jade smiled. "Simple. You just pretend to be someone else."

Ah, now that was something Emma *could* do.

Chapter 12

Emma sat sweating on the sofa, waiting for her breathing to return to normal. It was her third run in two days and she'd finally caught the fatigue she'd been chasing. Purposefully, she sniffed an underarm. There was a certain rawness about her odour that was true and just. She should go take a shower. That would require her to get up again, though.

Emma's flat wasn't a generous host to her perturbed state. Neglected and well aware of her preference for her father's house, it showed its resentment over her recent late nights with a heap of junk mail under her feet, a fridge full of stale, wrinkled tomatoes, and a bleating smoke alarm battery.

The long shadow of fear that had been following her crept into the room and Emma nearly choked on it. Today was Jack's wedding.

She didn't want to go.

"No good can come of this!" she cried. Feeling that wasn't quite dramatic enough to express her hopelessness, Emma threw her head back on the couch pillows and kicked off her trainers. With mild interest she watched one shoe land behind the television, the other under the window with the dust bunnies. She blew tiny spit bubbles through her pursed bottom lip and spent ten minutes seeing how many different sounds she could make by doing this. She tried to see how long she could go without swallowing. She counted how many seconds she could keep her eyes open before blinking. She counted the plaster roses in the cornicing of the ceiling.

She really didn't want to go.

Three hours' sleep combined with the onset of a truly earnest despair over the wedding this weekend had resulted in Emma making a few big decisions.

The first had been to go to a Platinum girl–approved hair salon and get long, thick caramel and chestnut brown extensions woven into her hair. Styling this hair that belonged to someone else was proving difficult for Emma. With some effort, she managed to scrape it all back into a decent ponytail for today's events. Not the same impact as she had imagined, but it was all she could manage.

Armed with new hair, Emma felt courageous (and panicked) enough to ask Ben from Anderson's to be her date. When he accepted her invitation (after she convinced him she wasn't making a joke as he had initially thought—this removed the courageous feeling and replaced it with more dread), Emma was pleased, though she couldn't shake the feeling she had talked him into it a little bit. Regardless, she had no time to marvel at his acceptance; she could only think of Jack and Susanna.

Jack's betrayal—and it was a betrayal—was not the first. Emma had come to view his behaviour with women as a separate entity to who he was. Compartmentalizing that aspect of her father was the only way Emma could keep it away from her, but it kept coming back, it would not die.

Cheryl Mercedes had warned Emma about this, saying men functioned on a base level that was much different than women. Cheryl told Emma many things about men long before she was ready to hear them, and most of her advice and endless stream of anecdotes on the laws of attraction, relationships and feminine wiles was never fully digested.

"Men are much easier to understand than you think," Cheryl told Emma one afternoon in her back garden. "This boy is being mean to you because he likes you."

"You don't pinch people if you like them," said Emma, spreading suntan lotion on her burned toes.

"Does he pinch anyone else?"

"No, just me."

"He likes you. Do you like him?"

"How could I possibly like someone that pinches me?"

"Why don't you ask him to stop? Be sweet, and tell him if he stops pinching your legs you'll hold his hand at lunchtime."

Emma was shocked. "Eeuuw! He picks his nose and never washes his hands. He always has grass in his hair. He's horrible. He's not my type, Cheryl."

"Oh, really? What is your type, then?"

Emma shrugged. "I don't know, but he's *not* it."

"Put him in a hot bath, brush his hair, and he could be good husband material, you never know."

"I don't care about getting a husband. I'm *never* getting married."

"Well, one day you will care. One day you'll have to figure out how to be independent, worldly, strong, have a career, marriage and still be sexy and manicured. Even if you pull all that off, some people will try to punish you for being sexy and manicured."

"Like who?"

"Men, women, grandmothers…" Cheryl smiled. "My advice for today, Little Miss Pinchy, is no matter what you choose to do with your life, never give up the things that come naturally with being a woman—your sexuality—you give that up, you lose your power."

Emma's ears pricked up at the word "sexuality." "How do you give up your…sexuality?" she asked.

"By pretending it doesn't matter. And it does matter. You're going to be a beautiful young woman soon and instead of boys with snotty noses, you'll have handsome, important men looking at you in a certain way. Don't be afraid of it. Never let anyone make you ashamed of it. Don't make a fuss when you're noticed for your beauty instead of your brain."

"Why?"

"It's normal; men like to look at pretty things."

Emma chewed this over.

"As long as you have self-respect, there's nothing wrong with it." Cheryl struck an exaggerated pin-up pose. "No man in his right mind could resist me in this bikini, but only my husband gets Cheryl Mercedes, mind, body and soul. I'm telling you, marrying Alex was the best thing I ever did! For him too— his friends are jealous because their wives don't care about looking cute or asking them how their day went. He feels more of a man since he married me."

"It all seems very complicated," Emma said dourly.

Cheryl pulled Emma into her lap and began to un-braid the intricate rows she had plaited in her hair earlier. "It's not. A man's power is in his ability to earn money. A woman's power is in...there!" She pointed toward Emma's crotch.

Emma felt apprehensive. What was it doing in there? How did you get it out when you needed it? Why would you ever need it?

"You see how hard your father works? That's because the more money he makes, the more powerful he feels."

Emma thought of Jack falling asleep on the sofa, too exhausted to read to her or play games, puffy, bruised bags under his eyes. "I think mostly he feels tired," she said.

Jack's car pulled into Nana's driveway.

Emma stiffened. She twisted around to look at Cheryl.

"Well, this is a nice surprise," Cheryl said, snapping a hair elastic around her wrist and squeezing Emma's shoulders.

Emma didn't like surprises, and ones that involved her father were rarely cause for celebration. "I better go."

"You're not going anywhere. I want to meet the father behind the fabulous daughter."

"You won't like him," said Emma.

"Nonsense," Cheryl said. "We're back he-re!" she called when they heard the car door slam.

Jack approached, suit jacket slung over his arm, designer sunglasses hanging out of his mouth by the stem. "You must be Cheryl," he said.

Cheryl gave an affable tut-tut. "I see my reputation has preceded me. Again!" She tickled Emma, who tittered nervously; she didn't know what Jack would think of this.

Jack kissed Emma on the forehead (he never did that!) and said, "Jack Gordon, it's nice to meet you."

"And you," said Cheryl, pushing her sunglasses up through her hair and shaking Jack's outstretched hand.

"Is this how you're spending your summer holidays, Emma? Soaking up the sun and watching the grass grow?"

Emma wasn't familiar with Jack's light-hearted tone, or how to respond to the playful wink she just received. Why was he pretending to not be surprised by a bronzed, romance-novel reading, bikini-clad woman embracing his daughter?

"Oh, she does more than just that," said Cheryl.

Jack raised an eyebrow. "I see she also has her own personal hairdresser."

"We were messing around," Emma said quickly. "Cheryl was about to take it out."

"Don't," Jack said. "It looks nice. It's pretty. Very exotic…" He was speaking to Cheryl, not Emma.

"It's not considered exotic where I come from."

"In Dulwich, it's exotic, take my word for it." Jack loosened his tie.

"Perhaps."

"I meant no offence by saying exotic—that's my anglophile foot-in-mouth disease—it's inherited at birth."

What on earth was this?

"What part of the world are you from, Cheryl?"

"Originally, St. Lucia, but I've lived all over the world, most recently Texas. I did spend a lot of time in Belize when I was younger."

"I've heard Belize is an incredible place. You know, Emma's mother was from Brazil—"

"How come you're here on so early on a Friday?" Emma asked. "I don't think Nana was expecting you."

"A place called Rio Branco, near Bolivia. Do you know it? She often spoke of how beautiful the land was."

"In places like Brazil, Belize, much of South America, the

beauty is breathtaking, but it's a very harsh place to live—I could never go back," Cheryl said. "The divide between the haves and have-nots is too great. There are few luxuries available if you're poor." She said to Emma: "Pumpkin, you know how I need my luxuries? Well, can you imagine I had to go outside to use the toilet when I was growing up? I had to crawl out of my bed in the middle of the cold night, though the long grass full of snakes and spiders and who knows what, with a tiny little flashlight to see where I was going. I was very happy when I moved to America!"

Emma didn't answer Cheryl. She was watching Jack, who was staring at Cheryl's legs and not being discreet about it.

"I'm sure America was very happy when you moved there, too." Jack said, setting his car keys down on Cheryl's wrought-iron garden table.

Emma wriggled free of Cheryl's grip and got off the thickly cushioned sun-lounger. "Jack, how come you're here on a Friday?" she demanded.

"Finished early. How have you adjusted to living in England, Cheryl? I hope London's treating you well."

"Jack, how come you finished work early?"

"Emma, adults are talking right now."

Cheryl said, "Very well, thanks. I prefer to live somewhere with a little history, America is such a *bebé* compared to Europe. I love the British sense of humour, and I love the accent, I could listen to it all day long." She sounded like she was coaxing a cat out of a tall tree.

Jack picked up the crystal pitcher. "Can I top up your drink?"

"An English accent and a gentleman, too? My, my. Emma, you'd better keep an eye on your father!"

Emma was way ahead of her. "Jack, why have your cheeks gone so red? Are you embarrassed?" She stomped off to find Nana who for once would be an ally.

Ben arrived early, when Emma was still in the shower. Hopes of being ready, relaxed and psyched up were dashed. She buzzed him in the front door and grabbed an old blazer hanging in the hallway as a cover up.

"Hello!" Ben said, smiling a wide cartoon character grin. He produced a very professionally put together bouquet of flowers from behind his back.

"Thanks, come in," Emma said, stepping back to let Ben in at the same time as he leaned forward to kiss her cheek hello. They executed a chicken-headed dance before Ben's lips connected with Emma's ear. Emma wasn't able to take the flowers Ben held out because she needed to hold the jacket—much too small for adequate coverage—closed. "You're early."

Ben looked at the puddle forming at Emma's bare feet and cleared his throat. "Do you want me to wait in the car while you get ready?"

"No, it's fine, really." She had soap in her eyes and it was starting to burn.

Ben looked *good*.

When Emma had invited him to the wedding, she didn't actually think he would ever accept, and then she reassured herself she would be able to manage bookstore Ben. But he was different away from Anderson's. No casual khaki pants or frayed flannel shirt? Ben's dark, lightweight suit was obviously well-made, his shirt stylish and subtle, with shoes she recognized as Jack's favourite brand. The flutter in her stomach turned to a flap.

They smiled at each other.

Ben took a look around the front room. "Get yourself ready," he said. "I can amuse myself poking through your book collection—looks like you've got half of Anderson's in here." He laughed and glanced up at her.

Emma noticed Ben's expression changed when he looked up at her—his eyes suddenly became like two pots of coffee on the boil. What would Cheryl make of it? She would remind her that she was standing in front of a man wet, and naked in just a jacket. She would remind her that men were visual creatures. Emma allowed herself to consider that Ben might be attracted to her. Perhaps today won't be so bad, the thought, heading down the corridor to get dressed. As she passed a mirror in the cluttered hall, Emma realized her jacket gaped at the waist, offering a mighty view of her freshly scrubbed chest. She gasped, sucking in a mighty breath and slip-sliding her way down the hallway into her room, shutting the door and pressing her forehead into the wood. As she exhaled she tried to send the air out through her bulging eyes until they exploded.

The Susanna-approved vintage bridesmaid's dress that Emma never got properly fitted for was still sitting in the closet of Jack's house, along with the rest of old Emma's life. The only things in her flat remotely suitable for a formal wedding were ghastly. (A long cotton skirt from a Sunday market nearby and an olive-coloured blouse with fabric bumblebee trimming on the neck—did she seriously used to wear this out in public?) She supposed they could race to Jack's and get her dress, but she had no idea where she'd left the keys to his house. Since she started her Platinum work, she'd rarely gone to Jack's—too much to explain, too much to hide.

Her heart, her head, her stomach, all were weighted with a dark, black trepidation. She couldn't bear it, she didn't know how she would be able to stand next to Susanna and watch her erase Imogene. This wasn't going to be a date she could escape from—one of the big glossy society magazines would be there to photograph every guest's every move, to immortalize in air-brushed perfection her new stepmother and all her glory. They lived for weddings like this, in the glorious English countryside, with a slew of imported A-list couples, celebrity chefs and designer-frock spotting.

Emma knew fitting in would be impossible, even if she wore the right dress and brought the right date. She could never pull it off. She brought Cheryl back to her mind. How would she carry herself, how would she handle this? With her head high, and a knockout gown that put the bride to shame, that's how. Emma had a thought of rebellious brilliance—she had that new dress she bought at the club last night, the one Bambi told her was a real "money-maker." It was a beautiful gown—a little flashy, with its gold beading across the chest, but all the better to show Susanna and Jack how independent of them she was, how well she was handling their union. She could picture it now: Ben, debonair and generously endowed with good hair and Italian import shoes, Emma, gorgeous and lush in attire, grace and elegance surrounding her every move. The church would whisper excitedly at their arrival. They would be sharing a private, intimate joke and—

Emma heard Ben trip over the stack of catalogues in her bathroom. (Catalogues were perfect for imagining the lives of the "normal" models whilst soaking away the evening in the bath.) It dawned on her what the flat must look like to an out-sider: the loo with its designer sink covered in nests of dental floss and old toothpaste moulded to the drain entry, tissues and newspapers overflowing in the small silver bin and the disorderly row of G-strings hanging to dry over the shower rod. Not good.

"The cleaner hasn't been!" Emma yelled out at the same time as Ben flushed the toilet. It didn't matter. She didn't have a cleaner.

She finished getting dressed, straightened and smoothed her long ponytail and dismissed any niggling warnings over her outfit as nerves. She hoped Ben's bookstore self, his mix of easy confidence and bumbling erudite charm would carry forth to the wedding because she had little space left in her head to create adequate conversation.

She met Ben in the hallway, weakly returned his smile. She wanted to cling to him and push him away at the same time. She wanted to tell him she was terrified and ask if that was a ridiculous or justified emotion. She wanted to know if this was it? Was this all she was, a little girl stamping her feet and pouting because her father had moved on, after years and years and years of nothing left to wait for? She wanted to move past it all but didn't know how. "Shall we go?" she said.

"One question," Ben asked. "Is collecting a wide range of fluorescent coloured thongs a hobby or are you just concerned with being able to be found in the dark?"

Emma opened her mouth, waited for a well-formed sentence to come out, knew that wasn't going to happen, and closed it.

They walked out to the car; she couldn't tell Ben that his shoe had a long piece of wet tissue trailing from it.

Chapter 13

"You and your father—are you always like this?" Ben asked after seeing Emma and Jack's self-conscious exchange when they were seated at the head table of the wedding reception.

"Are we always like what?"

"I don't know, but that was…awkward."

Emma didn't answer. She was staring at Jack across the table, who for some reason was acting like she didn't exist. That was fine. Right now, Emma barely existed anyway.

Held in Somerset, one of the most unspoiled areas of the country, a tranquil bowl of lakes, parklands and bright green hills, the wedding consisted of an elaborate yet traditional ceremony. The church, with moss meandering up its weather-worn stone walls, was perched at the edge of a wide lake with a moat encircling it. Candles and pink water lilies were set afloat in the water creating a mood of old-world romance. The area was private and secluded, so remote that it had no electricity supply and was over eight hundred years old. Emma was drawn in by the simplistic beauty of the church and the surrounding estate—a Grade II listed manor house with a watermill.

It was a fairy tale setting that moved many to tears, including Lottie, who sat to Emma's left on the bum-numbing pews, dabbing at her eyes with a silk handkerchief and sniffling throughout. Jack was sombre and staid during the reading of the vows—Emma had expected a joke, a wink toward his friends during the "richness and poorness" line, but he locked eyes with Susanna and never looked anywhere else.

The entire service and celebratory reception was far from the London registry office Emma was sure Jack would have wanted. He hated this sort of spectacle. He was "new money and proud." Surely he couldn't have wanted such pomp for a second wedding? The invitations came in a sheer blue silk envelope filled with rose petals. Susanna's dress had a twenty-foot train. She had twelve bridesmaids. Guests were requested not to wear white or lavender. Dinner was a six-course meal prepared by one of the best known chefs in England.

Emma had been invited to take part in far fewer photographs than she had thought she would be.

Ben cleared his throat.

Was he bored? Annoyed he had accepted Emma's invitation? Wishing he was with one of those pretty girls that always came to visit him at Anderson's? "Jack and I have one of those slightly cantankerous relationships," Emma declared, in lieu of anything better to say.

Ben raised one eyebrow. "Cantankerous? I think that's the first time I've ever heard that used in a sentence." He nudged Emma playfully. "Hey, do you think part of the reason there are problems is because you call him Jack?"

Emma dropped her shoulders. "Very funny. We've always used first names in my family—my mother insisted on it. My father and I have never seen eye to eye on anything."

"Fair enough," Ben said. "My father and I have opposing views on just about everything you can have opposing views on. He hates that I work at Anderson's—says it's 'beneath' me."

Emma started to touch Ben's leg in reaction and stopped herself. "Really? That is exactly how Jack feels about me— I mean, my job."

"What is it that you do at *Oxygen*?"

"Actually," Emma said, "I'm on a top-secret undercover assignment right now."

Ben thought she was joking and took the moment to get another glass of wine.

"Can I have everyone's attention please?" Jack announced over the noise of the jazz quartet who had launched into an energetic version of *Wonderful Tonight*. "I'd like everyone to raise their glasses and toast my brand-spanking new, perfectly exquisite ball and chain!"

Susanna nudged him with her elbow. "Ball and chain? Well, what did I expect?" she said, kissing him on the cheek. "Never change, darling."

"Join me in this celebration, enjoy the music, enjoy the food. We've got some kind of rare and ludicrously expensive animal on the menu..."

"I think it's yeti grilled over moon rocks," interrupted George, his magenta silk cravat slightly askew.

"...and enjoy the beautiful surroundings arranged by Susanna's wonderful sister Lottie and our wedding planner—"

"How the lovely Lottie has remained single, I simply do not know," said George, throwing back his champagne before the end of the toast.

"Shut up, George, you're drunk," said Jack. "Right, I'll keep it short. To my fantastic new wife, Suzy, I love you. Here's to our healthy, happy future together. Cheers all!"

Emma got up to find the bathroom. She had the sense of an unwieldy load of a thousand disappointments and a hundred regrets clinging to her shoulders as she walked; it took most of her energy just to get across the room. It was all she could do not to lay down on the peach-tiled floor and take a quick nap. She needed to get it together. She spent as long as she could in the heavily scented bathrooms, washing and drying her hands twice, re-applying her makeup, fussing with her hair. She stared at herself in the mirror. How little they knew about what it was like to live for so long under the radar, as a person without expectation. How little Jack understood what it was like to live with so many unanswered questions that you turn yourself inside out trying to make sense of it all.

The bathroom door swung open. Susanna and Lottie poured in, satin-fronted energies of pearls, perfume and not-so-hushed collusion about which guests looked atrocious at the reception.

"Hello, Ems!" said Susanna. "I'm so pleased with everything. Doesn't Jack look handsome?" She gave Emma a sturdy look. "I really, really love your father, you know that, don't you sweetie?"

"She knows," said Lottie going into one of the bathroom stalls and leaving the door open. "It's all over his face—it's pure love for you, Suzy."

"I knew you weren't going to wear the dress I got for you," Susanna said. "And it's ok. It really is. I understand your need to make your own choices, even if it *is* my wedding." Her voice cracked. "I'm not being funny—really. I'm fine. You look lovely. Your outfit is very...Las Vegas, isn't it? Lottie, you saw that fabulous vintage gown I had for Emma didn't you?"

"It *was* fabulous," said Lottie, looking around for some toilet roll.

"Would you please shut the loo door!" exclaimed Susanna.

"I did plan on wearing it," Emma said. "I had forgotten it was at Jack's and, I've been so busy lately..."

A squeal came from under Lottie's stall. "I know why she's in that slutty dress. She's trying to impress her new boyfriend!"

"Of course!" said Susanna. "I understand completely. God, when Jack and I first met we were so..."

"Like rabbits," said Lottie before flushing.

"We love Ben," said Susanna. "He is so..."

"He's fabulous," Lottie said. "He's like a great, big, tall, gentle giant. We're all getting on like a house on fire. He told the most hilarious joke at the church—"

"Very scrummy," interrupted Susanna. "We've got to have him round for supper."

"How in God's green earth did you get together with Sally Wright's nephew? Talk about eligible bachelors!"

"How *exactly* did you meet?" asked Susanna.

"Who's Sally Wright?" asked Emma.

"Did he ask you out, or did you ask him?"

"We met at a bookstore near *Oxygen*," Emma said edging toward the loo exit.

"Wait," said Lottie. "You asked him out, yes? You were the instigator—"

"See you both out there!" Emma called over her shoulder, letting the door slam shut behind her.

"We're not staying," Emma told Ben when she returned to the table. She finished his wine and then her own.

"It's sorted." Ben said. Floaty skirts and tuxedos flew by on the dance floor behind him. "Susanna already had a room booked for you at a B&B down the road, so I rang them and got myself added to the guest list. Separate rooms. Don't worry," he added.

"I'm not worried." Emma said. *Did she look worried? Did she not have things to think about more important than a B&B reservation?*

"Good, because they didn't have an extra room," Ben said with a smirk.

Jack started dancing with Susanna and Lottie, taking their hands and spinning them in to his chest without a care in the world.

Emma lifted up out of her seat and pulled her dress flat before sitting back down on it. "We're still not staying," she said, continuing to watch Jack over Ben's shoulder.

"You're a tough negotiator…I like that. OK, you win. I'll sleep in the car."

Emma counted to ten. "Ben, we are not staying. I want to go."

Ben's confusion sat on his lips. This was the first time he stood incongruous to the high-class wedding setting he was both comfortable and well-coordinated with. No rolled up shirt sleeves or chunky sports watch beeping on the hour for him today, no polyester blend Anderson's apron detracting from his impressive physique—it was as if he had been to a dozen such events last week alone. After what Lottie said in the loo, he probably had. Emma became quite sure Ben had accepted her invitation out of pity.

Ben stacked his knife and fork on his plate and pushed it away.

"Emma, I've been drinking...I can't drive back to London."

Emma checked the back of her neck to make sure her necklace was done up.

"You're a big guy; I don't think three glasses of champagne will fail a breathalyzer."

"When you said supper in the country, I didn't know it would be at your father's wedding reception!"

Emma was glad the alcohol she had had was subduing her grating conscience at being unfair.

"It was a last-minute thing...for me to bring a date."

"To a wedding? You didn't think you had to bring a date to a wedding?" Ben asked.

"It is my father," Emma said, in defense. "I didn't think I had an attendance quota to meet."

Ben knitted his eyebrows.

"I don't see the point in staying overnight."

Emma wished Ben would stay in the role she had cast him to play, as silent accomplice and supporter, but he was illustrating yet another error of her judgement. He had opinions.

"We've both been drinking is the point," Ben said. A waiter came over to collect some plates and Ben moved out of his way. "I didn't even know I was coming to a wedding. Isn't there some kind of a brunch in the morning? Lottie had mentioned—"

"Fine, forget it. I'll drive. Give me your keys."

Ben laughed. "You have got to lighten up. It's a wedding! Let's dance."

"What? No. I don't want to."

"Come on," he pulled Emma to her feet. "It's illegal not to have a good time at a party."

On the dance floor, Emma found it hard not to dance leading with her hips, not to undulate and roll her pelvis around to the music. Everyone seemed so straight and boring and regular. She imagined jumping on the stage with the band playing and performing, to have the room wrapped up in her spell in admiration. Before she realized she had the thought, she was kissing Ben, pressing her body as hard as she could into him, swallowing down the taste of tears in her throat.

Jack appeared. "I'm cutting in," he told Ben, and pulled Emma away to talk by the swan-shaped ice sculptures.

"Hey, we were in the middle of a song," Emma said, slightly garbled.

"Hey, you're acting insane," Jack said. "And you're embarrassing me. What are you doing in this fucking getup?"

Emma's last thread of confidence began to unravel, but she refused to show any emotions to her father.

"This is a very expensive dress," she said. "I thought you would approve."

"It's inappropriate. Why didn't you wear your bridesmaid dress? And where did you meet this one?" Jack gestured at Ben, who Emma saw had no trouble sourcing a dancing partner in Lottie.

"You hate it when I don't have a date, and when I do bring one, they're never 'satisfactory,'" Emma said.

Jack stepped in close to Emma and touched her hair.

"So different," he said. "Your clothes...why so different?"

"I fancied a change." She hoped she sounded nonchalant. She took a cigarette out of her dainty money purse purchased from the dressmaker at the back of the Platinum Club change room.

"You're smoking now? What next, a motorcycle and a leather jacket? You're rebelling about a decade too late, mate."

"It's just a cigarette." Emma's voice wavered. She wished it hadn't. She wanted to be strong and somehow defiant—she had done nothing wrong. (She had done nothing wrong!)

"I hope this shit isn't about me and Susanna," Jack said taking the cigarette out of Emma's mouth. "Because that would be so incredibly infantile." He dropped the cigarette in a vacant wine glass after taking a quick puff.

"Baby...?" Two manicured hands wrapped themselves around Jack's tuxedo and Susanna's sapphire tiara appeared over his shoulder. "Come and say thanks to the Morgans please, they have to leave early."

"In a minute, baby," Jack said. "We're just talking shop." He unhooked his chest from Susanna's fingers and kissed her hand.

They watched Susanna wander off. How wonderful it must be to live in Susanna's head, where green meadows and fluffy lambs co-existed with blonde frosted highlights and deep sea-salt facials.

"She looks really beautiful," Emma offered. She was breaking under the pressure of losing another parent, no matter that Jack was the reason she only had one; it was too hard to stand up to him. She made an attempt, it didn't work. To be completely alone in the world? It simply was not a possibility.

The doubt in Jack's eyes made Emma search the table for a glass of alcohol, perhaps labelled "Drink Me" in welcoming handwriting. She wanted to shrink away, to slowly slide under the table, where she would recline beneath the frozen swan and catch water from its thawing rump in her wine glass. She would never need to come out. She would stay there, with the misfired corks and lost car keys, until the building was put up for sale and bought by an eccentric billionaire who would marry her and never ask questions about where she got her tiny satin handbag.

"You're trying, Ems," Jack said, "and I know why. But shit, if you're going to do it, at least get it right. Knocking back wine like it's going out of style, dressed like a..." he lowered his voice, "hooker. What, are you trying to impress your new boyfriend? Just between you and me, kiddo, I think he's out of your league."

"You're being horrible right now, Jack."

"Don't cry now," he said. "I don't even want to see your pleading expression in *that* outfit. You're going out of your way to try and spoil this for Susanna and I. You can't even pull yourself together for one day. I admit, I've been on you to get your shit together lately, but your interpretation of my advice is, as usual, completely cockeyed."

"That's not true," Emma insisted. "None of it. You're wrong about everything."

Jack looked doubtful. "I know you," he said. "And I know that no matter how hard you try, it's always the same result. It doesn't matter that life never rewards those content to sit in the wings, hoping Jane Eyre or fucking Bridget Jones will rescue them from mediocrity—doesn't matter. The world needs background colour too, right? Everyone can't be the star. You're never going to change, and I have to accept that."

This must have been what he did to Imogene, pushed her and pushed her until there was nothing left of her, until she had to leave. Emma saw the futility in trying to change his mind; he had given up on her. What was she expecting Jack to do? Announce to the guests how fabulous Emma was for making him see the error of his ways, leave the wedding to hire a private investigator and make it his life's work to find Imogene so he could re-unite his family?

Jack was scanning the room, about to make his escape, and she began to feel the strong possibility she may do something she shouldn't to make him stay. She pinched her leg to stop herself. It didn't work. "Don't you ever want to know what happened to Imogene?" she said.

Jack turned, bringing the wind with him, and grabbed Emma's wrists roughly. "You never, ever, know what the right thing is to say, do you?"

"What is the right thing to say?" Emma pulled her hands free. "That I don't miss my mother?"

"You have no idea what you are talking about. You don't know shit, Emma."

"She loved you, Jack."

"She loved herself more." Now Jack had half the tablecloth crumpled inside his fist.

"So what? She had to look after herself while you were out having sex with secretaries."

Jack's temple fluttered. "Oh yeah? If you know so much, how can you be sure it wasn't you that she fucking left?"

Her chest gaping with humiliation and another feeling she couldn't find a word for, Emma ran onto the dance floor and snatched Ben out of Lottie's arms. In her haste to leave, she may have pushed over the table with the four-tiered raspberry and vanilla buttercream wedding cake. Oh, and it may have ended up on the floor.

Chapter 14

After Ben dropped her off, Emma rushed into her bedroom and got straight under her covers, shoes and all. She tried to sleep, but couldn't. She tried to read, but couldn't. She couldn't stop thinking about the unfairness of life. Jack got away with everything. He never had to pay the dues he owed for his behaviour. It seemed the consequences of his actions were set up to destroy those around him, never himself. Emma felt her life had been defined by Jack's choices.

When she was seven, and too young to have any control over her father's decisions, she and Imogene decided to surprise Jack at his office for his birthday, even though he told Imogene several times not to go there. (He would be too busy/it was not a place for socializing/no one else's spouses just turned up with some wonderful spelt bread from a new bakery that he just had to try.) They spent most of the afternoon making Jack's favourite foods: a rich, thick paella and cheesecake made from the ripest, reddest strawberries Imogene could find, and they were going to surprise him at his office for his birthday.

"Why does Jack have to work so late when it's his birthday?" Emma asked.

Imogene tugged a lid off a Tupperware container. "Because he has a job that doesn't let you have any fun."

"Why doesn't he get another job?" Emma asked, picking up the chocolate-smeared knife her mother had left on the counter and giving it a good lick.

"Because he thinks he likes this job," Imogene said.

"He's going to be so happy when we get there!"

Imogene nodded, still occupied with the container. "Uh huh. Emmalina, we don't lick knives."

Emma put the knife in the sink and practised doing spins instead. She was in her favourite red dress, the one with the white collar that Jack bought her for Easter dinner at Grandma's house. She had her hair in two braids with white ribbons that Imogene had woven through and tied in bows at the bottom.

They arrived at Jack's office and Imogene greeted the security guard with a big smile. "Hola, Ken!" she said. "How is your evening so far? Anything suspicious going on here?"

Ken stood up and turned the volume down on the portable TV he was watching. He tucked his work shirt in at the back. "Good evening, Mrs. Gordon. The only thing suspicious going on around here is two pretty ladies walking around with a big basket at ten o'clock."

Emma rolled her eyes but no one noticed. She tugged at her mother's hand. "Let's go, Imogene!"

"We're here to surprise my husband. It's his birthday, and we wanted to bring him a nice home-cooked dinner of his favourite foods."

"Go on up," said Ken.

Emma dragged Imogene through the lobby to the elevators and grinned at her in the mirror inside the lift. "You look pretty, Imogene."

"You look beautiful, Emmalina."

Emma started jumping, big ones, as high as she could. "This is what you have to do if the lift is going to crash."

"Stop that *bebé*, you're making me nervous. And what do you mean, if it starts to crash?"

"Well," Emma slowed down the jumps to explain. "If the lift is going to hit the ground and you jump at exactly the right time at exactly the right height, you'll live."

"Is that so?" Imogene glanced up to see what floor they were at. "And you know this for a fact?"

"It's scientific."

"Well in that case, I take your word for it," Imogene said, jumping with enthusiasm. The elevator shook violently. She screamed. "Maybe not!"

Jack wasn't in his office. They found him in a conference room, with the door shut. Imogene didn't say anything, she just put down the picnic basket and walked back to the lift, leaving Emma to watch the junior analyst pulling down her skirt and pushing Jack off of her.

Emma needed air. She forced the memory of Jack's infidelity and her mother's peculiar indifference out of her mind and charged out the front door, an expensively attired apparition, late for an appointment with the streets of London. She left the upmarket residential haven of Maida Vale's romantic canals with floating houseboats and weekends full of tourists in camera-face, up into Kilburn, through its neon-lit U.S.A. Nail shops and boarded-up market stalls, past Cricklewood and the broken glass on the pavement outside the pubs and chip shops. Trying to quench the inferno cooking in her lungs, Emma drew in great helpings of the cool night air.

When her ankles, already battered from too many nights at the club, couldn't go on, she stopped and went into a small, steamy café, chock-filled with people like her. People who couldn't run any further without a nice cup of tea.

A woman came out from the kitchen and rushed over.

"Sorry, luv," she said. "I didn't think there was anyone come in."

"That's alright," said Emma, taking a seat at a large booth at the back.

"It's always busy this time of night, so I was helping them in the back." The woman smiled and a hand of wrinkles fanned out from her eyes. "Oh, that's not my name," she said, after seeing Emma look at her name badge. "It's the only one I could find back there to put on. So today, it's 'Frank' at your service."

"What's your real name?"

"Miriam. And lovely of you to ask—no one ever does. Are you hungry? I can make you some soup or a sandwich, but we haven't much left."

Miriam wore a messy bun on her head the colour of a drenched Irish setter. She had sagging tights collecting at her substantial ankles, and a blonde shadow of a bleached moustache underneath her crooked nose. She had never been pretty, even as a little girl, but was always popular. Emma decided it was Miriam's personality that won people over; she loved to play the clown, using her self-deprecating humour as a way to make those around her comfortable. This was a noble trait.

"I'll have a milky tea, please," Emma said, feeling like climbing into this world. She could get a job here and spend the rest of her honest, hard-working life spreading mayonnaise on meat sandwiches and ladling soup to the late-night workers. She would never speak because she was a mute. Regular customers would try to get her to talk, but she would just shake her head and point to the specials board.

"How long have you been working here?" she asked when Miriam returned with a chipped teapot.

"Oh, forever and a day. My husband and I bought this place nearly thirty years ago. When he passed, bless him, I couldn't bring myself to sell it. I'm an amnesiac; I can't sleep nights, so it helps to work. Passes the time."

Emma stirred some sugar into her tea. She could be an "amnesiac" as well as a mute.

Miriam took a seat at the booth across from Emma. "It's none of my business, but I must say you look absolutely lovely."

Emma smiled. "I went to a wedding today."

"Near here?"

"Somerset."

"Posh one, then? Anyone close to you?"

"Yes...sort of..."

Miriam sighed. "I love weddings. I'm a real romantic. Did everyone look as glamorous as you? You look like you should be stepping out of a Cadillac!"

People Emma could be mistaken for: someone's long-lost cousin from Margate, or the piano teacher's daughter, but definitely not anyone glamorous. "This isn't how I usually look."

"You remind me of a girl that used to live down my road. Lovely girl, she was, with these beautiful eyes that were full of secrets and stories. Like yours—my, they're like a peacock's tail aren't they? Beautiful eyes, you have. Oh, this girl could have them eating out of the palm of her hand. She was a picture. She knew it, mind you, but she was clever about it." Miriam scraped at something stuck on the table. "Lovely, lovely girl. I bet you broke a few hearts at that there wedding."

Emma picked up her spoon and stirred her tea again.

"Look at your face! What did I say? Didn't it go well?"

"Well," Emma said, "some pretty harsh words were exchanged between the groom and me. He said some awful...he was really angry." A heavy raindrop fell out of her eye and splashed into her tea. "I also ended up being pretty rude to my date."

Miriam watched intently, her face awash with concern. "It can't be worth crying over, luv. It never is."

"Have you ever wished you could start over again as someone else?" Emma asked, wiping her eyes.

"Everyone does at one time or another, don't they?"

A smile started to crunch up the corner of Emma's mouth. "I was a bit tipsy—at the wedding—and I pushed over the table that had the wedding cake on it." A cackle rose from her throat and she laughed and cried at the same time. "It skidded across the floor—must have made it about ten feet before it collapsed and died on the parquet."

Miriam patted Emma's hand. "Well, good for you for livening up the ceremony!"

Emma blew across the top of her tea. "I think I meant to ruin it. I really think I tried to wreck it. I know that I did..."

They sat, suddenly silent, the orchestra of cutlery clattering on cheap plates and wind whistling under the doormat filling in for conversation.

"What was her name?"

"Who?"

"The girl you said I reminded you of."

"Oh, goodness, I'll never forget it. Phoenix. Very unusual name. She moved away, years ago, I'm not sure where."

Emma knew. Phoenix had moved to Hollywood. She was beautiful and confident, and dressed in colourful angora jumpers with tasteful diamond studs in her ears. She had expensive tastes and could speak four languages. After getting "discovered" by a film producer and acting in a few straight-to-video comedies, Phoenix found her calling as a makeup artist. All the actors she worked with fell in love with her chatty, relaxed personality and her raw ambition to make it on her own in such an impossible town. Leading men with schedule-packed lives, photo shoots and press conferences found time to seek Phoenix out at the lunch trailer to ask how her new puppy was adjusting to obedience training, or what her plans were for the holidays. Her kind but insistent rebuff to these advances only spurred men on to want her more, but she never agreed to so much as a quick drink or a movie, too afraid of feeling emotion for a man again after the painful loss of her fiancé in a drunken car accident. Her drunken car accident.

A chilly draught blew through the door as two men stumbled in. "I've got to get back to work," said Miriam. "You take care, and remember, we all have bad days. It's what you make of 'em that's important."

Emma wanted for company and wished Miriam had stayed. She hated her neediness for a waitress with a defective name badge, but she didn't want to be by herself when she couldn't figure out how to switch off her head, and the voices that had made their conclusions about her failures.

You really don't seem like a stripper.

Well, that was hardly surprising, Emma thought, reconsidering her conversation with Marcus, her nearly-customer. She was too connected to herself, running everything she said and did through her reality meter instead of detaching completely and focussing in on the job at hand. How did these women do it? How did they behave in such a sexual way for a man and not think of it sexually?

In the dressing room at Platinum, the woman she saw reflected in the mirrors struggled to marry up with the woman inside her head. How could she look so true to her environment, yet be such a pretender inside?

She wasn't like the other girls, came the answer.

But Emma fought against that—none of those girls had walked into that job knowing what they were doing. Perhaps Chanel was born with her baby feet flexed and ready for a pair of stilettos, but everyone else had to learn how to spin around a pole, how to close off that side of them that felt foreign. They learned and she could learn too. Their seemingly unashamed embrace of who they were, that aura of indestructibility, the single-minded pursuit of their goals.

As well as becoming less reluctant to prance around the club in a skimpy dress, other things had changed for Emma. Why had she started smiling at strangers on the tube? Why was she obsessed with how much money people made for a living? Why did she feel like she was really onto something?

Every night, Emma practised dancing in her heels and flannel night shirt, conjuring up favourite images for inspiration. Chanel tossing her head back, running her hands through her hair and across her neck before trickling her fingers down the middle of her cleavage. Jade rolling her hips slowly, eyes closed, as if she was in a world of her own, overcome by desire. Destiny climbing the pole like frost spreading up a window, until she reached the top and flipped upside down to walk on the ceiling.

Never before had Emma thought of her body as anything other than that—a body—but it was becoming a friend, a trusted ally. She was much more aware of how her body moved, how the curves and lines appeared if you stood a certain way. You had a choice. Once Emma could bear to look, dancing in front of a mirror changed everything. Seeing the stripes of her long, lean stomach, the sweep of her thigh, how much difference it made to stand with an arched back, your chest pushed out, how you could use your hands to direct someone's gaze, to suggest where they should be staring. The way Emma's legs looked with an arched foot in a high heel; a long, stretched, sinewy extension of muscle and sex; the exposed arch of her hip when she hung a thumb over her thong to tease it over her hip. And the command music had— how every song she now heard had her imagining the perfect dance to it.

The girls at the club owned their musical and physical personas—Jade's sassy, confident routine to "Hey Big Spender," using a top hat and white gloves; Roxy's high-energy, sexually aggressive postures rocking out to edgy R&B in PVC chaps and cowboy hat, choosing a different song every time she went on stage; a girl introduced as Kat, schoolgirl innocence played out in kilts and ponytails with classic rock songs released long before she was born; Bambi's allegiance to Prince and no other artist, her show strictly glamour and tease in lace and marabou.

Leave yourself at the door... pretend you're someone else.

There was a real comfort at Platinum in being somewhere where no one knew her. Emma Gordon was no one to them. In the club she could be anyone she wanted to be. Who was going to know?

Emma needed a refill, but didn't call for Miriam. She didn't want to jar the idea taking shape. It must have been floating around for weeks, in her bedroom, at the club, hiding inside her jogging shoes while she ran from herself, waiting until the time was right. At last it had drifted within Emma's reach. It caused a frisson in her stomach like a midnight motorcycle accelerating into traffic. It was unlike her other thoughts. It was the most urgent, raw idea she'd ever had.

A girl that could have them eating out of the palm of her hand. Smart with it. Eyes that told a tale—like yours.

It was possible that the girl Miriam spoke of never moved to America. She may have come to a different fork in a different road. A girl, orphaned, abandoned and left to create her own destiny, with simple desires in life: food, shelter, love, but in five-star luxury terms or not at all. A girl who chose to protect her inner thoughts by using her outer gifts to get what she wanted. A girl with a fiercely competitive streak, and little time for wasting. The kind of character that Emma would love to read about—the undying independence of Jane Eyre, the limitless, ruthless abandon of Macbeth's ambition and the courage and spirit of adventure that Alice had when she jumped down the rabbit hole. Someone with a soul that welcomed their fate, regardless of the consequences.

The best thing of all about this character? She doesn't know anyone named Emma Gordon. Has never, ever heard of her.

False face must hide what the false heart doth know.

MACBETH

meet
phoenix

Chapter 15

The REAL Platinum Club House Rules

1.   Don't trust anyone.
2.   Have a drink, get a little loaded up—it's much easier to approach a person you don't know with the false sense of confidence alcohol can give.
3.   If you're a bit tipsy when giving a private dance and accidentally knock a guy in the face with your ass, he'll blow at least another hundred on you because you touched him.
4.   The best-looking girls don't make the most money; the girls that tell men what they want do. No matter what it is, just tell them. You're already getting naked for money, there's no point in having pride now. Promise to meet him outside the club, tell him he has sexy eyes, tell him you're wet for him—learn how to lie convincingly. If the man is in the building, you can take his money. He has a wallet, doesn't he?
5.   The easiest money comes from drunken customers. You can tell them you've done dozens of dances and they have no idea if it's true. If you double-team them, one of you can distract him while the other lifts his wallet.

6.   You need to have a regular or two. The only way to get a regular is by phoning them, so figure out how to get their number without being seen taking it.

7.   It is OK to view men as pathetic, weak and one-dimensional if they are nice and in love with you and come in all the time to give you money. If they are rude to you or expect "extras," it is OK to view men as objects to be loathed that make your life difficult. Remember why you're doing this job and stay focussed.

8.   If you get in a fight, try to hit the heel of your hand in your attacker's nose. That usually drops them to the floor and ends the struggle. If you have time in advance, take off your earrings so they can't be ripped out and tie your hair back.

9.   You will be told a hundred times a night that you are beautiful by well-spoken, well-travelled, powerful men. You will be showered with gifts, and all eyes in the room will watch you walk across a room. You never have to do your own hair or nails and you get to go shopping for cute clothes any time you want. You will forget this is just entertainment and it will become a lifestyle.

10. You will be told you are too beautiful, or too real, too fake or too ugly. Asinine losers will think they have a chance with you and grope you on the way to the bar. Your feet, legs and back will ache constantly. Your skin will age prematurely from the UV lights on stage, late nights and cigarette smoke. You will be told you are better than this. You will be called a slut behind your back, and to your face.

11. You will become mentally drained trying to figure out whether you are a goddess or a whore.

12. When you quit, the Platinum Club will keep your application and your locker key so that when you return to work here, there will be less paperwork.

Chapter 16

Breathless, Emma collapsed into the nearest chair and pulled her hair up off the back of her neck. She grabbed a club flyer off the floor to fan across her face and dropped the costume she had shed onstage to her side. Crisp, white shirt, prim and proper black pencil skirt. Add a silky knotted scarf at the nape of the neck, black lacy underwear, garter and stockings, hair stacked on top of her head with a pencil, tortoiseshell glasses, pearls. Bookish met boudoir and it felt just right. She had made money with her stage show. Men had come forward to the stage (one from as far away as the restaurant bar!) to tip her.

She had chosen Michael Jackson's "Dirty Diana," a song full of layers—angry, loud guitars where she could rip open her shirt and throw her head back, low, humming strings perfect for lowering her glasses to intensely look into a man's eyes or peeling off the strand of faux pearls around her neck and dropping them cheekily into a customer's drink. As the tension in the song built to a climax and then suddenly dropped out to just a haunting cello, Emma debuted the move she had been practising for weeks after hours: a reverse-mount onto the pole. With the pole at her back, Emma reached behind her and placed her hands above her head and kicked her legs up over her head, open into a V. The momentum of the lift spun her slowly around the pole. After holding the pose for a moment, she brought her legs in, one at a time, and wrapped them around the pole. She let her upside down body slide head first down the pole to the floor, where she coiled up like a snake, pushed off her skirt and sat up shaking out her hair from its loosely pinned-up do. Playing this role came easy—as soon as Emma got into character, she had known exactly what to do, what to say.

After setting up the next dancer, Mike stepped out of the booth to grab some dinner. "Great show," he said. "You really had 'em out there."

Emma grinned, didn't say what she was thinking: *Just you wait, I'm only getting started.*

Answer phone message 1: "Emma, Sylvia. Call me."

Answer phone message 2: "Jim here. From *Oxygen*. But you know that, of course. Anyway, where the hell are you? Let us know you're alright so we don't have to get the stripper police to go find you. (*Lower voice*) Sylvia's pissed. So if you're sleeping, I suggest you wake up and do some face time in here."

Answer phone message 3: "Hey hon, it's Bambi. I need retail therapy I'm stressing out with life, so hit me back. I heard you made good money last night and that your stage show is rocking. I'm *so* fuming that I didn't come in, but the freakin' flight from Paris was delayed and I was so tired, and remind me to never go on another trip with Adolfo—he's such a woman. Anyway, call me!"

"Hello?"

"Hey, you're there!" said Bambi. "Uh uh, why are you screening your calls?"

"Don't ask. So what time do you want to meet?"

"Please, wait." Bambi said into Emma's phone, picking at a loose thread on her dress. "Please, just wait up for me, babes?"

Emma finished buckling her shoe strap and gestured for Bambi to hurry up and get off her phone.

Bambi slammed the phone shut. "I swear he is cheating on me," she said. "If he is up to something I will cut his nuts off and…and…after that I will do something really bad. I really will."

"Why do you think he's cheating on you? There's no reason for him to want to be with anyone else. He's not dim-witted."

Bambi looked blank.

"Stupid. He isn't stupid—I'm saying he knows you're the best thing he'll ever have."

"I'm sure of it, though. I know he is."

"How do you know? You don't know."

"I do. Oh, it's so *embarrassing*…" Bambi moaned.

A girl with bloodshot eyes, a surgically enhanced chest and short plum fingernails strolled over. She had a large tattoo of a rose on her wrist, a cigarette in one hand and a drink in the other.

"What's embarrassing?" she asked, opening her locker and discreetly pouring something from her handbag into her glass.

People with addictions surrounded Emma, and it wasn't just the women. Many of the men were serious gamblers, alcoholics, sex addicts or God knows what. Platinum was a palace built on lies. Tricks and lies. Tell a cute guy you never get to dance for truly sexy guys like him and you're so excited, tell an overweight man he's cuddly and you want to snuggle him like a teddy bear, tell an ugly man you find his intelligence an incredible turn-on, or take a deep breath into his neck and say you love his cologne. Deeper than the soft lights that made your skin glow to perfection, so much more than the parade of immaculate women adaptable to any fantasy, the deception knew no bounds. The club was like wonderland—everyone happy, everything easy-breezy. But Emma was surprised at the hoax unravelling in front of her every night. Few girls genuinely had it together. They were with boyfriends who were threatened by them or who took their money or hurt them. They had stretch marks, hair that didn't grow from their head, scars under their breasts. They were spending the best years of their lives as hedonists concerned with nothing more than their beauty and their earning power, hijacked by the Platinum Club.

So why did she love it so much?

Bambi crinkled her brow. "I swear Scott is cheating on me," she said. "I know this is going to sound dumb, but I know I'm right. He's not attracted to me anymore."

"Go on, what happened?" asked the girl. She turned to Emma, "Alright?" she said. "Hi, I'm Kat."

Emma caught herself before she told Kat she knew her name already.

"I'm Phoenix," she said.

"So, listen to me," Bambi said. "When we were in bed, I farted. A really big, noisy one." She covered her face in her hands.

"He probably didn't hear it," offered Emma.

"It was so loud it woke me up from my sleep! I sleep really deep—through anything, I really can. I know it's put him off me, I just know it."

Kat said, "I bet it was just a little tiny one and he probably thought it was cute. He's not gonna cheat on you for that."

Emma nodded. "I really don't think that's the reason he's cheating. Not that he *is* cheating. He is definitely not cheating."

"Now I'm completely stressed. I am so para—I can't relax. I'm mashed because I can't sleep anymore." She reached for one of Kat's Marlboros. "Can I bum a fag?"

Kat handed Bambi her dying cigarette to use as a lighter. "Babe, I fart in bed all the time. Why should I hold it in? I'm not going to suffer and squeeze my colon into giving me cancer for any man."

"A little decorum wouldn't go amiss," said Emma. "I think you should be discreet—you have an image to uphold, right?"

"Have you ever farted in front of your man?" Bambi asked Emma.

"You have a boyfriend?" said Kat.

Emma thought quickly. "Yes. I've never done that, but I truly don't think he would mind, he's very laid back."

"Aww, how sweet! I bet your man is gorgeous," said Kat. "Totally buff, super fit body, right?"

"How did you guess?" said Emma.

"I can tell," Kat said. "I'm good at reading people. Doesn't he mind you doing this job, though? I'm glad I'm single." She dropped down to the floor to stretch.

Emma knew how to answer this now. "He finds it sexy," she said. "The idea that I'm at work teasing all these guys but I'm coming home to him."

Bambi nodded, cocking her ear to the ceiling to check on the next stage call. "Scott used to be that way. He used to want me all the time, no matter how late I got home from work, you know? He *worshipped* me. Now when I get home he's fucking snoring."

"What you wanna do is control the noise, not the actual fart," Kat said.

"I'm listening…" said Bambi.

"The fart noise is caused by, I dunno, your butt cheeks vibrating or something. So when you've gotta let one out, just grab your ass and pull your cheeks apart and it will come out silent—just air."

"In spite of the absurdity of this conversation, I think Kat's onto something," Emma said.

Bambi ground out her lipstick-stained cigarette into a locker and flicked the butt into an ashtray. "I can't believe Scott's cheating on me. After all we've been through."

———————————

"It's pretty harmless," Emma said to Toni in the office kitchen.

"Sure it is…" Toni was looking closely at Emma's head. "What have you done to your hair?"

"I have extensions in."

"Can I feel? I bet they cost a fortune."

"They're not cheap."

"They're really bad for your hair, you know. A friend of mine had extensions and half her hair fell out when she removed them."

"Well it's just for a short time." Emma was sure the whole office was listening.

People don't like it when you change. Unhappiness is irrelevant; they would rather you stayed as you always had, ticking the box they had you categorized as. If you want for more, or try to do something different, it seems more uncomfortable for them than it is for you. When Emma came into work now, her presence announced itself down the hallway and around the office. She caught women appraising her guardedly, like suspicious mother birds protecting their territory. The men were more predictable, smirking during conversations when they would casually ask questions they never used to—if she had the name of the file they needed from an old issue of the magazine, for example, or staring at her chest when they thought she wasn't looking.

Toni added a slice of lemon to her regular meal of hot water. "Seriously, though, I can just imagine the state of the girls in there...really trashy, hey?"

"You'd be surprised—"

"I'm sorry, Emma, but I really can't believe you go up on stage! That tacky, giant phallic symbol of a pole? How can you not feel gross taking your clothes off in front of leching blokes? I could *never* do that."

Of course Toni could never do it. Toni was someone who preferred reporting on other people's lives because she didn't have one herself. Wasn't that the true nature of a journalist?

"I don't feel gross."

And she didn't. The first time, it was surreal and peculiar, but there were so many other things she had to keep track of in order to do the job, it was, ironically, the most straightforward task. At Platinum you were revered for your naked chest—nudity was everywhere, from the dressing room to the dance floor. Somehow it becomes the norm. Emma had jokingly said to one of the security men working the private rooms that he must think he's got the best job in the world. "Sure, in the beginning," he said. "But now, I could give two shits. They're just tits. You've seen one, you've seen 'em all." Emma had been quick to write that down, but it didn't seem so outrageous a quote now. In fact, she couldn't remember if she actually had written it down, or if she meant to and never got around to doing it.

"I'm not ashamed of my body," she told Toni. "And the club is very strict with enforcing the no-contact rules. Anyway, don't you sunbathe topless on holiday?"

"That's completely different. No one is paying me to do it!"

And they probably never would, Emma thought. Toni probably went on vacation, got drunk and danced (for free) on tables in a miniskirt, loving the attention. Emma had heard Toni discussing her vetting program for the men she dated, with rules about what a man had to do before she would even consider sleeping with them—expensive dinner and presents. She wondered what was worse, or even if the two situations were not much different.

"I'm not saying you should be ashamed of your body, but it all seems so tragic…"

"I'm on an assignment, Toni. I'm working on an article, undercover, getting a story. I'm not actually an exotic dancer for a living, remember?" Emma hated saying those words; she was betraying the girls at the club.

"It's a lot to ask though, don't you think? It's not like trying out a spa treatment." Toni lowered her voice. "Your reputation…I don't know how far this is going to advance your career."

"I'm not worried about my career or my reputation," Emma said. "I'm more concerned with people judging me over something they have very little familiarity with. Or don't have the fortitude to do themselves."

What a hypocrite Toni was. Emma wished she didn't have to come into the office at all. Her three-day-week freelance schedule had turned into one day a week, and even that was starting to grate. Any other work she had to do for *Oxygen* paled against the vibrant energy of the club. If she did try and write about her experiences, she struggled to find the right words—something that had never happened to her before. Walking out onto the floor dressed like a star, music all around you, joining a roomful of women that all held this energy— being part of it; the importance her sex carried, how much power women had just in their bodies, the strange existence of an underworld both sordid and fantastical—how could she ever explain that?

Emma never thought much about money until she started getting it folded over her G-string several dozen times a night. Now she can see why the girls are obsessed with its power. Instant gratification, fast, tax-free (shhh!). With every dirty bill she makes, she buys a higher status, an oddly gratifying game.

Emma spent a lot of time thinking about her potential alliances at the club, and of their fragility. Status and the unspoken hierarchy ruled Platinum—and how quickly you could move up a grade or two with a few well-chosen moves. A good breast enlargement, for example. Or even dying your hair from brunette to blonde. A stage show that didn't copy anyone else's tricks, persuading a big spender to take a VIP room with not just you, but several of your friends, a fight happening because of your actions—these things could change your standing almost overnight.

Emma's cellphone began humming in her pocket. It was a text message from Kat: R U STILL SLEEPING? MEET ME 4 LUNCH? JADE CUMING 2. BOND STREET AFTER! CHAMPS AND SHOPPING, U KNO U WANT 2!

She was in. She'd never seen Jade or Kat outside of the club before. "I'll catch up with you later," Emma told Toni. Elated, she grabbed her jacket and legged it before Sylvia saw her.

Chapter 17

Mike waved Emma over.

"The gaffer wants a word," he told her.

"Why?"

"Must be all those customers you've been giving your number to."

"Don't make jokes like that, Mikey," Emma said. "We're paranoid enough as it is."

The club was currently under investigation by the local council for breaches in their licences. Charges of prostitution and customers being offered drugs were among the scarier accusations. As a result, Eileen had told everyone to be very careful with customers—anyone caught giving out their number or telling a customer they would meet them later would be instantly fired. It was so serious, some girls were convinced the club would be shut down and were auditioning at other, lesser clubs in the city. Police officers were coming into the club acting as punters (the girls spotted them a mile off) trying to catch out girls by asking them where they could buy drugs or if they could "hook up" later. She remembered Bambi saying that to sleep with a customer was a stupid move—it destroyed the carefully constructed market value of the club, for one. Emma knew many dancers—herself included—implied things to customers in a roundabout way: they were interested in dating them, they were getting so into the dancing they wished they weren't in a club, but with them somewhere privately—it was part of the game, right?

Trey was in his office and on the phone, so Emma lingered outside the door sucking in her stomach and fretting about what she could have done. Trey hardly ever spoke to the dancers, but Emma would sometimes see him standing by the side of the stage, arms folded, watching a performance derisively. She hadn't forgotten his experience with Kat. (When Kat first started, she got drunk and slept with Trey. Why? "Just because." Afterward, she was so embarrassed she would hide from him at work. No matter, he ignored her and still tormented her for fun by doling out random fines for late stage calls that had never happened or making her dance for his friends for free.)

When Emma made good money she was sure to tip Trey as well as the doormen and the DJ, even though she didn't want to share a single pound of it. She saw how Chanel handled management generously, and she never forgot that. Every time she banked for the club she was ensuring their loyalty. She tried to give the impression that Phoenix was at Platinum for a purpose, that she had goals, and was serious about work. Emma didn't want to be put in whatever category it was that managers of strip clubs put dancers in.

Trey hung up the phone. "Come in," he said picking up his cigar. "Don't stand there like a lemon."

Trey's office was a tiny hole next to the stockroom, with cases of beer stacked against a wall badly in need of re-plastering. Behind his desk, the closed-circuit screens flashed black and white images of the club floor and private rooms.

"Alright?" Trey asked.

"Yup."

"You sure?"

"Why wouldn't I be?"

"You girls are so suspicious," Trey said.

"I'm not suspicious."

"You've not done anything wrong, so relax." Trey balanced his cigar on the edge of his desk and picked up a yellow flagged file. "Look, two things. We don't have a signature from you for the Rules and Conditions form, so please sign your life away here. Also, we've got some footie players coming in shortly and they'll be straight into the VIP. They don't like the trashy type and I don't want them getting attacked by the vultures on the main floor. Take Bambi and Destiny with you."

Like hell. She was taking Kat and Jade. "OK. Thanks Trey." Emma signed the coffee-stained form and set her face on relax. "I appreciate you telling me about the VIP, cheers." If Chanel was in tonight, would Trey have told her instead?

Trey squeezed his deep-set eyes and yawned, showing more gold fillings than teeth. "No problem. I know the kind of girls these guys like—they'd set up shop at Tigerz and never return if I sent some cokehead like Kat to entertain them."

Emma bit the inside of her cheek.

"When you started I knew you were going to be my little money-maker. No one else believed me, of course, but I kept saying, 'give her some time and she's gonna be running it.' Man, I've been in this damn scene for too long."

"How long have you been working here?"

"I don't know...forever. I've seen some shit, let me tell you. It's always drama in here. I've had it with strippers. You girls make so much money and all I ever hear is bitching and complaining. I'm sick of it. Anyway, don't start doing any stupid shit and you'll be fine."

Emma wasn't sure if Trey was being kind or how she was supposed to answer. She also wanted to tell him they hated being called "strippers," and preferred "exotic entertainers" or "dancers," but that would probably wind him up.

"That whole mysterious 'I've got a secret' look—guys love that shit. The 'I'm not really supposed to be doing this' naughty-but-nice shit. You've got that down to a science. The secretary-librarian stage show? Pure class." Trey looked her over. Ve-ry slow-ly.

Emma was silly to think that Trey would see she wasn't like the other dancers—not when she was sitting here alone with her cleavage on show, persona for hire, in an office with the door closed.

"Got enough body glitter on?" Trey scoffed. "Fucking hell."

Emma cleared her throat. "On stage I look luminous."

"Sure you do."

"These aren't the right lights," Emma insisted.

Trey turned back to his computer. "Try to leave those boys with enough for cab fare."

———————————

"Well, hello there," he said, watching bemusedly as Emma took his cigarette from him and crushed it in the ashtray. "You are fucking gorgeous."

"If you've got that in your hand, I can't get very close to you, now can I?"

He smiled. "I don't recall asking you to start dancing yet."

"I'm not dancing," Emma purred. "I'm just going to get very close to you and take all my clothes off."

He laughed. "No one is going to say no to you."

He settled back into his chair, widened his legs, relaxed. A man that made ninety thousand pounds a week to kick a ball, a man who could (and did) have any woman he wanted, was about to willingly hand the controls over to her.

It wasn't hard to be Phoenix anymore, it was so easy. She wouldn't be intimidated by him, or act impressed. She didn't watch football, she would confess, looking sweetly apologetic. She would cheekily say, "Aren't you all a bunch of hooligans? I think I prefer cricket players..." and then the next minute bite her bottom lip and let her eyes sit for a moment too long below his waist and find a way to let him know he was different from the other men she had danced for; she was *truly* attracted to him. And the more she was attracted to him, the more powerful he would feel, the more his ego would preen its feathers until he felt so good around her that he wouldn't care about the money—he would give her whatever she wanted. Like he said, no one can say no, not to her.

———————————

Twenty minutes. Emma's legs were starting to burn. Every time she pushed back off the armrests of the chair and stood up, he ordered her to come straight back. "Don't you go any further away than this," he said when she returned to breathing inches away from his face, her hot air sitting on his lips.

The energy in the room had changed. There was an evocative, licentious charge wrapping the two of them up warm and tight—the air was electric. Emma could almost taste the champagne and tobacco on his breath. His heavy-handed designer cologne made her think about him getting ready to go out with the boys—a quick shower before the splashing of scent on his neck and chest, brushing his teeth and meticulously applying a gel to his hair, unwrapping a shirt from its dry-cleaning bag, going to the bank machine, hearing the whoop of his deactivated car alarm, pulling out of the driveway, music blaring, to arrive at Platinum, feeling the familiar recognition and admiration of the women and men as he crossed the club floor, disappearing into the VIP section, finishing here, with Emma, holding a glass of champagne out for her to take a sip.

But she didn't take a sip. While he watched, Emma took the glass and dipped a finger in. She slowly licked the champagne off her finger and smiled. Then she sucked on her finger to make sure she had gotten every last drop of alcohol. She could not believe how sexy Phoenix was.

He leaned further back in his chair, and Emma came forward with him, as if she was going to his lips. At the last minute, she moved her mouth and sighed into his ear as her hair fell onto the side of his face.

He cocked his head and whispered into her ear: "Tell me something. Do you ever have times when you're dancing and—"

"Yes," Emma said, quickly. "Sometimes, yes."

The music changed.

He threw his head up. "I love this song!"

"Me too!" Emma said. She'd forgotten she was at work. She'd forgotten that she was pretending to like what she was doing. She felt like she was holding a slippery, wet balloon that was about to burst. She was dancing in her underwear, her head spinning, her mind racing, her heart thrashing.

"*You're leavin' on a seven-thirty train and you're headin' out to Hollywo-od!*" they sang, loudly and out of tune. He gave her the champagne glass again, and she obliged his request to watch her drip it on her body. She also took a large swig, and passed the glass back to him. His heavy eyes stayed on hers while he tipped the last of the bubbles down his throat.

Emma put her hands against the wall on either side of his head and whispered, "Isn't it amazing how easy it is to get caught up in a moment, and get completely locked into a space where there is no one else on earth but us?" The buzz of the club seeping in, the yawning security man, the waitress popping her head in every so often—they did not exist anymore.

He moved his face a second closer to Emma's, his lips refreshingly damp on her cheek: "You knew exactly what I was talking about, when I asked you that question before, didn't you?"

Emma nodded. Her skin sweat-sticky. A blazing bead of heat left the nape of her neck and trickled down her spine, to dissolve in the lace of her knickers. She pushed herself off the wall and stood up, tall in front of him, aware of the rising and falling of her salt-beaded chest under the soft lights.

"You look incredible," he said. His shirt had risen up; the inch of skin above his belt made him seem as naked as she was.

The way he watched her. His eyes travelling all over her body taking a long, frequently detoured route round before they came back to meet her eyes. The way he was entirely focussed on her. That she was showing him her body. That he was paying for that privilege. The understanding between them. Heady, intoxicating, intensely arousing.

Emma turned around and took her time bending over, keeping her back arched, giggling at the upside-down person between her legs. She ran her hands down her legs, then back up over her thighs. She shook her behind in time to the music.

"Come back," he said. "I told you I don't like you so far away."

Emma obliged and kept dancing, although she was moving so slow you couldn't really call it dancing. "Do you want me to keep going?" Emma asked, as the next song began seeping through the speakers. She already knew the answer.

"Stay," he said. "Stay. You can't stop when they're playing Prince." He sealed his legs around Emma's. The contact made her jump. "This is great music to fuck to," he said.

She nodded, exhaled like there was gravel in her chest. Why wasn't that offensive to her? Somewhere in her head she knew that was rude, but it made sense when he said it. It made perfect sense.

"I could fuck *you* to this," he said.

A shiver rose up from the small of Emma's back and leaped across her body. She had stopped moving completely, and was standing in front of him, hands covering her breasts, hair melting on the back of her neck.

They stared at each other.

"Oi, mate!" One of his friends stuck his head in the private room. "We gotta go." He sat up quickly. "Yep, coming!" he yelled.

Emma picked up her dress and sat down. She glanced over. He smiled sheepishly and reached for his wallet. "Damn...I gotta go with my boys. You know how it is. How much do I owe you?"

It had been under an hour, but Emma didn't want to ask for what seemed suddenly like such a small amount. At the beginning of the night, she would have been very satisfied with what was an incredibly expensive forty-five minutes. She hesitated.

He took her hand and pressed his credit card into it. "I don't care about the money," he said, running his arm around her waist and pulling her up against him. "Take as much as you want. I *want* you to have it. Now, how much do I owe you?"

Emma jumped in with two feet. What did she have to lose? "That's for me to know and my friendly swipe machine to find out, isn't it?" She grinned and pushed him away, handing his card to the waitress hovering by the door. "Put a thousand in Platinum chips on this please," she said.

"Is that all?" he said, winking. "Worth every penny."

Chapter 18

Emma understood a part of Jack now, and it was more than just the heady satisfaction of making money (even when you had all the money you needed), it was being master of your destiny. The harder you worked, the more you had; if you could be smarter than the competition, you would win; and being smarter than the competition felt good, really good. Making another person a puppet in your show, instead of the other way around, had a strange gratification. So did getting a dance from someone who just turned down another girl (even if it was a friend of yours), having other dancers chasing you for lunch dates or catching men watching you in the private room instead of the girl they'd paid for.

Why had Jack always pushed Emma away? Was her existence a constant memento of his inadequacy to his wife and family? Emma could remember the time Imogene forgot to pick her up from school because she was in the middle of reading her theatre texts and couldn't put them down until she knew all her lines; or the time she refused to make cake for Emma's birthday party, insisting that the kids eat a fruit and vegetable platter instead of the chocolate and fizzy soda they were expecting. Emma seemed to recall there was a time when her mother went to a work function with her dad dressed in a head wrap and army boots that caused a very big fight. But never had she doubted her mother's devotion to her or her father.

Emma's favourite bedtime story:

A girl named Imogene Lina Martinez had just returned from a backpacking trip through South America, where she helped to build an irrigation system in a peasant village (Peru), taught English classes in a rural school (Colombia) and had her heart broken several times (Ecuador, Argentina, Chile). Back in California, Imogene was living with her aunt, working at the Sunshine Bar and Grill and writing her third screenplay. She was nineteen.

A boy named Jack Gordon, imported from the U.K., fresh out of grad school, was sent to work in San Francisco for three months. It was his first bit of responsibility and though he tried not to show it, he was jumping with excitement. Not one for patience, he felt he had done his share of sitting in the office as a lowly intern, head down, making numbers add up that shouldn't, while his superiors went to meetings, flew around the world and earned big money. He was cocky, but intelligence and ambition worked in his favour. (The first deal he ever worked on was so pressured he didn't go home for five days, showering at the gym and catching a few hours sleep on the sofa in the canteen.) Jack was high with the adrenalin that comes from a vision of wealth and power, and he was determined to set a standard none of his peers could keep up with.

But California was a disappointment. Jack was doing exactly the same thing he had always been doing, only with people that made fun of his English accent and didn't understand his sense of humour. Lethargy and disillusionment were creeping in. Jack wanted to be the master of his future, and was doing all he could to succeed, but there was a hollowness about his life that he couldn't comprehend.

When Imogene came to take his order at the Sunshine Grill, Jack knew he was going to hit on her, he just didn't know how to do it. He ate his steak as slowly as he could, well aware that the extra hour he was spending at the restaurant would probably amount to another three hours in catch-up time later that night in the office.

Another Saturday night in the office.

The thing was, Jack couldn't stop staring at her. She was like that feeling right before you sneeze, tickling and uncertain. Her black hair was cut short and boyish, framing her sharp face, and her pointy cheekbones rose up like little ramps under her eyes. And her eyes—huge masses of green, choking for air behind curtains of eyelashes. Her mouth never stopped moving: singing under her breath, laughing to a co-worker, smiling at the customers, always moving. Her skin glowed like sand in a desert sunset. When she took a food order, she sat down at the table with you, listening like it was the first time anyone had ever ordered a chicken sandwich.

He couldn't stop staring. She knew, and it didn't make him embarrassed.

At ten-thirty, Imogene finished work and came out the back door where Jack had been waiting, tetchy with nerves, for an hour. She wore a thin, white cotton shirt and a patchwork skirt that was too long and carried a dirty hem of purple lace. She stopped unexpectedly, her skirt running around her ankles, revealing a flash of grape-painted toes in worn leather sandals. She switched her big denim bag to her other shoulder and said, "I guess you want to go for a drink."

She was nothing like his usual choice, too opinionated for a start, but under the poetic streetlights of San Francisco he fell in love with her right then.

She knew the power she held, but tried to forget it, even when he would shower her with gifts she took straight to the charity shop, even when he would stay up all night listening to her read James Baldwin when he had to be at work at six-thirty the next morning. She tried to start arguments but they turned into debates that turned into discussions that turned into hand-holding, which turned into love-making. Jack wanted to know everything in her head. He wanted to never have met her. She was not part of the plan. She was too granola, too artsy. She was wild. He couldn't stop saying her name.

They lived like this in California for three months, then six, then a year. Then Jack had to go back, he really had to, if he was ever going to make VP in under six years. He had to go—this was their future. So she came with him, and they found a flat in Clapham and she decorated it with her paintings, Duke Ellington records and Hemingway novels. Of course she didn't like his friends, didn't like his aspirations of hostile takeovers of small, shaky companies to make a profit. But she loved the way he looked at her when she was telling him about her childhood in Brazil, and she loved the way he stroked her hair while she read to him. It seemed like enough.

Emma's years of practice creating fairy tales to cope with her circumstance was turning out to be the winning ticket to survival at Platinum. After devouring everything from the classics to Cheryl's romance novels, Emma began using bus and tube journeys looking for escape before finally discovering the delights of the airport. A long ride out to Heathrow on the Piccadilly line meant numerous passenger changes: a quick loss of the tightly packed day-trippers heading to the madness of Leicester Square, or the sale-seekers jumping off at Knightsbridge to buy an olive green plastic shopper from Harrods. It meant luggage started to build up on the train from the people that couldn't afford a cab, or who didn't want to pay to park their cars at the airport or, more captivatingly, people who didn't have a friend or loved one to wish them a good trip.

Airports were the best places to find people full of dreams and excitement of purpose; Emma loved them. The influx of activity was continual. Families with sugar-high children tearing around the Body Shop while mum looked for a last-minute shower gel before the self-catering challenges of a two-star apartment in Tenerife; group-booked lads on their way to Barcelona for the Olympics, to drink good wine, eat tapas and cheer on the British cycling team; and new couples on their first romantic getaway, eager for the unknown pleasures to be found in the cobbled streets and red-lit canals of Amsterdam.

Instead of studying for her GCSE's, Emma went couple-hunting. She focussed on couples, not because she was a naive romantic, but because to find one with a good story was a real challenge. At a seat near the check-in or the entrance to the departure lounge, Emma watched carefully for subtly mismatched pairs bursting with texture and originality—not your standard white-haired gent with the bottle-blonde companion.

Couples like the slim man with melted chocolate eyes, tall, dressed in a pair of dark trousers and Nirvana T-shirt, holding the hand of a pretty (but not too pretty) girl with a wavy curve in her hair. Emma knew they weren't going to last long after their holiday. For starters, the girl didn't have her ears or belly button pierced (fear of needles brought on by early childhood rabies scare) but her boyfriend had both ears and an eyebrow sporting metal artwork (he worked on a market stall selling leather cuffs and belly chains). He had tried several times to get her to just have something small done, a tiny little stud in her nose, or even a banal ear piercing like every other woman in the free world, but she wouldn't do it. He told her it was sexy—he found it really sexy—she still said no. Deep down inside, she hated his piercings, she thought they were trashy. She'd seen the photos of his ex-fiancée, no thank you, she wasn't going to end up like a pin cushion.

Emma hoped they could work it out, but she knew it would be over in a month, right after he sold a piece of jewellery to a girl in an up-and-coming rock band who left him a demo tape with her phone number on it. This girl had a voice like a dozen Jack Daniels over ice and he couldn't stop imagining the thin metal ring through her bottom lip as she said the words, "Do you sell gold studs?"

But back to Emma's more recent stories—she needed several: for the punters, for the girls, and for herself.

She'd decided that Phoenix was born and raised in London, the youngest of four sisters and thus used to being spoiled and getting her own way. Men liked hearing about her having four sisters. The first thing they would ask was if they all looked alike.

Her oldest sister, Jenna, was a successful lawyer and loved to be in control. She went to work in power suits and wore her hair up, worked long hours, and took expensive vacations. Tania, the second oldest, worked as a school teacher; she was the good, sweet one always staying late to mark up papers— every child's father had a crush on her, but she never noticed. Her sister Morgan was the earthy type and loved to travel; right now she was in Australia learning to surf. Before that, Morgan had lived in a ski chalet in France, and studied art in Italy. As for herself, when Phoenix stops dancing (not yet, she loves it!) she is going to open up her own boutique selling gorgeous little purses, jewelled bags and designer clothing. (The truth about Phoenix? She had no interest in having her own shop, but she didn't want to tell men the truth, that she was working at Platinum to finance her dream of travelling the world in a private jet, with a man in every port.)

If they asked how she started dancing, Phoenix would dip her eyes and giggle before confessing she'd always been a bit of a show off, and she loved the attention. She made great money, met lots of famous people, and got to explore her wild side. She always said "explore" in a suggestive way.

Emma experimented with various plots, and using a hard luck story was a no-no; if a customer felt sorry for her, forget it. Acting distant and untouchable like Roxy wasn't the right match, and being blatantly sexual like Kat felt too forced for Phoenix. Men loved the persona she had settled on—innocent on the outside, vixen on the inside. The high-rollers wanted the works—a girl they could sit with and have dinner and conversation as well as dances. In town on business, bored or lonely, most had little intention of taking things further than a sexy dance and a flirt. And what if the customer's only interested in dances? Bambi was right about dumbing it down and letting them put their vision, their fantasy, on you. If a man asked

Phoenix what she did with her spare time, she would put on a mock serious face and say, "Shop!" or, "Well...I usually meet my girlfriends for lunch and we'll get a facial or something. Then maybe shopping, or the gym." If it was a man who wanted innocence, she would tell them she spent the afternoon curled up on the sofa watching a romantic comedy or babysitting for her sister while she was at work.

Men actually believed her. They believed that in her whole day, every day, she had no applicable life problems; she never had to go to the post office or deal with a messy kitchen.

Crazy, right?

It was easier than Emma had imagined, and so pleasing to take on the persona of someone so dynamic, so focussed. She pushed the limits, to see how far she could take it, and guess what? People believe anything you tell them—especially if you believe it, too.

Chapter 19

"I wanted to tell him I didn't have the time." Jade ran a hand over her slim thigh. "I can't deal with shaving my legs today, how can I be meeting you for dinner *again?*"

Emma was sitting on the main floor with Kat and Bambi, listening to Jade complain about a regular, Gabriel, that called constantly and was always in need of attention.

"The baby was up all day yesterday, he didn't have a single nap. He's so sick, poor little guy. Throwing up *Exorcist*-style— gale-force vomit. I used the last of the baby wipes on myself because I didn't have time to shower. I'm on the verge. I am on the verge. I can't deal. Look at the stubble on my legs!"

"Don't worry about it," said Bambi. "They aren't looking at your legs, girl."

Jade smiled. "For real, though, this dude's driving me mad. I got a man and two kids at home. My *one* night off, Gabe's blazing my phone wanting me to get all dressed up go to some flash restaurant, just to make him look good. I'm like, I'm going to bed at ten tonight. Even if I was awake, why would I want to be with you? Come on. I just can't do it *no* more."

"You have to do it," Bambi told her. "If he's paying you to eat, you go."

The other girls agreed. Jade had the best regulars. This one gave her crazy money—a grand for dinner and drinks before he'd put her in a cab home—but he was a drain on her mentally, wanting to chat three times a day, needing constant validation that Jade wanted to see him for more than his money. He came to the club frequently and liked watching her dance on the stage, but would never ask her to dance in one of the private booths. He was too shy.

"I wish I had someone like that," said Kat.

Kat could have that, could make a lot more money, but she was silly with her time. Emma had seen her sitting and drinking with guys for hours (guys Emma knew weren't paying her) or she would sit around in the dressing room, gossiping.

"Think of all the designer gear Gabriel gives you!" Kat said. "How you gonna give all that up? I thought you were after that new handbag."

"Ohhh!" Jade slid down in her chair. "That Gucci...Why must I suffer for the Gucci?"

Emma knew Jade was older than the other girls—at least twenty-seven—but she showed no signs of quitting. After a few late nights, the burnout was beginning to show through her incredible beauty—you could see it reflected in the darkness under her eyes, in the purse of her rounded, pouting lips. It was a shame, because when she was up for it, Jade was one of the best girls to work the floor with—she wouldn't take no for an answer. If a guy was rude and said, "Sorry I don't like black girls," she simply would flick her braids over her shoulder and tell him, "The blacker the berry, honey," or "That's okay, I don't like white guys," and drag him off, returning twenty minutes later with a big wedge of his cash, and he would be smitten, his eyes on her all night. No other woman would be able to get a penny out of him.

"Love that trick," remarked Kat, watching a girl named Honey dancing on the bar stage.

Honey was a standoffish beauty who used to tour the world doing backing dancing for pop groups and now had an addiction to Platinum's lifestyle and wages.

"She looks high as a kite," remarked Jade. "Tony'll fire her before the night is over."

Honey finished a tight turn around the pole and absent-mindedly caressed her cleavage. "Her eyes look like a shark," Kat said. "You know when you see a nature program and a shark swims past the camera, with big, black, dead eyes? Shark eyes."

"You kill me," Jade said, with a laugh. "If bored eyes mean you're over it, I think we *all* need to quit."

"Why make eye contact with any of the guys in here?" said Roxy, joining them at their sofa, squishing in next to Emma. "They'll only steal your soul."

"You know you've been dancing too long when..." Jade tipped her head in Roxy's direction.

"...You have to set your alarm to go to the bank?" said Bambi, nudging Jade. "I'm looking at you, girl."

"When you can fix any outfit, including heels, with a bottle of nail polish!" said Kat.

"You know what?" Jade laughed to herself. "This is bad, this actually happened to me. I introduced myself to my husband's boss by my stage name."

Bambi gave a hoot. "People, we have a winner. Jade has been a dancer for too long. She wins a free G-string from the lost-and-found pile."

Chanel arrived. It was nearly eleven o'clock, three hours later than the start of the night shift. She headed through the restaurant toward the back entrance to the dressing room, trailing a small monogrammed leather suitcase behind her like a well-heeled stewardess. A snug white dress hugged her hips and large sunglasses hid her eyes. Bambi jumped up and waved, following her.

"Off she goes."

"Whatever, Roxy." said Jade. "She's gonna make big money tonight."

"Why the fuck does Chanel get to waltz in here at this time—through the front—when the rest of us are fined if we show up two minutes late?" Roxy spat out cigarette smoke. "It's pure bullshit."

"Roxy, you get fined because you're always drunk and cursing out the customers like some kind of project-dweller, not because you're late," Jade said. "Don't hate on Chanel because she's making money."

"Piss off, Jade," said Roxy. She set her silver-shadowed eyes on Emma. "What do you think of Chanel?"

Emma was marvelling at both Chanel's audacity to wear sunglasses at night as if the paparazzi were stalking her every move, and Jade's attempt to act like she wasn't bothered by Chanel. If anything, Jade was the most concerned with Chanel's comings and goings. Second in seniority to Chanel, but with far less influence or control, Emma wondered why Jade hadn't made a play for Chanel's place, or even Bambi's. What was she afraid of?

After Emma saw Phillip tipping Chanel, Roxy had told her that Jade usually didn't usually stick around to watch the action. She would hide in the kitchen making conversation with the chefs so she didn't have to hear the DJ, or see Chanel flushed and wild-eyed, rushing into the dressing room covered in fifty-pound notes, money falling out of her bra, her underwear, crammed in her fists. So much money that Chanel's friends, India and Bailey, and a bouncer had to help to collect it. Jade stayed in the kitchen because it was the only place in the entire club that wasn't piped in to the DJ. You could be sitting on the loo, but if they call you to the stage, you needed to know about it, so the speakers were everywhere. Hearing, "That's what we like to see, gentleman—show the girls what you're made of and tip your favourite lady!" or "Put your hands together for Platinum's top girl, the incredible Chanel!" was soul-destroying. No one was immune to it.

"We've never spoken properly," Emma told Roxy. "Chanel seems alright." A week ago, Emma was chatting to two suits by the bar, and Chanel breezed past, giving the men a cursory assessment. "They have no money," she warned loudly in Emma's ear as she swept toward a private room, her fuchsia pink robe following her like a cape. Emma took it as a compliment, until she realized Chanel had said that for her own ego, not as a gesture of sisterhood.

"You don't know squat if you think she's alright," said Roxy, pursing her lips.

"Oh stop it," Jade said. "All you ever do is talk about Chanel and how much money she's making and where her dress is from and whatever juicy details Bambi decides to throw our way."

"Me? Jade, you're the biggest gossip here! I'm just trying to warn Phoenix to be careful, that's all."

"Why should anyone be careful of Chanel?" asked Kat, her eyes wide, pupils eating up all the blue. "She barely talks to us."

Emma took a long drag of her cigarette and passed it to Kat. "Yeah, why should I care about Chanel?" she said, as blasé as she could. "I barely know her."

"She's definitely noticed you," said Roxy. "Watch yourself."

"Me?"

Jade gave her consent: "She has. You're cute, you're starting to rinse customers properly now. Plus, Bambi sort of adopted you."

"Yeah, that's true," said Kat. "She won't like that."

Emma had to work to suppress a grin.

"Chanel's a veteran," said Jade, getting up for her stage call. "She's gonna have her people watching new girls that are starting to earn."

Perhaps that was why Bambi had been so friendly with her.

Jade continued, "She's not above the threat of other girls taking her money, right? No one is. Now, speaking of threatening, I'm about to kick the shit out of the pole, so everyone please feel free to tip your featured entertainer."

"You need to take everything Jade says about Chanel with a grain of salt," Roxy said, after Jade left. "She's not exactly unbiased."

"What do you mean?"

"Let's just say her and Chanel have a bit of a past."

Kat leaned forward and the club lights pooled in the pockets of her collarbones. "Is that true? That shit about Ronnie?"

Roxy nodded.

"Tell me?" Emma said.

"About two years ago, this girl named Ronnie was the queen bee—hardcore queen bee, too, you didn't want to mess with her—"

"Was she pretty?" asked Kat.

Emma put her hand on Kat's arm to tell her to be quiet.

"Sure she was," Roxy said. "But I'll tell you, she was a bitch. She was strictly business. All about the money. She never got involved in politics. She had the most incredible hustle. Every night she'd have a sit-down, and we'd all be standing at the bar with our arses dragging and she'd be chilling with a bottle of champs."

"Were you friends with her?" asked Emma.

"She didn't really have friends, more like hangers-on. She was too para about someone trying to take her spot. And then Jade came along and it all went balls-up."

On cue, they all turned and watched Jade dancing on the stage for a minute. "Go on," Emma prompted.

"Anyway, Jade was Ronnie's dedicated prodigy. She kissed up like you've never seen, she was like her freakin' doll, like her best friend in the whole world. She used to send her customers, buy her drinks, act like she worshipped her. Meanwhile, Jade's working her way up the ladder, earning good money, getting in with management, right? So here's the kicker—all of the sudden, Jade cuts her off. Acts like Ronnie doesn't exist. Ronnie totally loses it. She couldn't believe it. She tries to get her fired, talks shit about her, but no one gave a crap by that point because Jade was like, the new queen. She had her own little crew of ass-kissers. Classic move."

"What's that got to do with Chanel?" asked Emma, taken aback by the level of the stakes at play.

"A couple of months go by and Chanel arrives. She used to work at some club in New York or somewhere, so she's already big time. But her and Jade knew each other from somewhere—"

"Chanel's got something on Jade," Kat said. "No one knows what it is, but as soon as Chanel showed up, Jade backed off. She just let Chanel take over."

"Way to let me tell the story, Kat," Roxy said. "Jade's had it and lost it and she sure as hell isn't going to tell anyone why."

"What do you think it is?" Emma asked.

"Dunno. I reckon it's something real foul to do with her man—like those kids aren't his or something," Roxy bit her lip. "It'd have to be big for Jade to back down. The whole point is, if I say you should watch out for Chanel, I know what I'm talking about. Shit will go down and you'll know it came from her, but her hands will be clean as a whistle."

Emma tucked a leg underneath her, the velvety fleece of the sofa tickling her ankle while she considered the Chanel situation.

"Do you want to go for lunch tomorrow?"

Emma accepted Roxy's invitation as if it was the most natural thing in the world, but she knew how rare it was to be asked. Why now? "Sure," she said. "I'll give you my number later, my phone's in the dressing room."

"Cool," Roxy said. "Me and Honey are going to go to some new wine bar in Chelsea around three."

"A bunch of guys just came in," interrupted Kat. "By the bar."

"What, those *children* over there? Go ahead, you can have them," said Roxy.

Kat stuck her tongue out. "Whatever."

"I'll go with you," said Emma, getting up and following Kat's lazy wiggle to the group standing at the bar.

Dressed in suits: good sign.

Drinking beer: bad sign.

Under twenty-five: terrible sign.

Most of the group were blatantly ogling Jade on the stage or scanning the room with their faces lit up like Christmas. Emma wished she had stayed sitting, then reprimanded herself for thinking that. She wasn't here in the same capacity as the other girls. Funny how she would forget that sometimes.

"Hi, boys!" Kat sang out loudly, putting her arms around the nearest two. "This is a real treat, so much talent in one room!"

Emma smiled and said hello in a more demure fashion. "What's your name?" she asked a man on the edge of the group.

"Danny," he said. "Look we just got here, and..."

"I'm just saying hello," Emma said, keeping her smile on full wattage. "Sometimes a gentleman can be shy introducing himself."

Danny wasn't listening. He was looking at Kat, who had lifted up her skirt to show off the new tattoo on her buttock. "It killed!" she exclaimed. "Do you like...?"

Emma took Danny's arm and pulled him out of the circle. "So, why are you guys so dressed up?" she said.

"We've just come from a funeral," said Danny.

Emma wasn't sure if he was joking and hesitated.

"Really," he said. "We've been out all day and none of us fancied going home, to be honest."

"When I asked why you were dressed up, I thought you'd been out to a work do or something."

Danny nodded, took a sip of his beer. "It was a friend that we went to college with. It's been pretty rough."

"Enough small talk," Kat said loudly. "I'm ready to get naked now, who's coming with me?"

"I suppose that coming to a strip club will either be really depressing, or a good idea to take your mind off things."

"That was the plan." Danny looked over at his friends, "but most of these guys are just going to get drunk and annoy the women. I don't think anyone has any money."

"It is a strong possibility the lack of money may irritate the women, yes."

This was probably a lost cause—Kat had just walked away with no wiggle and no dance, but she wanted to prove Roxy wrong. "So what do you do?"

"IT," Danny said. "Not very exciting, I know, but it pays the bills."

"Sounds like a smart move to me," Emma said. "If you work in computers, you're never out of a job."

Danny's tie was flipped over and Emma could see the Tie Rack label, and the loose grey thread barely keeping it attached. That kind of thing would drive Jack mad—a cheap tie was bad enough, but to have the label advertising the thriftiness of its owner was unacceptable. Jack was far too judgemental. No one knew how this death had affected Danny. Maybe he was so upset about his friend that he forgot to bring a tie, and had to borrow one from an elderly steward at the funeral home. Maybe he didn't care about what tie he had on that day because he had more important things to worry about. Emma pushed Jack out of her mind and turned Danny's tie the right way round. She gave his arm a gentle squeeze. "I'm very sorry for your loss," she said.

Danny stared at her. He put his beer bottle down on the counter and took her hand. "Come on," he said. "Let's go and have a dance."

Chapter 20

Lee spoke into her ear. "So why don't we meet up sometime?"

She smiled, made her eyes sparkle. "I'd love to see more of you, but..."

"But what?"

"Well, it's just that...I don't want this to come out the wrong way."

"You're not interested."

Emma feigned shock at her new customer's deduction. They had shared several private dances and a long chat over a bottle of wine about his job in the music industry and she wanted to get him to come back and see her again. "Of course I'm interested, silly. You're lovely! But I never go out with men I meet at work, it's a little rule I have."

He relaxed. "You can trust me. I'm not a stalker or anything like that." He put his arm around her waist. "Have you got a boyfriend?"

"Put it this way: if my boyfriend was taking care of me the way I deserve to be taken care of I wouldn't be working here, would I?"

"Then let me take care of you."

"You are so sweet," Emma said, putting her hand on Lee's and stroking his wrist. "I need to get to know you better first. Surely you can understand that I have to be careful if I meet someone in the club. Not all guys are as sweet, or as cute as you."

Lee fluffed up, smiled.

Emma found it hard to believe that line could ever work, but it did. Especially on men like Lee—attractive enough for it be true, and arrogant enough for their ego to agree. They had come to the end of his credit card limit, and as she had thought he might, he was really pushing seeing her in the real world.

"I'll behave. We can meet wherever you want. I'm sure you get asked this all the time."

"Maybe. But I don't usually take it seriously..." She let a look of deliberation cross her face while she traced a figure-eight on his forearm. "Maybe if you come and see me here, at the club a few times, then I can get to know you in a place where I feel comfortable." The easy part was pretending she had just thought this idea up, under the guise of spending more time together in a safe, protected space. The hard part was convincing them you weren't after their money, but it was crucial. Emma got around that by imagining that the things Phoenix said were true.

"That means every time I want to see you, I have to spend three hundred quid to sit in here where I can't relax without some bouncer staring me down or spending eighty pounds on champagne. I'd prefer to take you out for a nice meal and a bottle of wine."

"Are you saying I'm not worth three hundred quid?" Emma pouted, and unwrapped his arm from her waist.

Lee pulled her back. "You are worth ten times that. That's why I want to take you out of here."

Emma chewed her bottom lip and looked into Lee's eyes. "I really do want to get to know you. But I have to take my time. I understand if you don't want to because it's...too expensive for you..."

"It's not too expensive. I make good money. I can afford it."

Time to go for the kill. "Let's not make this about money. I'm not trying to hustle you—it's not me, and you'd see right through it. I knew as soon as we met that you weren't like the other guys in here, you're way too smart to get ripped off and fall for the lines."

"Christ, you don't know how badly I wish I met you in a regular bar. Please, can I see you again? Can we meet somewhere?"

"Come back and see me next week. I'd love to see you again. I really want to get to know you better. You know we'll have a fantastic time."

"Take my number and we can chat over the weekend," Lee said.

"I can't do that here, everyone will see! I could get fired— I can't lose my job. Listen, just let me get to know you a little and then we can go wherever you want whenever you want. I promise. Come and see me on Wednesday."

"...OK."

"Promise?"

Lee shook his head and grinned. "I promise."

"Yay!" Emma made a show of clapping her hands and giving him a hug. "You've made my night!"

Emma knew better than to drink and dial, but thanks to Lee and a few other well-chosen customers, she was the club's top earner that night and had a few (just a few) glasses of champagne to celebrate.

Susanna answered the phone.

Emma could hear laughter and music in the background. "Have I crashed a party?" Emma asked.

"Ems!" said Susanna. "No, I've got Lottie round and we've had a little too much bubbly, I'm afraid. My sister is demonstrating how not to dance in high heels on a slippery floor." She screeched, "Get up woman!"

Emma picked at some glitter stuck underneath her fingernails. "Is Jack there?" She cast a glance at the pile of money on her nightstand and grinned.

Susanna didn't answer; she had started coughing from laughing too hard.

"Is Jack around?" Emma asked again, stumbling into the kitchen to get some water.

"Singapore sweetheart. He's off in the land of...Lottie what is Singapore known for? No, that's Japan, you ninny. Ems honey, I wish you'd come over and see us. The wedding—I have forgiven you, I have. And whatever else has been said between you and your father, this is silly...why don't you come for supper tomorrow and we can chat about it? Oh, and I need to show you all the photos from our honeymoon! My tan bloody well disappeared a week after we got back, I'm not kidding."

"Susanna—"

"Jack can be a stubborn goat sometimes, but he does miss

you, sweetie. One little fight isn't enough reason to disappear from our lives. It's terrible."

"Why is it so terrible?"

"Because you *need* him, Emma."

"You need him!" Emma snapped. She racked up a quick tally of all the reasons Susanna was needier than she:

1. She forced Jack into marriage;
2. She was getting older;
3. She was desperate for a baby;
4. She hated being alone;
5. She forgave too easily;
6. Etc.

"Of course I need him," Susanna said. "And so do you. I've seen you when Jack is late or doesn't show up when he says he will, you get all panicked and funny."

7. She was paranoid.

"Caring about someone is different from needing them," Emma said. "I can function entirely well without Jack. You're the one that can't live without him." She tried to remember what it was she wanted to speak to Jack about in the first place.

Susanna slipped off into a daze. "I know...I couldn't. He means that much to me...We have a fabulous relationship. I love him so, so dearly. He makes me a better person. But it's not one-sided—we need each other, there's nothing wrong with that. Promise you'll come by?"

Emma made excuses and hung up, forgetting her wish to apologize to Susanna for ruining her wedding, too afraid she would admit things she didn't want to.

The next morning, when Emma had sobered up, she was shocked at her behaviour, at her brazenness in ringing her father—to say what exactly that could fix things? She was relieved he wasn't home and, as time continued to pass, was validated by his silence. He didn't even care.

———————————

Emma and Kat went into the last stall in the loos for customers, a place guaranteed to be empty; there were rarely any female guests in the club.

Kat started building a tiny mountain range of cocaine on the toilet seat. When she was satisfied, she pulled a twenty out of her garter. "Be my guest," she said, handing it to Emma.

"No, you first." Emma didn't know what she was supposed to do, not properly—only from television or watching at Jack's parties.

Kat rolled up the twenty. The stark track lighting cast heavy shadows over the dirty tiles and Emma saw Kat's back had a long red scratch across it and there was a wine-stained blur of a bruise under her ribs. The gold swan tap with the drip that could never be shut off dribbled quietly into a pile of tissues in the sink. Oh, and there was an exotic dancer on her knees with a twenty-pound note up her nose. Was this really happening? She could not do this.

Kat stood up and Emma replaced her on the floor, her heart blowing through her temples. She steadied her hand and glanced quickly over her shoulder. Kat was leaning against the toilet paper holder with her eyes closed. Emma swept as much of the powder off the toilet seat onto the floor as she could. She caught a quick look up at Kat.

"You cool?" Kat asked. "Hurry up."

There was still too much left on the toilet for Emma to leave behind. Kat would notice. It would be uncomfortable.

Just this once?

Damn it, she would never do it. Who was she kidding?

Emma crouched over the toilet seat and wiped the rest onto the floor, quickly.

"Let's go make some money." Kat said, whipping the stall door open. "I caned it last week and my rent's due tomorrow."

They hit the club floor and had a look around. Everything had changed in the minutes they had been gone—so much so that Emma questioned whether she had really knocked the cocaine onto the floor or taken it. Not crossing that line made her feel heady with control over her character and no detail in the club was lost. She soared, an alert, ravenous hawk above Platinum's lush, money green forest. Every table was full of prospects. The music pumped louder, funkier and was part of her. No matter who she approached she would make money. She was the hottest bitch in there. She thought that was the first time she'd called herself a "bitch," like the other girls did, and was about to laugh, but the thought was gone too fast. "I'll catch up with you in a minute," Emma told Kat, after hearing her stage call.

Emma wondered if she should take some time off for a rest. Jade had told her many girls subscribed to the two-nights-on, one-night-off schedule, but Emma hadn't wanted to confess Platinum was the only place she wanted to be. She loved having a place where it didn't matter what she'd done or where she'd been. As soon as she saw someone on stage, felt the music in her body or watched the buzz on the floor for a minute, she would be back there. Like everyone in this underground network united by sex, fights against council shutdowns, and middle-aged idiots that talked dirty, you had to love the life.

And she did. This job was a privilege Emma shared with her extended family of wait staff, bouncers, floor managers, cashiers, dancers, cloakroom assistants, cleaners, costumers, DJs, bartenders, chefs and doormen. The only ones that understood, they were a subculture all their own, united in their corruption and suffocation of the night, in their reconciliation to live in the underbelly of society. To them, it was just life.

Emma returned to the floor and convinced a foreign businessman to buy her and Kat a drink while they watched another episode of The Money Skirt.

"What does she have that I don't have?" Kat whined. "I'm way prettier than her."

"Have you ever thought about why Phillip does it?" Emma asked, thinking aloud. "He's doing it as much for himself as he is for Chanel."

Either Kat wasn't buying it or she didn't understand it. She remained silent, waiting for Emma's conclusion.

"He could give her that money at a table, privately, instead of making such a scene, right?"

"It's more fun that way, innit?"

No, it was about so much more. Emma found herself wishing she could talk to her father about this. Jack could offer valuable insight to the Money Skirt. He would know exactly what made Phillip tick.

In a flash, she understood. "It announces his position to everyone in the club," Emma said. "It's a power thing." Being raised on a diet of ambition, greed and rank was really going to come in handy.

Leaving the floor, they exited to dressing room to find Chanel standing at the ironing board counting bills out of a champagne bucket. Bailey was in assistance. "How much do you think you got this time?" she asked.

Chanel shrugged, slowly getting her breath back. "Looks like the usual," she said. "I hate when Phillip comes in so early, I never feel like working afterward. Bailey, babe? Would you take this and take care of Mike and the usual suspects?" She smiled at Emma and Kat. "Gotta keep everybody sweet, right?"

"Of course," said Emma. "Bet everyone expects a big payout from you on nights like this?"

"God, yeah," said Chanel. "Back in the day I used to tip out half of what I made to get in the good books." She chuckled and began wrapping an elastic around a pile of bills.

Emma took the opportunity of the bright lit room and her proximity to Chanel to scrutinize, looking for bruises on her legs from the pole, or badly blended hair extensions, a broken nail—anything. But she was immaculate, her costume box fresh, her makeup bold and beautiful, the jewellery on her wrist sparkling like sunlight on the ocean.

She had seen enough.

Emma was going to do something about this, starting with introducing herself to Phillip.

Chapter 21

"Emma?"

"How do you know where I live?" Emma asked as Ben greeted her at the front door.

"I picked you up for the wedding—remember?"

She did, now. Emma hoisted her bag back onto her shoulder. "Of course I do, I was making a joke of sorts." Why did she say the things she did around Ben?

"So many different men you've lost track I guess?"

Emma didn't answer.

"I'm joking. Your absence at the bookstore has been noted. You're greatly missed."

"I know. I've not been in since..."

"Since...?" Ben stepped up into the doorway, blocking the flood of sunlight streaming in. "I don't hold it against you, you know."

Emma stopped picking up the mail. "Hold what against me?"

"The wedding—would you just turn around? It was obviously a difficult time for you and all. So I understand if you're a little…Hey, I'm not trying to be rude—I'm glad you brought me—in spite of being dragged back to London twenty seconds after a three-hour drive. I wanted—"

"Ben, why are you here?" Emma asked.

"You know why I'm here."

"*I think if all the world hated you, and believed you wicked, while your own conscience approved you, and absolved you from guilt, you would not be without friends,*" she said, quoting Jane Eyre, and then became painfully aware she had just done the thing that used to make everyone in the world look at her the way Ben was looking at her right now. "My conscience approves. Look, what I meant to say is, I don't really know why you're here." She twirled her key ring around her fingers a few times trying to look casual. It slipped out of her hand and hit Ben in the crotch.

Embarrassed, Emma picked up her keys, ignoring Ben's exaggerated cry of pain. "Sorry. I thought after what happened at the wedding…why exactly did you say you were here?"

"I'm stalking you, obviously," Ben said, annoyed. "Your message the other day? Asking me—"

Emma suddenly remembered, and wished she didn't. She had left Ben the worst sort of message a girl could possibly leave a boy: the drunken late-night message, dictated shortly after the drunken late-night phone call to Jack, thankfully fielded by Susanna.

"…something about how cute you thought I was and how glad you were I came with you to the wedding—"

"Okay!" Emma tried to cut him off before he continued. She clearly could hear herself saying something about "making it worth his while" while in champagne-Phoenix mode. "I forgot about that call. I've been really busy lately."

"Can I come in?" Ben asked. He stepped forward again and tried to tuck a strand of Emma's glossed, coloured and artificially lengthened hair behind her ear. It took a few tries, but he finally did it. Emma stood perfectly still, her stomach hovering just inside her throat.

"I want you to know," he said, "I don't make a habit of seeking out women—the lawsuits and restraining orders are too costly, for one. But after getting that steamy message…I knew my luck had turned." He laughed. "Oh, come on, let me in."

Much as Emma wished otherwise, Ben still did it for her. She thought of him often—both sober, and obviously otherwise. His scent of cedar chests and mint chewing gum; his silent support at Jack's wedding when he stepped over the squashed cake and went to start the car; how small her hand seemed in his when he reached to help her into the car. But (and she steeled herself firmly to this thought) if a guy like Ben (no matter how confidently he wore his odd socks and wrinkled shirts) came into Platinum, Phoenix wouldn't bother to go over to his table. "Probably not a good idea," she told him.

Ben nodded in mock seriousness. "I promise not to make any jokes about your thongs."

Emma laughed, in spite of herself. "No, seriously, Ben."

"Seriously? I'm coming in," he said, and pushed past her into the flat.

Emma was stunned. Ben had never been forward or assertive with her before. She followed him inside.

"I guess the cleaner came," Ben said, sitting down on the sofa.

"I don't have a cleaner."

"Oh? Last time I was here, I thought you said the cleaner had the day off or something."

"Right...yes. I meant I don't have a cleaner anymore..."

"Because...?"

"I fired her."

"Why?"

"She stole from me."

"She *stole* from you?"

"In any case, I'm getting another one soon—I'm not really into cleaning up."

Ben nodded. "I hear that. Dishes are my worst enemy. I think I'm going to just buy paper plates and eat off those. I hate to clean my place."

"I would never have guessed," Emma said.

"If you're implying my appearance gives the impression of a disorganized oaf, you would be correct."

"Call it intuition."

"Mystic Emma, what else does your crystal ball say about me?"

If Emma had a crystal ball she'd be using it every night before leaving the dressing room. She certainly didn't need one to figure Ben out, that was easy enough.

"Okay, forget the crystal ball," he said. "How are Jack and Susanna?"

"I wouldn't know."

"So things haven't improved, then?"

"Let's not talk about my family, Ben."

"Susanna's good fun. Lottie's quite close with my aunt, did she tell you?"

"I haven't much in common with Susanna or Lottie," Emma said. "We try to tolerate each other."

"It didn't seem that way to me," said Ben, relaxing back into the sofa. "Lottie told me Susanna adores you."

Now Susanna was getting her sister to do her dirty work? Emma sat down on the sofa to take this in. "You were discussing me with Lottie?"

"Susanna says you remind her of herself when she was younger—shy and bookish."

"I'm nothing like that! And why is it a mark on my character because I like to read?"

"She said you prefer books to people."

"That's ridiculous." Susanna had never understood Emma, no matter how much she tried to wheedle her way in with false support and shopping invitations.

"I thought it was an interesting observation, that's all. Books are better than people—no backtalk." Ben shifted a little closer to Emma. "Don't worry, I set her straight on the other stuff. Would a shy girl invite a man to her father's wedding as a first date? I think not."

"That's different."

"Speaking of which, *why* did you invite me to your father's wedding? All those times I spoke to you at Anderson's and I had you pegged for someone else."

"How do you mean?"

Ben hesitated, didn't seem to want to answer. "Doesn't matter. You're very different now—it's a good thing."

What was the bad thing before?

"Change of subject," Ben said, holding up a book. "How could you *possibly* consider turning me away from your door, when I've come fully prepared to talk of Victorian thunderstorms, orphans and happy endings? Voila! Miss Brontë's romantic masterpiece in Penguin Popular Classics paperback—

as left on the floor of my car in your Cinderella-like midnight dash the last time I saw you—now finally read in its entirety, by yours truly."

"You've never read *Jane Eyre* before? You work in a bookstore." Unbelievable.

"I've always been more of a non-fiction man…biographies, travel guides, comics, that kind of thing."

Emma was thrown by Ben's admission. She had never pictured Ben as a non-fiction reader. How could she have been so wrong? What else was she wrong about? "What did you think of the book?" she asked against her wishes.

"It was alright. Jane's so moody, though, and defiant for the sake of being defiant. 'I will not do what you ask,' et cetera. And the convenient inheritance of money at the end? Bit too Hollywood for me."

"Are you serious? She's suffered throughout her entire life, so of course she's morose! By the time she comes into money, she's survived the loss of everything she cares about: her family, true love, career. The money she receives will never take away from that."

"Not buying it. Sorry. Anyway, how can you identify? You've obviously not had to worry about money before, or live out on a moor in the cold with nothing to eat—look at this flat, it's wall-to-wall designer furniture and ostrich feathers. Marilyn Monroe could live here."

Emma swallowed an annoyingly dry lump developing in her throat. "Jane struggles for independence her entire life. Her inheritance means she's finally, truly liberated and the master of her fate—that's the purpose it serves. She doesn't have to do anything she doesn't want to. Having money gives you control and choices—two things women never have enough of."

"Sorry, who are we talking about? Jane Eyre, or you?"

Emma folded her arms. "Don't read into things that aren't there."

"Hey, I'm all for women being in control. Read whatever meaning you want to in that," Ben said, grinning. "Let's make a deal. I won't read into things that aren't there if you stop pushing me away."

Emma excused herself and went into the kitchen. She was furious that she had gotten into a discussion of this sort with him. Ben had accepted her invitation to Jack's wedding out of pity for her, she was sure of that now—how else to explain his change in direction when he saw her looking like Phoenix? And why was she talking about Jane Eyre? It didn't matter what Ben read, that had nothing to do with her. She didn't care what he thought. If anything, he was right, Jane had nothing to do with her, not any-more, perhaps not ever. Emma was beyond Jane's experiences, she was living alone, truly alone and self-sufficiently in a way no one could understand. She dropped her teaspoon on the floor and the sight of sparkling diamantés on her newly pedicured toes reinforced her determination. Phoenix was the best thing that ever happened to her.

Phoenix had so much going on around her that Emma wanted to tell someone, but who? She wished she could talk about what it was like to have men tell you secrets no one else in their lives knew, confessing with desperation that they were bankrupt and using the company credit card to come and see a girl they were in love with: "Girls like you don't want to be in relationships because it's too complicated. I told Kat that I loved her and she said, 'as a friend?' She can't love me...she's with the next one the next night. The other morning, in bed, I stared at the tattoo on her back for three hours thinking, I *fucking* love this girl." Or admitting they want their girlfriend to use a strap-on and take them in bed. Or confessing: "I'd really like to...you know, get another man off. Is that wrong?"

It made her head spin.

Emma wanted to tell Ben so many things—how she'd fallen in love with the magic of the dressing room, the irresistible femininity of perfumed bosoms and mascara applied with open mouths. Watching the girls arrive in jeans and running shoes, no makeup, hair under a baseball cap, to swiftly transform into perfectly coiffed, glamorous showgirls filled her with a sense of contentment she hadn't felt since watching Cheryl Mercedes put on her "face" in her pink, fluffy bathroom.

She couldn't talk to the girls about it—couldn't seriously discuss with Bambi the guilt she felt over the lies and tangled tales she told a man to get his money, or discuss with Jade why women were vilified for working in the industry, but men suffered little recourse for blowing the budget on dancers. If she asked Kat whether she thought being a dancer ruled out ever being able to view men in a normal way again, it would endanger their friendship. Emma found it so delicious when a man begged for more after a dance, and she wished she could ask Roxy if she thought that made her a sadist, loving the moment a customer opened himself up to her, knowing she had him in the palm of her hand.

The things she heard them say about men? Jack would have loved to hear them.

Destiny: "Men are so stupid. My boyfriend and I had a dance one time in Blackpool, and he was so excited afterward. He was convinced that she was into us. *Both* of us, he kept saying. I'm like, 'Uh, honey? We just *paid* her to be into us!'"

Bailey: "I hate them. I really hate them."

Roxy: "I feel sorry for them. I seriously pity them."

Kat: "I know I shouldn't, but I love slipping a guy my number, and hooking up later, letting them believe it's the first time I've done this...And they'll always remember you as the sexy little minx they turned on so much she had to break the rules. You don't know how good the sex is when a guy thinks that."

Honey: "This is exploitation. For the men! Now that's girl power."

Jade: "Anyone that comes in here is fucked up. Think about it."

Bailey: "So what does that make us?"

Roxy: "This shit is starting to mess with me. Smiling in some fat fucker's face when he asks me why 'a girl like you is doing this job' (because guys like you make me rich, jackass!), and no I don't do 'extras,' (I make two grand a week not letting losers like you touch me...) I just want out."

Bailey: "Make him feel sexy, cane him for all he's worth. What else are they good for?"

All these experiences and emotions, and Emma was just as alone as she ever had been. Perhaps she could have—should have—told her father about it, at the beginning. She could have sat him down and asked for advice, made him feel involved. Even though she knew Jack would hate the idea, at least he would have known. Maybe she would have caught him on a good day. Emma's mature, measured discussion about the opportunity at *Oxygen*, and her desire to experience something new and exciting would impress Jack, and he would put his doubts aside and bid her well.

"I've got a lot to do today," Emma said when she returned. "So I think you should go now."

"In a minute," said Ben. He flicked through *Jane Eyre*, stopping several times before settling on a spot. He read: "'...a tale my imagination created...quickened with all of incident, life, fire, feeling, that I desired and had not in my actual existence.' What do you desire, Emma?" he asked. "Do you know?"

"I'm familiar with that passage," Emma said, snatching the book from Ben. "And it's none of your business."

"I think you need a little more adventure in your life," Ben said, grabbing the book back and holding it out of Emma's reach.

"This is childish," Emma said. "Give it back!"

Ben put the book up under his shirt. "What would Jane do about this little predicament? Would she run away, clutching her tattered skirts and seek out justice? Does anyone care? Not this guy. I want to know what Emma's going to do now that her book has been relocated. I hope her fingernails aren't too sharp."

"Just keep the book, Ben."

Ben readjusted his position, and leaned further back on the couch, putting his hand on the book under his T-shirt. "The cover's a little slippery, I fear the book may move in a southerly direction. The sooner you rescue it, the better."

"I don't know what the hell you're doing," said Emma.

Ben rested his head onto the back of the sofa. "Yes you do. Come and get your book, Emma. I don't bite."

"No."

"Have you ever wondered why is it always about someone else with you?" Ben asked. "All these books you read and talk about. Why are you only interested in finding out what happens to other people? What about you?"

"What about me?"

"Come here."

"No."

"Come here, Emma."

"I can't." She took a step forward.

"Why?"

"It's been nice having you come round, and I appreciate you letting me know you've noted my absence in the book store—"

"Stop it! It is incredibly frustrating to talk to you with your irrational comments like you're totally oblivious to the real world."

Emma through Phoenix's eyes: "We're not right for each other," she said. "You're not the kind of man I want to date. We have nothing in common. I simply don't find you attractive—in any way. I thought all this was obvious, but I guess I haven't made myself clear enough."

In Ben's haste to leave, the book fell on the floor. He kicked it so hard, it went skidding across Emma's newly polished floor, and crashed into the wall.

Chapter 22

Emma was very drunk.

She dropped down into a chair in the dressing room and tried to focus on her reflection so she could check her makeup.

A girl sitting nearby approached her. It was obvious she was new; everything about her said featherless bird fallen out of the nest. She was wearing the wrong dress and had a brown velvet scrunchie in her hair. "I can't do this!" she said.

Emma dabbed some concealer over the dark half-moons under her eyes and acknowledged the girl with a fake smile.

"It's just too hard! How long have you worked here? It's my third night and I just can't stand it. I'm not making any money and…" The girl sat on the counter and wriggled her bottom back until she was leaning against the mirror. "I'm Kelly," she said. "I mean, in real life I'm Kelly. In here, I'm Diamond." She threw up her shoulders. "I keep telling people I'm Kelly."

"Hi," Emma said, widening her eyes and studying them in the mirror.

"I *love* your outfit," Kelly said.

"Thanks."

"Have you been working here long? I'm so nervous. I can't do this." Kelly had a lilt that made every sentence she said seem like a question. "And I love your hair. Mine is so . . . blah. I hate it. No one likes brunettes. I was just out on the floor, and there was this group of guys and they were so drunk, but I thought because they were drunk it would be easier to get a dance from them, you know? But they were all really rude, saying really nasty comments. And then one of them kind of tripped or something and he tipped half his beer down my leg." She lifted up the hem of her dress. "Now I smell like beer."

Emma pushed back her chair and went to have a rummage in Eileen's drawer for eye drops. She found some, and some body spray, which she offered to Kelly. "I'm a brunette," she said. "Well, I used to be. But you can make money as a brunette, trust me." She felt generous and wise. A hardened, money-making, generously wise and completely sloshed exotic entertainer.

Kelly went into the loos and came out flushed and in despair. "I just got my period," she said. "Now what am I going to do?"

"Eileen will give you a tampon."

Kelly's eyes widened. "I can't! I've never used one before and I don't think I can do it."

"You're aware of the irony of not knowing how to use a tampon when you are working in a strip club, right?"

"I guess so."

"Listen—you should leave young guys alone," Emma told her. "Go for the old ones."

"Yuck, I don't like the old ones, they're so gross and pervy."

Emma finished with the eye drops and set to applying some lipstick. She was starting to look better now. "Ninety percent of guys that get sex regularly when they go out don't pay big bucks for a fantasy girl that won't touch them in here. Old men do. When you're first starting out, at least pick the unattractive ones, if they're not old."

"Okay, thanks."

"Do you want to go around the club with me tonight?" Emma asked.

Kelly's eyes lit up. "Really? Wow, thanks...you're so nice."

"Diamond's a good name," Emma said. "You can tell guys that few can afford you, but that you're a superb investment."

Bailey met Emma by the stage door. "I saw you going into Trey's office the other night. What did he want?"

Emma spun her lock open and kicked off her shoes. She needed to change out of her dress, which was much too clammy to keep wearing after a long stretch of private dances and stage shows. "Nothing really," she said, unhooking her bra.

"There's got to be a reason."

"It was just my application from when I first started. They needed me to sign some rules thing." Emma pulled the stretchy neckline of her new pantsuit over her head and began to put on her earrings.

Bailey made a point of looking Emma up and down, stopping at the thin diamanté chain she was wrapping around her waist. "Nice belt. Where'd you get that, then?"

"Bambi's regular bought it for me." Emma couldn't resist.

"You go out with Adolfo?"

"No. Sometimes when I go out with Bambi, *she's* with Adolfo."

Adolfo was a regular of Bambi's. He held a fully fledged hope of sleeping with her, if not today, one day very soon. Bambi made false promises; she planned on stretching things out as long as she could until he figured out it really wasn't going to happen.

Emma thought it might take Adolfo a really long time to work this out. He was in his late forties, with polished hair and a pockmarked face. He liked to talk about all the famous women he'd "bagged." He kept checking his Japanese-import mobile phone to see if there were any messages for him. There never were. Emma liked him straight away.

"See, I told you he exists," Bambi said to Emma while they waited for Adolfo to get fitted for a suit in a tailor off Savile Row.

"I never doubted you," said Emma.

That was a lie. Emma had never believed men like Adolfo existed.

"I thought we were shopping for me, Dolfi," Bambi whined, flicking through the suit racks.

Adolfo and the tailor smiled to each other. "We are. Pick anything you like," he chortled, cigar waggling. "Don't you give me that look. Go take a walk nearby and I'll find you when I finish here."

Bond Street buzzed with high-priced sunshine and afternoon shoppers without jobs to rush back to. Older women in bouclé suits left lacy perfumes floating on the air, and delivery vans pulled up on double yellow lines, ejecting rustling plastic-wrapped cargo on thick wooden hangers.

Emma and Bambi were buzzed into a purple scalloped boutique and were soon surrounded by well-dressed sales assistants. "Try something on," Bambi told Emma. "They love me here—look, here comes the champs."

Emma meandered along the pretty wall of shoes, catching a glimpse of herself in the mirror behind the shelves. Her reflection gave a flit of excitement. She fit in here, spending money and having a girly day out with a friend and her unconsummated sugar daddy. Her hair, pulled up in an overpriced hair clip, looked the right combination of casual and styled, a few tendrils falling at the sides of her face. She reached in her purse and patted some lip gloss on her mouth. She wasn't in a costume anymore.

She belonged.

During lunch, Bambi poked at her dessert and refused to raise her eyes past the level of her water glass. She was having another one of her mood swings and wasn't bothering to answer Adolfo, who didn't need encouragement to express himself.

"It is overrated," he said to Bambi. "But you have to do Palme d'Or. You have to be there. Now, because I am the client, these people have to look after me, but they don't know the first thing about how to do that. And you would love these clubs—so exclusive, full of beautiful girls like you and their men friends like me."

"What do you mean by that?" asked Bambi, stabbing a raspberry with her fork.

Adolfo prodded Emma in jest. "She knows exactly what I mean. She likes to pretend, but it's fine. Why are you so grouchy?"

"I'm not grouchy," said Bambi. "I just really wanted those shoes, Dolfi…"

Emma couldn't help but smile. She knew this situation was outrageous (*truly* outrageous), but she felt completely comfortable, almost serenely calm and at peace being in it.

"Oh poor baby, you going to pout all afternoon about these shoes? I didn't like them, they didn't suit you—they looked cheap. Adolfo will get you a much nicer pair from a different shop."

Adolfo turned to Emma.

"Phoenix, how long have you been working at the Platinum Club?" he asked.

"Long enough," said Bambi. "Right?"

Emma smiled. "Right."

"It's a nice club." Adolfo folded his napkin into a precise square and set it on the table. "A girl like you must make good money there."

"It's been shit lately," said Bambi.

"It's the summer, all the businessmen have to take their wives and families on vacation. I'm sure you two are fine, no? You're both beautiful girls, and the way some of those other ones carry on there—so unclassy, so pushy..."

"You know who he's talking about, right?" said Bambi.

Of course Emma did. It was getting pretty vicious on slow nights at the club. Girls weren't waiting for guys to sit down or have a drink before they began their unrelenting onslaught.

"That infuriates us too, Adolfo," said Emma. "If you hate it, imagine on our side of things—you see someone come in that you know, that has come in to see you, and they are hit on by—"

"Hootchies!" said Bambi. "You can't get near them."

"Hoo-what? Where do you learn these words?" said Adolfo. "You watch too much MTV."

Bambi rolled her eyes and wounded another raspberry.

Emma pretended she didn't want to accept the gifts from Adolfo, but she was delighted to carry around her free designer bag and other prime goods. It meant she'd hit another rung on the ladder. She played it modest, but she deserved those gifts; she'd done most of the work with Adolfo that day, chatting to him and making conversation while Bambi pouted her way through the afternoon. Emma would handle Adolfo very differently if he were hers.

It might not have been so smart to bring her prime goods to work and then taunt Bailey with them, but too late now. Bailey was staring at Emma contentiously, without blinking. "That catsuit is fucking fierce," she said, snapping her gum. "Real fierce. That's not from our dressmaker, is it?"

"I don't really remember," Emma said, getting out her deodorant and spraying a big cloud of it, hoping to disperse this Lycra-clad mosquito. The carryall that Adolfo had also treated her to fell out of the locker and deposited its contents at her feet. A pile of new dresses, a dainty eggshell blue jewellery box and Adolfo's business card put the conversation further at risk, as did her Louis Vuitton CD holder.

"Looks like you're trying to go VIP in that getup."

"She's livin' in the VIP!" sang Kat, joining them. "Can I borrow your phone, babe? I've got no credit left on mine."

Emma passed Kat her phone and gave her a firm look. "I am not 'living' in the VIP. And why don't you pay your bill like everyone else does?"

"I saw you rob that footie player last week! Why you lying? Those boys spent three grand on drinks alone. I swear they bought me about a hundred shots of tequila. So, how much did you get, you jammy cow?" She leaned against a locker for balance.

Why did Emma have to notice things the way she did? It had happened before, people defiling the idea she had of them. Kat, for example. Emma had found her fascinating and beautiful in her simplistic approach to work; she admired her ability to focus on the job at hand, have fun and never question herself. But after a while, she started to notice that, well frankly, Kat was a bit thick. Emma thought it was an act, or was because she was young and left school early, but Kat was not going to get smarter as she got older. She was just thick. Diamond's frequent bruises weren't from her scandalous sex life in bondage and satin, they were because her boyfriend used her as a punching bag. Jade, a woman with a university degree in politics, was so high the other night that she went on stage with two different shoes on. The other day, Emma heard a girl say she was going to help her younger sister get into stripping as soon as she was old enough. Destiny was pregnant—four months pregnant and still working, her belly becoming a question mark in the men's eyes. Destiny's continued drinking making Emma feel strangely tearful. And Bambi, who was so polished and so well maintained? If you looked closely, you would see her dresses had loose threads and missing sequins. Sometimes she didn't reapply her lipstick often enough, and would sport only a lip line, or a half-eaten mouth. Today her dress had the chalk ghosting of deodorant marking the armholes. Emma was no longer sure Bambi, Jade or Chanel weren't sleeping with their regulars. Something wasn't adding up. She hated seeing these things; they irritated like mascara under a contact lens. She tried to ignore them, but they were everywhere.

"Are they coming back, do you think?" asked Bailey.

"Don't know," said Kat, dialling a number into Emma's phone. "One of them said they might come back next weekend. Oh, Phee, your one was so cute, I hate you! v...i...p...Who sings this song, do you know?"

Emma caught Bailey looking at her again, but this time she held her gaze and didn't look away. "If you want, I could call the one I made a fortune off and ask him. He did give me his number. I'm sure he'd have some doubles."

"I don't need fucking charity, Phoenix." Bailey lowered her voice. "I know now you're doing well, and looking good and all that, but some of us have been in this game for a lot longer than you have. So just remember that, and just remember that I don't need help from you. I was the one who gave you the newbie tour, have you forgotten already?"

"I'm just saying, if you want to come, come."

A tall girl in a pair of white patent leather boots came out of the DJ booth and stood by the stage door waiting for her call.

"Can't believe they hired another black girl," said Bailey. "It's an invasion, I swear."

Kat scrunched up her face. "Bailey, please let me hear you say that in front of Jade. Please? You're so fucking ignorant."

"She'd agree with me, mate."

Kat handed Emma her phone. "Where is my new man? That's the third time I've tried to call him tonight." She linked arms with Emma. "C'mon, let's go make some more ching-ching."

"You coming, Bailey?" asked Emma. "Or have you got anything else you want to say about Jade and all the others like me and Bambi, too? We don't sunbed to get this colour, 'mate.'" She was pushing her luck now, definitely.

"Mind yourself, Phoenix," said Bailey, before turning away and opening her locker.

Something was starting, but Emma didn't know what. What was Bailey challenging her for? There was a very conspicuous edge in the air. A low-lit bulb of warning popped into Emma's head, but tending to it would have to wait.

Chapter 23

He was looking at her. He was definitely looking at her. On the edge of the floor by the private rooms, a well-dressed man sitting with Bambi was staring at Emma as she walked through the club weighing up the customers. Emma slowed her pace and watched him watching her until she reached the bar, where she preened, pretending to oversee the club activities.

As soon as Bambi got called to the stage, the man waved her over.

Before approaching him, Emma took her time, picking her cigarettes up off the bar, opening and closing her purse, checking her jewellery was done up.

He invited her to please sit down. She nodded toward Bambi's lipstick-stained glass and the bottle of wine they were sharing. "I can see you have company," she said.

"Join us. Please," he insisted, taking a chair from the table next to them.

Emma sat down and paused for a waitress to pour her a drink.

"As soon as I saw you, I wanted to talk to you. You're beautiful."

This was a predicament. He had money and must be in the middle of a sit-down with Bambi, who wouldn't be having a drink with anyone if they weren't paying her to. Emma wanted that money. The unsaid code was simple—it said you couldn't approach a customer when he was with another girl. If girls broke the code from time to time, usually they were new, or the night was so slow it was open combat. But Emma hadn't approached this customer, he'd called her over. He wanted her, not Bambi.

"Are you paying for Bambi's time?" Emma asked the man, taking in his diamond-encrusted watch. "Because..."

"No, not yet," he said. "We began to talk about it, then she was called to the stage. Nothing's been arranged, so you can stay. I insist you stay."

Loyalty was a novel concept to Emma. With few close friends in her life she was loyal only to herself and knew no other way to be. Bambi had helped her so much, but for whose benefit? Emma was quite sure she had only been helped so she could be added to Chanel's stable. She half-heartedly tried to sell both herself and Bambi to him, but who was she to change his mind? He was the one paying.

"I'll get rid of her," he said.

Bambi returned, glowing after her efforts on the pole. "Hi..." she said, smiling at the customer and looking quizzically at Emma.

"Hey..." Emma said. She tried to convey an expression that said she was innocent and had been summoned over against her will. It didn't look like Bambi understood. "He called me over to keep him company while you were on stage," she said quietly. There was nothing worse than two girls fighting over a customer. She hoped Bambi wouldn't make a big deal out of it—these things happen.

The man began speaking in Bambi's ear, but when he finished she didn't get up. "We agreed," she said to him through her teeth.

He huffed and reached for his wallet, thrusting some money in Bambi's hand.

"Right, she's gone," he said when Bambi left.

"How much did you give her?" said Emma.

"Forty quid."

"Oh." That was embarrassing and Emma didn't want to think about it. "Now, what kind of trouble are we going to get up to tonight?" she whispered, soft as silk.

Emma emerged from a private room after a lengthy string of dances with Bambi's customer to a very freaked-out Kat.

"I've been looking for you everywhere!" she hissed. "It's all kicked off, Phoenix. Where the hell were you?"

"I just came out of the VIP—you just saw me walking out the door," Emma said. She put her hands on Kat's shoulders. "What's happened?"

"Jade…" Kat said, her voice thick, "…just got the shit beat out of her because of you."

In a rush of words, breaths and death threats, Kat told Emma: "Bambi came into the dressing room with Chanel, cursing your name, saying you just stole a customer from her—you didn't, did you?—and Jade told her to chill out and that you would never do that and then Bailey and India got into it, slagging you off saying how you're trying to take Adolfo from

Bambi, too, and before you knew what was going on, they started fighting, Bailey and Jade and then Bambi jumped in—it was two against one—and I was diving in, and India held me back telling me this wasn't my problem, and I was trying to get her off me and all the time they're just laying into Jade—she was on the floor just kicking at them. You know Jade can hold her own, right? So she gets one of her shoes off and slices Bailey's face with her heel and it was bleeding everywhere, and she was trying to get up off the floor and then I got away from India— and you know the whole time Chanel is just sitting there watching, she's not moving a muscle, like she's too good to fight when she's got her little slave girls to do it! Eileen comes in and separates everyone and decides Bailey needs stitches so she sends her off to the hospital with India. And Jade's okay, but her lip is bleeding and her hair is a mess and she's gone home, and the whole time I'm thinking how I never trusted Bambi or any of them that are tight with Chanel, you know? Everyone was in there and no one got involved, they all just freakin' sat there. I swear, I've had it with this place. But Phee, you didn't nick Bambi's customer, right? Tell me you didn't do that."

Emma hurried down the stairs—no, wait—she should be descending, gracefully poised, but she wasn't. Emma was clutching the banister tight, holding on for dear life, instead of letting it graze her soft, little hand, instead of letting her freshly polished nails tap the shiny, wooden rail to the music rising from the cave below.

Phoenix wouldn't be emotional. Phoenix would remember a time when she had faced a similar challenge and come out alright, like the time she was booked to perform at a big club in Las Vegas and the car she was driving in…no, that wasn't it. It was the time Phoenix had her heart broken by a man she thought would never betray her, a man that…no, not that either. *Damn it.* Emma couldn't keep her thoughts together.

She felt sick about Jade. It was her fault. It made her want to crawl out of her skin.

Emma had nearly stopped walking. Each step she took, the lights were dimmer, the stairs steeper. She was sliding into the pit that fed on self-indulgent illusion. If she kept going, she would slip and fall to the place where the idea of her was worshipped, before the woman in her could ruin it.

She opened the doors to the main floor and went in. The rush of atmosphere, inviting and seductive, enveloped her and drew her close, just like it was supposed to. She swallowed the sensation, took a great big gulp of its air-conditioned reassurance. She put on her cloak of indifference and reined in her emotions, reminded herself that Phoenix was not Emma.

She saw a group of dancers sitting at the bar with their legs crossed high, thighs shimmering in the club lights, drinks in their hands, a thousand secrets in their hearts. They were beautiful. They ran the world. Above them, Roxy was dancing on the bar stage, running her hands down her body to take off her dress. She tossed her hair to one side, and when she saw Emma watching, her expression changed—suddenly she pulled a face and rolled her eyes. That face meant, "You understand, don't you?"

Then Roxy kicked off her dress and went back to focus on the man who had been watching her from the bar, licking her lips and throwing her head back. If you didn't know better, you'd think she was in ecstasy.

Chapter 24

"Blackjack!" screamed Kat with delight, jumping up and hugging Emma. "I can't believe it!"

Emma couldn't believe it either. She didn't know how Kat was still standing. They'd been in Vegas for two days and hadn't been to bed yet. She could barely see straight, let alone do the math to count to twenty-one. "Nice one," she said, as Kat collected a stack of chips and began doing a victory dance around the slot machines.

Leaving a group of male admirers behind, with the promise of meeting at a posh bar later that evening, they decided to go and spend Kat's sizeable earnings in the glass-and-iron strip full of designer boutiques and shops at their hotel. Most of the shopkeepers knew them intimately already.

The jetlag and tiredness were worth it. Emma hadn't wanted to take time off, but when Kat suggested the trip, she couldn't say no. Her back ached constantly, her joints were becoming loud, cracking accompaniments to her dance routines. She was waking early in the mornings, drenched in sweat, disoriented, like she used to do after Imogene left. Things were getting hot at Platinum, and Emma needed a breather. The stress of wondering who the "secret shoppers" working undercover from the council were—and how much the club knew about her trips with Adolfo, or her small collection of business cards from customers she built into regulars—was getting to her. Things had been going missing from her locker—nothing valuable, but enough to let her know she was being messed around with. She was sure she would suffer some consequence for taking Bambi's customer. She'd lied to Kat and Jade about what really went down that night—she couldn't get the image of Jade's bruised face out of her mind. And the idea of Jade letting that attack go without retaliation? Never.

Emma sensed a breaking point on the horizon, but for who, or when, she didn't know. She needed to get it all under control, and she needed a time-out. She was becoming more and more irritated by many of the girls Bambi associated with—classless, clueless girls who Bambi took under her wing undeservedly.

The other night, two of the door security men carried a quadriplegic man down the stairs in his wheelchair, and placed him where he jutted out cumbersomely from the black lacquered table. His wheelchair had a computer screen and keypad attached and when the waitress came over, Emma found it excruciating to watch him pound out his request with a folded, feeble hand. He was too much of the real world to be in the fantasy of perfection at Platinum; she could see it written on the other customers' and dancers' faces.

India was summoned.

India was exquisite. She had slate-grey eyes and straight black hair cut into a heavy fringe. Her manner was so gracious—she carried herself as if she was of royal blood. She wore a beaded cap with crystal and pearl droplets elegantly dangling down into her hair and had two golden brown freckles dancing on her left shoulder. She made Emma understand how men were seduced at Platinum—when they couldn't get enough of a dancer's looks, so pleasing that they were content to stare for hours and all they wanted to do was to make them happy.

A good friend of Bailey's, India's real name was Karen and she was from Bristol. She had a funny body odour—like stale bread—because she couldn't be bothered to wash her costumes and left them in a locker overnight. India wasn't a very nice person, and she certainly wasn't as sweet as she looked. She picked her nose in the dressing room and gave dirty private dances.

India kept making eye contact with Bailey and Bambi, who snickered and whispered to each other. The man in the wheelchair typed a message and turned the screen for her to see. She smiled, answered quietly, and he typed again. This went on for ten minutes, her diffident response, leaning forward to see the screen, holding her hair back from her face, and then as soon as he looked away to type, opening her eyes wide to her friends in embarrassment. Emma felt like murdering her.

It wasn't all about the tension Emma felt tightening the walls of the club; the long flight was worth it for the sense of warmth and security Emma felt being around her girlfriends. She'd never felt like she was part of something before, been so accepted at face value. She would protect these current friendships now no matter what—they were all she had.

How different a woman would Emma have been had she had her mother around for longer? If she'd been able to bond with others instead of watching from the outside? Life had never failed to show her that as soon as she made a connection, it would be broken. Even Cheryl Mercedes (a painful, unexpected loss), broke their association, something Emma could never forgive her for.

It was late one balmy evening in August, and Emma had overheard a conversation between her grandmother and Cheryl. Startled from her sleep, Emma crawled out of bed and crouched under the window overlooking the driveway. She put her ear next to the inch of air she was allowed to have her window open (at night the temperature dropped and you could catch your death).

"Mrs. Gordon, I don't mind her spending time over here. Not at all—she's a very sweet girl."

"Yes she is." Nana's voice sounded like a squeaky drawer. "And I think it's very kind of you to entertain her. I know you have many interesting stories about your life as a beauty queen."

"I wasn't a beauty queen. Until very recently I was the head of a successful cosmetics company—"

"It's probably not a good idea for Emma to be next door as often as she is, or to be reading such fanciful romance books as you do. They are inappropriate for her age."

"I agree. I have to say, she's very advanced, with an incredible imagination. She reads voraciously. We've just started reading some of the classics—she loves *Jane Eyre*. And really, I love having her over—she keeps me company and we have loads of fun. She's like the daughter I would never wreck my body to have!" Cheryl's laughter stopped quickly when met with Nana's hostile silence. "I'm happy for her to come over. I know her father's very busy with his work and that she gets a little lonely—there aren't many children on this street."

"Emma doesn't care much for friends," said Nana.

Emma's stomach felt like someone had trod on it; her heart was beating harder than in the *Tell-Tale Heart*. She pressed her hands as hard as she could on her chest to try and quiet the banging.

"With all due respect, Mrs. Mercedes..."

"Please call me Cheryl."

"Emma's father is of no concern to anyone outside this family. I have nothing against you, dear. I'm sure you're a lovely woman. I have Emma's best interests at heart. I don't think it's a good idea for her to develop a relationship with a woman of your age." Emma knew her grandmother's facial expression would be one of tasting sour milk.

She had started to shiver violently in her thin cotton night-gown. She wanted to scream out the window—to run to Cheryl and get in her big car and drive with her to America. She wanted her grandmother to leave them alone.

"I appreciate that Emma's mother isn't a part of her life anymore." Cheryl's voice was fading in the air, like she was already in the car pulling away. "I've spoken to her father about that—really, I'm just trying to help. I want to help. She's such a wonderful girl and I feel she has so much inside her that needs to come out."

"There is much, much more to this story than you realize," said Nana. "In any case, Emma will be back living with her father in the fall, so it makes little sense to create a bond that she will have to break in a month."

"I see."

Nana lowered her voice, and Emma strained to hear it. "Until fairly recently, Emma would be physically sick every single time her father would leave her—for any reason—to drop her off at a sleepover, to leave her here for the weekend. When her mother left, she woke in the night for over a year, calling for her. I don't want her to become attached to another person who won't be in her life permanently."

Before Emma could identify her feelings for Cheryl, it was too late. Jack came for her, and they were living alone in a soulless loft conversion in the Docklands.

Emma struggled trying to figure things out for herself. She developed much earlier than her friends and struggled to hide her changing body in the schoolyard. Getting a bra was a nightmare—she didn't know her size and she was too embarrassed to ask Jack for help. He never remembered to give her money for her "time of the month," so she would have to go to Boots with her allowance money, and hide the girly pink boxes in her school bag. She could have asked one of Jack's girlfriends, but he didn't have them stay over very often, and none of them seemed to be that interested in her, except for that one who had said she "clung" to Jack. (So untrue.)

She kept her first boyfriends a secret from Jack, though there wasn't much fun in it: sneaking home late to find an empty house; condom wrappers discovered by the cleaning lady instead of her father; and birth control pills handed out by the pharmacist who didn't ask for a parental signature.

Coming to Vegas on a whim for her birthday was good for her. Since she was eighteen, Emma had stopped bothering to celebrate. She had always been disappointed by birthdays— Jack was never one to make a big deal out of them—but her eighteenth was the worst. She was certain her mother would reappear—how could she miss it? Eighteen was a big deal, and Emma was sure, if she knew Imogene, that this would be when she would choose to come for her, woman to woman, adult to adult, now that Jack could lay no more claim to her. She woke on that morning half expecting to find Imogene kneeling by her bed, watching her sleep, like she used to before her other birthdays. "Good morning one year older," she would say, and before Emma could croak a greeting, Imogene would shower her with kisses, tickles and her special before-birthday breakfast present—always something extravagant, their "secret" from Jack: a pair of emerald earrings, a gold charm bracelet or a lusciously soft angora jumper. But nothing. She couldn't hide her disappointment and was grateful Jack was thousands of miles away on business, leaving her a card and hastily scribbled promise to make it up to her.

On that birthday, Emma swore it would be the last time she hoped for Imogene, the last time she picked up her mother's favourite books and flipped through the pages, inhaling the smell of sandy beach holidays and school vacations, of leaving biscuits for Santa and overstuffed Christmas turkeys, of sleepover parties and fluffy rabbit slippers, of lavender shampoos and hundred-strokes-a-day hairbrushes, of first-kiss descriptions and first-breakup tears, of graduation ceremonies and wedding dress shopping; it would be the last time she cried.

"I reckon we should forget about those boys from the casino and go on a rampage tonight," Kat said, bringing Emma back to the designer mall. "I say we crash all the strip clubs and check out the competition."

"Mmm...I'm going to need a power nap before we go out tonight," Emma said before answering her vibrating mobile phone.

"Emma?"

Shit. It was Sylvia. She had forgotten she was screening her calls. "Oh, hi!" she said.

"I got your message. Smart to ring and leave it after hours when you know I won't be here to answer the phone." Sylvia sounded angrier than Emma thought she would be. "You can't resign on my answer phone a month before I'm expecting to run this—"

"I'm sorry," Emma said, nodding as Kat held up a cute snakeskin handbag. "Get it," she whispered.

"Where are you? Come down to the office now so we can talk about this properly," Sylvia said.

"I can't. I'm not in London...I really apologize for the message, Sylvia, but I thought it would be easier."

"For who? What's happened? If you didn't want to do this assignment you could have just told me. That would be the fucking professional thing to do. Where's your respect?"

"I did want to do the assignment. And I do respect you. I just feel like I'm moving in a different direction with my work now and *Oxygen* isn't the right place for me."

Kat brought over a swishy cashmere minidress the colour of a ripe lime. "What do you think?" she asked. "I'm going to try it on."

Emma nodded and flicked through a few of the well laid-out racks of clothing. "I've put together all of my notes and my work so far," she said. "You can still run the story." It was true, Sylvia could put something together, something good. An intern could do it, Emma was sure of that. Well, nearly sure.

"If you ever want to work in this industry again—"

"I don't."

Sylvia was silent. And then the line went dead.

"Phee," called Kat. "Are we shopping or what?"

"We're shopping," Emma said, putting her phone back in her purse.

Chapter 25

"I don't understand why they have to have these stupid meetings after work," said Kat, rubbing her drooping raccoon eyes and yawning.

"Me neither," said Diamond, massaging a kink out of her shoulder.

Emma sunk further into her chair. She could barely keep her eyes open. The flight back to London from Vegas was long and Platinum didn't care how tired they were, tonight's meeting was mandatory. This was surely the longest day in the history of the world. Now she was stuck with the rest of the Platinum staff, from chefs to chauffeurs, on the main floor waiting for Trey to address them.

"Why don't they have these meetings in the daytime?" Diamond asked Jade, who was sitting on her right.

Jade finished tapping out a message into her phone with a hyper-flexed finger to protect her polish. "Would you come to work early for a meeting? They've got to do it now when they already have us here. Why so quiet, Phee?"

"No reason," Emma said. She still felt guilty when she spoke to Jade, and had vowed to make it up to her, even though Jade acted like nothing had happened. It was clear that was not the case—the girls were clearly divided up in factions on either side of the stage. Emma, Roxy, Jade, Kat and Diamond on this side, Chanel, Bambi, Destiny, Bailey and India on the other. Chanel and Bambi were engaged in a heated discussion.

"What's the meeting about, do you know?" asked Kat.

"Probably the bullshit with the council and the court case," said Jade.

"Thank God that's sorted," said Diamond. "Those worry-warts who all quit last month must feel like idiots now."

Jade nodded. "I knew it would blow over. It's not the first time it's happened. No biggie."

Emma didn't admit how concerned she had been about it.

Trey climbed up onto the main stage. He waved off the hoots and catcalls from the girls and straightened his tie. "Thank you for the applause, but I will not be performing tonight, you ladies cannot afford this. I know everyone wants to go home, myself included, so I will keep this short. We've had a rough couple of months what with the council trying to take our licence and shut us down, and we had our last day in court Friday. For those of you who don't already know, the ruling came through that we haven't been up to anything shady, so the Platinum Club lives to see another day and rob a few more punters!"

"Yay!" said Kat. "I was so worried I'd have to go audition somewhere else and I hate auditions. I was going to try and go to—"

Trey held up his hands. "Hang on. Shut up for a second, you guys. I'm not done. First, I want to thank the people who came down to the tribunal and testified on our behalf: Terri, Honey and Max—everyone give them a round of applause. Honey, you get a month's free house fees, and Terri and Max get the next two weekends off with pay."

Emma took a long look at her fellow workers sprawled under the burnished lights of the formidable main floor. Girls curled up on sofas in the centre of the floor counted their money under cover of their bags, mouths giving them away as they calculated. The waiters huddled at the edge of the floor, and the bouncers stood in a tangled mob of black suits and two-way radios. Seemed there should be a violin or a string quartet documenting a sweeping view across the plains of the floor.

"Also, I want to make a point of saying that we know it's not been easy lately with the extra strictness of the bag checks and the extra bouncers on the private rooms, but it was for the club's protection, which is for your protection, too. We had our 'secret shoppers' out, trying to catch you girls out, and everyone behaved themselves, so congratulations again there…I need to make a special announcement about one of the girls. It's important for all of you to see how serious we are about maintaining our licence, and looking after the girls that play by the rules. Because it just takes one girl on that video footage that the council reviews every quarter, to ruin it for the rest of you. Now, it is unfortunate that we have to do things this way, but I'm going to have to name and shame…"

The mood in the room became like an elastic band tightly stretched around finger and thumb at point-blank range. The girls looked at each other, alarmed and uncertain.

"Ohmygawd ohmygawd ohmygawd!" said Kat. "I swear, I'm totally innocent."

"Shush, babe," said Jade.

"She has been seen outside the club with customers. She takes business cards from guys in the club. And we found drugs hidden in her locker that we've been told she's selling to other girls. All the warnings we have given to you guys that we are not joking around, that we will be heavy-handed—some girls just don't seem to care. And to the rest of you, you should be pretty pissed that someone in here wouldn't care about leaving you in the street with no job, having to fight with over two hundred girls to get an audition somewhere."

"Holy shit!" whispered Kat. "Ho-ly shit…"

Trey continued, his voice hard and empty of warmth. "This girl is Jade. Jade, that you would so blatantly disregard this club and its policies when everyone else is working so hard to play by the rules is truly disappointing." He set a look of disgust on her. "Now get the fuck out of my club."

As Jade was escorted off the premises, screaming her denials, Chanel and Bambi blew Emma a great big goodbye kiss.

Chapter 26

Emma hadn't mentioned to anyone that she had carefully been approaching Phillip, saying hello, even buying him a drink when he was at a table waiting for Chanel and sending it over through Max (giving him strict instructions to "pretend" he wasn't supposed to tell him it was from her).

It was a busy night, and Emma saw Phillip sitting alone at a table near the back of the restaurant. He was wearing an expensive black suit, baby blue tie and his trademark matching monogrammed handkerchief in his pocket.

He was alone.

Emma flipped her head upside down and shook her hair out. She adjusted her cleavage and popped a breath mint in her mouth.

Time to go to war.

"Hi Phillip!" she said, kissing him on both cheeks.

"Phoenix, my lovely, how are you?"

"Wonderful, thank you. Have you just arrived?" She hoped she wasn't slurring her words.

"Yes, I just got here. What would you like to drink?"

She raised her hand, "I can't, I've had too much to drink already."

"What, you can't have a soft drink? Some juice? You must have a drink," Phillip said, waving to Max and ordering a mango juice.

Emma tried to keep track of her thoughts, which a minute ago had been clear and unembellished, easy to follow, but she found now if she tried to hold on to one idea, the others would fly past like a fast train on another track, speeding away from her. She knew she had made a decision to do this, but she wasn't sure how to pull it off. She tried to clear her mind and reassured herself she knew all she needed to.

"Are you alright, Phoenix?" Phillip smiled at her. "Sit down." He wasn't attractive, not to Emma. But he had a certain charm tied up in his well-placed poise and the lilting foreign accent that no one could place. His economic success soared above him like a cloud of confidence.

Emma knew Phillip had thousands of pounds in cash as well as a black American Express card in his hand-stitched pockets. Her mind was working overtime. She bit her tongue to stop herself from asking why the Money Skirt was only for Chanel, and not other girls. She choked back her all-consuming desire to beg Phillip to choose her, to demand that he elevate her to such status. Instead, she glanced over Phillip's shoulder in the mirror behind him.

"Looking for Chanel?" he asked.

"Of course. I don't think she would be very happy to see me sitting here with you." That was the understatement of the year, but Emma had to tread very carefully here, couldn't say a bad word against Chanel.

"Bah!" Phillip said. "She doesn't care. She will come to me when she's ready. She's off entertaining some twenty-year-old boy somewhere. She knows I'm here to see her."

"How long *have* you been coming to see Chanel?" Emma concentrated on saying Chanel's name like she was her best friend and favourite dancer (the *stunning and beautiful* Chanel, Platinum's *top* girl!).

"A year or two," said Phillip, turning one of his rings the right way up. "I was doing a lot of work with foreign clients, and I would bring them here to entertain. Chanel was very good to me. My clients loved her—she's a very well-educated lady—and they would always debate politics while she charmed them. She took good care of me when we would come in. She said she knew I was the one in charge, she could tell I was the only gentleman of the bunch. You know—all the things I wanted to hear," he chuckled. "Chanel's very good."

Emma nodded. Looked again in the mirror. A striking, sexy woman named Phoenix was staring back. She could focus again, she could see straight. This was a good sign.

"I remember when you introduced yourself, you were like a little mouse, so timid. Now, you're like a lioness!"

"A lioness?" Emma couldn't help laughing. "Far from it!"

"Oh, but you are. You've gone from this timid girl who no one noticed—and I know, I notice all the girls, I remember *all* the girls that come work here. And now you're the queen of the jungle, elevated, removed from the lowly wildebeests."

Emma ducked her head, feigned shyness as she laughed. He liked her. Now what? She stayed silent, let him give her more to work with.

"Many girls here are just trash," Phillip said with disdain. "Trash on the inside, trash on the outside. No brains, going home with men for less than I spend on dinner tonight. It's not easy to find a classy, intellectual woman you enjoy spending time with."

Chanel must be the best. She'd made Phillip think she had a brain and a personality.

"Chanel was right about you," Emma said. "You're a true gentleman, and you stand out a mile here." Not least because he was the reason for Chanel's mythical status at Platinum. The real reason Chanel was the queen was down to what Philip had created. The more money he spent, the higher she rose. But he must know that.

"Many of the men here don't understand what this club is about," Phillip said.

"What is it about for you?" Emma asked.

"Many things," Phillip answered, pausing to take his mobile phone out of his jacket and turn it off. "Obviously, I like being able to enjoy a drink and conversation with a beautiful woman, and I love to see her take off her clothes for me—of course..."

Emma smiled. "Of course."

"But I also like to watch the men in the club. How they act, what they're spending, who they're spending it on."

Emma saw a window opening. "None of them compare to you," she said. "You're Platinum's favourite client..."

Phillip swatted that away. "Yes, the money I spend brings them much joy, I know."

"It's not just your generosity with the club," Emma said. "No one tips the stage like you do."

"When I am up at the stage, giving all that money to Chanel, I'm waiting—I'm wishing another man would step up and take on my challenge and try to out-tip me. A little competition, you know? Imagine that. But I look around, and no one has the balls. It's only gratifying to be on top when you've had to fight to get there. Do you understand what I mean?"

"More than you know," Emma said. "I don't think many men can compete with you, Phillip. That's probably why they just don't bother."

Phillip raised his eyebrows and nodded slowly. "Phoenix," he said, "flattery will get you everywhere."

"That's the name of the game," Emma said, smiling. She toasted his glass. Phillip wasn't stupid, he knew what she was trying to do.

Phillip waved to Max. "Can we have another menu, please?" he said. Then to Emma, "You will have dinner with me."

Emma tucked her chin to one side and let her hair fall forward onto her face. "I am hungry..." she said, looking up at Phillip with her eyes on full sparkle. "But I can't."

"I know what they disguise as food for your dinners in the dressing room," Phillip said. "I'm sure you have supper all the time with other customers that come to see you."

"Sometimes I have dinner with *friends* who come in to see me," Emma said. "I'm just thinking, perhaps Chanel will want to eat. I'm sure she's been working hard tonight and I don't want her to go hungry..."

"She's a little rabbit. She eats nothing but salad leaves."

Speak of the stiletto-heeled devil, here she was.

"Hello, baby," Chanel said to Phillip, leaning over and putting her bottom in Emma's face. She kissed him and whispered something in his ear before turning to face Emma. "Thanks so much for looking after my Phillip. I hope he behaved himself."

"A perfect gentleman," Emma said.

"Of course he was."

Phillip took a sip of wine. "My dear Chanel, you look beautiful this evening."

Chanel ran her hands down her shiny silver dress. "Thank you, sweetie. And now I'm all yours. I promise I'm not going anywhere." She flicked her hair, gave Emma a fake smile. "I think you should give Phoenix a little something for keeping you company while you were waiting for me...it's only right..."

Chanel shouldn't tell Phillip what to do. Because that was just rude. Nor should Chanel be offering Emma a way out of the situation, an easy exit—*with cash*—not if she wasn't worried about something. Emma couldn't believe it—that something was Phoenix. How extraordinary.

"Actually, Chanel," Emma said, waving Phoenix into the home stretch, "if you don't mind, Phillip and I were about to have some dinner. I'm absolutely starving!" She opened her menu and began looking through it.

Chapter 27

Emma checked her stage outfit in the mirror and adjusted the straps of her black lace bra. She pulled out her "stage" glasses, an overly stern tortoiseshell pair, and put them on. She quickly checked that the thin black line that ran up the back of her stockings was aligned properly, slipped her feet into a pair of towering black patent leather platform heels and popped her head into the DJ booth. "Hey Mike!" she said, giving him a kiss on the cheek. "How are you?"

"Hey good lookin', what music do you want?" he asked, taking off his headphones.

Emma leaned her head on Mike's shoulder. "Hmmm...you know what I fancy?" she said. "Can you play 'In The Air Tonight'? That would be perfect."

Mike pulled away. "Babe, you know that's Chanel's song. For Phillip."

"Please?"

"Pick something else."

Emma took out two fifties and put them in the pocket of Mike's trousers, giving his thigh a squeeze. "Please? I *really* want to dance to that song…"

"What are you up to?"

"Just play it for me, okay?"

Mike put his headphones back on. "You better put on a good show," he said. "It might be your last."

Emma took her time walking toward the pole at the front of the stage, letting the music seep in around her, waiting for the smoke of the dry ice machine to drift gently around her.

One of two things would happen: Chanel would hunt her down and try to kill her, or Chanel would send someone to hunt her down and try to kill her. Either way, she didn't care. If she was going to do this, she wanted to take it all the way, regardless of the consequences. She'd openly declared war on Chanel and there was a fairly good chance she might win.

No turning back now.

She'd never felt such a head rush of pleasure like this before. Goddamn it, she had worked so hard for this, had given up so much for Phoenix, and wasn't she worth every bit of it. Her life had a tangible, measurable set of intentions and she was authentically pursuing them. Or to put it another way, she totally rocked. She was the shit. The bomb. And all those other words the girls used that she used to scoff at. She got it now.

I can feel it coming in the air tonight, oh Lord…

Emma rolled her head slowly from shoulder to shoulder, flicked her hair back off her face and spun around the pole, gripping it between her legs to slow down before landing. She circled her hips around in a languid figure-eight and ran her hands down her legs.

When Emma saw him, she had to fight to stay upright.

Phillip had come to the edge of the stage. He was holding a thick roll of money in his hand, which he began to unwrap. He cast some casually at her feet where they settled like a dirty scarlet newspaper. He threw some over Emma's head and they fluttered down around her like tickertape butterflies.

Carefully. Slowly. Delicately. Elegantly. Emma knelt down in front of Phillip and ran her hands down her body, lowered her chin, and looked up into his eyes.

"Hello," he said.

She smiled, took her stage glasses off. "This is a surprise."

"This is *my* song," Phillip said, tucking two notes under the strap of her bra. "And it's never sounded better than it does tonight."

"I'm glad you think so."

"Dance for me, Phoenix," he said. "Let's see if anyone will challenge me tonight."

Emma turned and climbed the pole to the ceiling where she perched, surveying the club. She felt invincible; she was one with the music, a cinematic moment brought to life. Her body and mind were absorbed by the rhythmic atmosphere of song and the power of her movements—she had the audience under a spell, wrapped up by the scenes unfolding. Emma rolled her head back and gyrated to the music before hitting a difficult pose in mid-air, heady with this perfect moment. She slid down the pole with her legs in a scissor-kick in one smooth motion and finished dramatically, arching her back. Chanel was standing at the back wall of the club with her eyes set on cold steel. She hadn't bothered to put her dress on after her last dance, and it hung around her neck like a shiny, sequined python.

Simultaneously, Emma felt a rush of exposure and of question—it was as if there was something out there, as if she was being hunted. She wanted to tilt her head and sniff the air like an animal sensing danger. She was panting from the exertion of her dancing, but now it felt more like anticipation. Her mind was getting away from her again—Emma always had a way of creeping back in when Phoenix was in charge.

Emma returned to Phillip, wanting to drink in every detail of the experience, to never forget the intensity locked into the walls of the club, the blinding colours of money and sex and success. Could this really be happening?

She extended her gartered thigh for Phillip to fold some money over it and couldn't help but take another voracious look at her audience. Kat had stopped dancing on the bar stage and was staring with her mouth hanging open. In the restaurant, Trey raised his glass to her and went back to his dinner. Bambi was standing outside the dressing room door smoking a cigarette like it was her last. A handsome man sitting in a booth with Destiny and Bailey was staring at her so intensely it gave her a chill. Why was he looking at her like that? The answer was immediate and horrendous: because the man was her father.

... All pretty girls are a trap, a pretty trap, and men expect them to be.

THE GLASS MENAGERIE

get me a
cab
now

Chapter 28

For just a split second, Jack thought he'd found Imogene. For just a moment, he really did think he could see her right there in front of him. The world stopped spinning. He actually felt something way deep down, like hope. Then he felt something like angry, blue-black, fist-crunching recognition.

It wasn't Imogene. It was Emma.

And then hell.

Jack leaned his throbbing head out the window of the taxi to spit a gob of blood into the road. Those security bastards threw him out of the club like he was a fucking yob. He hadn't realized he'd left his seat. Barely noticed the chairs he knocked over or the champagne bottles that smashed as he charged the stage like an unhinged bull in Pamplona. Thank fuck he'd stopped short of strangling that slimy bastard by the stage with all the money. He just wanted to cover her up. Get her off the stage. He shuddered.

Jack tried to control the vertigo whirling inside his head. Did Emma need money? Impossible. Had she met some drugged-up pervert outside a tube station that had her conned, pimping her for cash? That idea made Jack nearly tear a hole in the cab seat.

He'd have known if she was in trouble, she would have come to him. Didn't he always try to rally round her if she needed help? He tried to think of a time Emma had come and asked him for help. He couldn't.

He mopped his forehead with a jacket sleeve and racked his memory for signs of Emma slipping away. There was that time she told him to use an escort service for dates. That was ages ago, there was no way. Was there?

"Excuse me, mate?" Jack called to the driver. His voice sounded strangled. He swallowed the acid start of bile rising in his throat and tried again. "Don't take me to Holland Park… Here's the thing, though. I don't know where I want you to take me." He sounded a complete twat and the cab driver's facial expression confirmed it.

He did not sign up for this. Fucking Imogene—she'd ruined his life, she really had ruined his life. How was he supposed to raise a daughter? How was he supposed to know what to do? She must have known he would fail. God, the years of being blamed by Emma for her mother's mistakes; the years of his mother nagging in his ear about what a screw-up he was. How hard he worked—through stomach ulcers, insomnia, living through the black hole of unanswered questions—so he could give Emma a life to be proud of, and for what? For his daughter to end up exactly like her mother, working as a fucking stripper.

He had to calm down and get a grip on himself. He took a breath so deep it burned his chest, held it and released it.

With a jolt, Jack remembered:

- clients: abandoned.
- credit card: left behind the bar.
- wallet: mercifully still in his pocket.
- briefcase: dumped at the coat check.
- *daughter*: dancing on the stage.

Okay, fuck calming down. Murderous rage and overwhelming embarrassment were the appropriate reactions in this situation.

The phone rang and he checked the display. Susanna. Jack stuffed the ringing phone back into his pocket and loosened his champagne-drenched tie. He couldn't go home now, not to look Susanna in the eye and have her see him laid out on the floor. That would do irreparable damage to their relationship.

In an instant, Jack's love for Susanna seemed laughable compared to his love for Imogene. His stomach rolled over at this.

He should have told Emma the truth about her mother, but wasn't it bad enough already? She broke something in Jack, and he'd be damned if he let Imogene break any more of his daughter. He would never understand. What kind of woman leaves her child behind? Leaves him to explain? She must have known they would never survive without her.

Jack couldn't admit it to himself, how hard he had loved Imogene, so how could he explain it to Emma? He couldn't admit that he loved the tragedy in Imogene's existence, that he was attracted to her all-consuming, overwhelming need to be loved, her overambitious want for beauty and pleasure and deliciously fine things, her good heart buried under the years of street life and abuse and God knows what that she'd gotten away from—it made his dick hard that he could fix it all. He wanted to be her hero. He felt ashamed remembering the rawness of his emotions over another person, but oh, she had him whipped in a minute. She made him feel like he could do anything. Her luscious, pouty mouth. Her caramel toes. Her beauty, so pure it made him ache to be near her. Her rounded, growing belly, full of a gift he never gave to her. He was stupid in love with her. Still?

It was as if he had seen Emma for the first time tonight. That she could harbour such secrets was as impressive as it was terrifically horrifying. The fruit never falls too far from the rotten, empty tree.

Didn't she look beautiful, though? This made something else start in Jack's chest, a sense of pride he had never experienced in having an attractive offspring. But that was Imogene's doing, he couldn't take credit for that.

They weren't great together, but still, he and Emma had their moments. There was that Christmas they went skiing in France and he'd pissed off that woman—God, what was her name? Well, he pissed off whoever he was with, and she fucked off back to England, and he and Emma got so drunk that she knocked over all the skis at the side of the chalet. She kept saying, "I am in tumult!" over and over, and the more she said it the more the skis fell like dominos. He was so buzzed he tried to help but he just ended up falling over with the skis. They laughed for hours, and he loved her that day, he knew that he loved her, even with all the shit she was putting him through missing school and disappearing for days.

She was fourteen and starting to look the spitting image of Imogene; Jack tried his best not to notice this. He had followed

Emma once to see where she was going, to try and understand what was going on in her head, trailing her into the tube station, keeping a herd of young skateboarders with silly hair between them down the escalator. On the carriage behind her, Jack watched as Emma took the Circle line around and around, never getting off, never speaking to anyone, just occasionally glancing up from her book to stare fixedly at a person opposite her. After two hours, Jack got off the train and drifted around the grime of King's Cross until he had the energy to go back to the office. How do you fix it?

Emma.

One thing Jack has learned about times like this: amazingly, incredibly, somehow his life continues. Financial markets drop out of the sky, people lose millions of dollars, but the sun still comes up the next day. Wives leave, love is bludgeoned to death, but the earth keeps on turning. Tomorrow Jack will go to the office, finalize his presentation and fire someone for putting his career in jeopardy. And then he will come home to a late dinner with his beautiful, adoring wife. He will be thankful for these things.

And Emma?

This wasn't his mess to clean up, and there was no recovery from it, even if he wanted to fix it.

He was her father, but this was asking too much of him.

Well, at least now he could get his briefcase and credit card back, Jack thought. He stared at the drinks menu waiting for a game plan to form in his mind.

Nothing came.

He waved for a waiter and ordered an expensive bottle of wine.

"In the champagne section you must buy a bottle from this list—at least one an hour, sir," said the waiter. "You can pay cash, or use your card. The rules are printed here." He pointed to the folded menu on the table.

"Oh right. Let's have that one then," Jack said, sharply. "And a double Scotch on the rocks." He was willing to kill for a drink right now.

"Very good choice. Would you like a cigar? We have several quality imports in the humidor I can recommend."

"Sure, fine. Just bring whatever cigar you think best. And one for the lady."

Emma and the waiter looked at each other.

"For the lady, sir?" the waiter looked like he was tired of calling people sir. Jack resisted the urge to punch him.

"Right, no. Of course not. Sorry." Jack adjusted the knot of his tie. "Just get the damn drinks, would you?"

Jack felt like everyone in the building knew he was sitting in a strip club with his daughter. Why had he come back? He'd half expected she wouldn't sit with him, more than half hoped they'd tell him there was no such girl here, but she had come, she was right here in front of him. One thing he knew for sure, he would never set foot in another strip club as long as he lived. He would rather die. In fact, he would happily lay down and have a leg removed than ever have to step foot in another place like this.

He found if he looked at Emma very quickly, in small lightning-quick increments, he could deal with the visual apparition of his ex-wife in front of him. Jack never thought of his failures, refused to accept their possibility, because if he did, he would never have the strength to get up and go to work every morning. He focussed his attention on a girl who had just come on stage. She was struggling with her show, in that wrong-shoes-wrong-hair kind of new girl way, but Jack could tell she loved the attention of the guys at the tip rail. She grabbed at the pole and swung her hips a little too fast, out of sync with the music as she sang along to every single word of the song, feeling like a star under the lights on that stage. She thought the song she'd chosen meant something, she thought the music mattered. But all the guys wanted was for her to hurry up and show them her tits.

A girl poked her head around the side of their booth.

"Hey," she said, coming in.

So much for privacy. Jack gave a passing glance at the huge security man standing in the doorway, arms folded.

"Just wanted to bring these in for you," the girl said, putting a pack of cigarettes down on the table in front of Emma.

"Cheers, Diamond," Emma said.

Cool as a cucumber, Jack observed. Or was she? Her crossed leg was jangling, and judging by the way she tore open the cigarettes, she had been suffering for the relief of one.

"Am I being charged for this?" he asked Emma. He couldn't help it, he wanted to make things worse. Jack was quite sure he wanted to see his daughter cry. "Just let me know your rates. I assume you take credit cards?"

He saw Emma flinch.

A moment passed between them. "I usually charge three hundred pounds an hour to sit with someone in a private room," she said.

Where did she get the balls? Jack felt overcome with an almost murderous rage. This was a woman he did not know; this shook him even more than seeing Emma on the stage an hour ago. He prayed for calm. He prayed to the almighty gods of mercy: if anyone deserved some mercy, ye gods, it was him. He composed himself. He was a pro at the power play, and if Emma wanted to do things this way, so be it. Pushing another wave of nausea down, Jack reached into his wallet and counted eight fifties, slow and steady, on top of the ashtray. "Let's start with this then, shall we?" he said.

Chapter 29

Emma had not expected the anger.
Embarrassment, but not this much anger. How had she not expected anger? Jack's scarcely guarded fury horrified her; his fists clenching and unclenching, the whites of his eyes set to ferocious. How did he get back in? Once security had thrown someone out they had no chance of returning that week, let alone that night. Jack must have greased several palms with more money than she could imagine; he had paid for one of the expensive private booths upstairs next to the restaurant.

After they saw each other, she had stayed, unmoving on the floor of the dressing room, money scattered at her feet, tears in her throat. Diamond and Kat had come in with a champagne bucket of bills; she promptly vomited in it. And then, in what had seemed less than a minute, Eileen was telling her a very high-rolling, high-paying customer had requested her in the VIP.

Jack had come back.

And so she somehow stood up to this challenge, which she now regretted dearly. Asking Jack for "sit-down" money tore out her throat and hit her limit. Neither of them had spoken since. Remember, this is your territory, Emma told herself. Not his.

Their waiter, Max, returned with the drinks and Jack downed his quickly.

"What are you doing here?" Emma asked.

"What are *you* doing here?" Jack responded, moving on to his glass of champagne and taking a large gulp.

"Isn't it obvious?" she said.

"Don't talk to me like that. Tell me what the fuck is happening right now!"

Emma didn't answer.

Jack reached over and took Emma's hand. "Why? Why are you working here? What is going on?"

Emma peeled Jack's fingers from around her hand and flicked her hair. She wasn't really ready to speak and needed to stall for a moment. She took a deep drag of her cigarette.

Jack's moment of microscopic tenderness was gone. "I can't stand the way you're acting right now," he said.

"You never liked the way I acted before," said Emma.

"Your mother used to act like this."

"Like what?"

"Attention-seeking." Jack's face crunched even further in disgust.

"How would I know what's fact or not if I know nothing about her? You reject her, you reject me, fine." She was shivering. She told herself it was because of the air-conditioning.

"You're so deluded, Emma."

"I may be deluded, but I am a different person now. I'm not dependent on you anymore—"

"You? Independent? You're having a laugh. I'm paying you to sit here!"

Emma felt torn in two. Her moment of glory, sweeter than she could have dreamed in a million imaginings lay on the carpet of the dressing room where she had left it so she could return to the floor and agree to sit with her father. Phoenix was the one who gave her the strength to get to this chair, but what now? Phoenix was the victorious one with Phillip. What about Emma?

Who was she really? There was the troublesome rebel, breaking things just to stop the screaming in her head; there was the withdrawn, folded-in version of herself to keep Jack from suffering any further; and now there was Phoenix, a multidimensional, contradictory caricature that was taking over her life and erasing any union to the person that had been. It used to be fun—disappearing. It used to be a safe place to go. But now she had become stuck inside this story.

"It was *Oxygen*," Emma said, suddenly weary and confessional.

"What was?"

"How I became...how I ended up in here."

Jack leaned forward in his chair. "What do you mean?"

Perhaps not everyone was meant to have a story. All those people she gave lives to—the escaping husbands, the lost phone numbers found in a back pocket leading to romance—perhaps they really were just regular people, with no stories. The woman on the tube taking her child home was just a woman on the tube with a baby, nothing more.

"It was a feature—a feature article for the magazine. An undercover story."

Jack didn't understand.

"I came in here to write an article, Jack. It was an assignment about strip clubs. I was doing a story."

Jack's face went through an array of changes. "I get it," he said, but he didn't look like he did.

"I was going to tell you."

"Wouldn't that be something I might like to know? Wouldn't that be something we should talk about?"

"You were busy. I didn't want to say anything until I had done it. There was no point in mentioning something if I hadn't done it."

"I never liked that magazine. Pure exploitation—they're using you, Emma, they're using you so they can...I don't know, so they can get a story. They don't give a damn what happens to you in here."

"They do care—they did...I'm not being exploited. No one forced me to do this."

Jack spat out his words: "Did you think you were going to get the Nobel Prize for literature doing this shit?"

"Lots of jobs require you to make sacrifices, Jack—look at your job. Doctors, lawyers, celebrities—they all give up parts of themselves. This is like that."

"And why you? Why did they pick you to do this? When you said you were getting more involved at work, I just figured it would be, I don't know, like a recipe column or something daft," Jack said, craning his neck to watch a girl climb the pole. "Can you do that?" he asked. "No—don't answer. When I think of all the time, and all that shit we went through with the wedding..."

"I know."

"When does it finish?"

"When does what finish?"

"This article. When do you get to leave?"

"I don't have to be there anymore. I missed my deadlines and then I quit. I come in and work at the club because I want to…I know you'll never understand, but I like it here, Jack. I feel like I belong here."

Jack's nostrils flared. "You like it? You've no right to be here in the first place." He threw his hands over his face and back through his hair. "This is so, so fucked up, do you know that?"

"Well, whose fault is that?"

"It's my fault you're a stripper? Good one. I had nothing to do with this. You've got more chance of blaming that on Lottie, mate. Blame me for making you a spoiled adult or blame me for not buying Malibu Barbie when you were four, but not this."

"You wanted me out of your life. You passed me off on Nana, you sent me away to school—you wanted me to just grow up, to just go away and disappear and stop bothering you and interrupting your all-conquering plans. You wanted me to be successful and ambitious and focussed—a big money-maker like you. And I am! Aren't you proud of that?" Emma didn't care that she sounded like a child. She didn't want to be here any more, everything was ruined. She wanted to take her makeup off. She wanted to go home. She felt like she had aged ten years. "You can't all of a sudden try to be my father and tell me what to do!"

"All of a sudden? All of a sudden I'm *trying* to be a father? I stuck around, remember? I stuck around to take care of my sullen, unsociable, live-in librarian of a daughter. But now, because I don't want you working here, you of all people— a girl in a woman's body, prancing around with no clothes on—you say that crap to me? I have worked and sacrificed things you do not know."

Emma could really see her father now. Under the provocative lighting that put your best face forward, she could see his willingness to wash his hands of any responsibility simply because he stayed. Just because he stayed was enough for him.

Jack flung the last of his Scotch down his throat. "Something has gone seriously wrong for you to end up in here. You don't know who you are, Emma. That's your problem."

"You're one to talk. You're three different people—Jack the harried husband, Jack the executive asshole and Jack the absent, fucking father."

"Enough of that absent father shit, that record is getting old. And swearing like a sailor won't impress your punters. I'm the one that's been there—I'm the one that cares about you, Emma."

"None of it matters anyway. I can't be who you want me to be."

"Who is that?"

"I don't know. But I can't be her. What does it matter? It's better for you now that I can look after myself. You don't have to pretend to care anymore."

I know I should think well of myself; but that is not enough; if others don't love me, I would rather die than live— I cannot bear to be solitary and hated.

Perhaps for Jane Eyre, but Emma knew this wasn't true. "I can bear the solitude, Jack, I really can. Rather than compromise myself for others' attention, I can stand alone. How many people can truly say that?"

"I don't understand you," Jack said. "You're not making any sense. Please. I'm fucking begging you. I am begging you— this isn't the place for this conversation. Let's go, please, let's leave now."

"Did you ever read *The Glass Menagerie*?" Emma asked.

"Imogene's favourite," Jack said. "No. I never did. Let's go now."

"It's a story told by a man named Tom Wingfield, who works in a shoe warehouse and is terribly unhappy with his life. He wants to find adventure, and write poetry, not give his soul to a factory every day." Emma reached up and tucked her hair behind her ears, leaned forward. She really wanted Jack to listen to her now, she needed him to hear her. "After work, Tom stays all night in the cinema watching movies and magicians instead of going home. Tom lives with his mother and sister—his father left years ago. His sister is kind of a non-entity, really frail, she's given up on her dreams. Tom's mother is almost tyrannical in her disappointment with him. He's miserable. Jack? Are you listening?"

"I'm listening. Tom is really, really miserable."

"Tom has this line," Emma said, after a moment. "He's talking about a trick—this escape he saw a magician do—that left him mesmerized. He says, 'It don't take much intelligence to get yourself into a nailed up coffin—but who in hell ever got himself out of one without removing one nail?' Do you know how impossible that is to do? To escape a life that's fated to be unsatisfactory and not leave a trace?"

Mike's voice came over the PA announcing a two for the price of one dance special.

"I've been thinking," Emma said. "What if it's not your fault? What if it's other people who decide your life is to be unsatisfactory—what then? And I was also thinking, what if no one would even notice you had escaped? How hard could it really be? I thought I was the only one, but I'm not. There are so many people like me, knocking out nails and never coming back."

Emma tilted her head to the ceiling, waited for her eyes to absorb the tears. "How could she leave us, Jack? I don't understand. She started something in me, and then she left. How could she just leave?"

"I don't know, baby," Jack said. "She started something in me too."

Emma got up to go to the loos, she needed a moment out of the confrontation with Jack, with the truths she felt starting to thump inside her head. The day Imogene left followed every step she took toward the bathrooms, it replayed in front of her eyes as she reapplied her lipstick with a shaking hand and dabbed at her moist forehead with tissue.

She was eight. When no one came to pick Emma up from school—again—she assumed Imogene was just late. She was busy lately with her acting classes and sometimes would forget. Or maybe she was trying to finish the sweater she was knitting for Emma to wear for picture day. She was always losing track of time.

Jack came to pick her up from Victoria Buckley's house. She'd been asleep, her hair in wet worms stuck to the side of her face. Groggily, she followed Jack out to his Jaguar, shoelaces trailing on the pavement.

Jack didn't speak, he just put the key in the ignition and started the car. Before the inside light went out, Emma saw he had a deep scratch running from his ear to above his eyebrow. She wanted to ask how he got it, but something made her afraid to. Jack was mumbling something to himself, his chest rising and falling sharply. Emma's book bag slid off her lap toward the floor of the car, the zipper scraping against her skin as it descended. She felt prickly, but didn't move.

"How was that English test of yours, honey?" Jack asked.

"What English test?"

"I bet you got the highest mark in the class. Didn't you? You're the smartest girl in that entire school."

Emma sat unmoving in her seat, her bag and its zipper having made its complete descent down her inner calf to rest at her ankle.

All the way home, Jack hummed along to the radio, which was turned up too loud, playing music she knew he didn't like. Then he started changing radio stations, punching buttons one after the other, over and over. He tapped the steering wheel out of time.

At the house, Jack pulled into the driveway, put the hand brake on aggressively, and turned off the radio. He reached across Emma, got the house keys out of the glove box and hopped out of the car. He took the stairs two at a time and went inside.

There was something Emma liked about seeing the house from there, with all the lights on, knowing her parents were inside waiting for her. Imogene would be on the sofa, the quilt half-wrapped around her, yarn all over the floor. Jack would come in and say, "Don't give me that look, she's fine." Then he'd go over and kiss her forehead. She would pretend she was mad, but she would look up in his eyes and let him.

Emma leaned over to turn off the ignition, but she turned the key the wrong way and the noise of the engine gunning made her jump.

When Emma got inside, the silence in the house enveloped her. A knitting needle lay on the floor of the lounge, ready to roll under the sofa. Emma searched the room until she found its partner spearing a ball of grey wool next to a knocked-over tea cup, the West London Theatre Company logo stared up at the ceiling. Magazines lay scattered on the floor like stepping stones across a parquet lake. Emma hopped from one to the other until they ran out and she was stranded in the middle of the living room.

She waited for Imogene or Jack to come in and tell her to get ready for bed, but no one came, so she went and changed from her school clothes into her pyjamas. Then she washed her face and brushed her teeth. And flossed. She went to her parents' bedroom door. It was locked.

She sat outside it, pulling her stretchy cotton nightgown over her knees and tucking her feet underneath. She tried not to think about how hungry she was. Where was Imogene?

Putting her ear to the door, all she could hear was wood, and the sound of her head resting on the door. Before she fell asleep there, she thought she heard Jack laughing. Rather than making her smile, the sounds Jack was making made her very, very afraid.

Since then, it had always upset Emma to see her father in pain. When her grandmother died last year, she often found him up late, staring into the fireplace, his Scotch untouched and eyes distant; she tried to hug him but he was angered by affection and denied that he was even bothered. It took months before he agreed to help go through Nana's personal things so the house could be sold.

"Can't we just hire someone to do it?" he had said.

"She was your *mother*," Susanna said.

"I'm not a monster," Jack said. "I think she'd hate the idea of one of her family, especially me, going through her personal things, that's all. You know how pedantic she was about privacy and reputation."

"Wherever she is now, she sure doesn't care about who clears out the attic," Susanna said.

"You'd be surprised."

"I'll help you," Emma offered. "I could meet you after work and we could go down together. It won't take long."

Emma told Susanna they spent several hours there, but the combination of dusty furniture (dust was really just old skin, Jack said), ants in the kitchen and Emma's discovery of a walnut trunk filled with photographs of her grandparents in happier, more naked times, had them out of the house in minutes.

Wasting time in the pub afterward, Emma tried not to laugh as she watched Jack trying to recover. "I am so sorry," she said. "I never...I mean...that's the last thing I expected we would find. I thought it would be jewellery or love letters..."

Jack grimaced and put his arm around her. "What's today's lesson? Having a heart gets you nowhere but covered in old skin and needing years of therapy. Now, I think you owe me another pint."

It wasn't as if they were unable to connect, she thought. It was just so very rare, so pushed aside by the rest of their lives. She didn't want it to be that way.

Emma returned to the booth determined to find that connection again. Jack looked exhausted and unwilling to do anything more than lay down on the sofa and pass out.

"Let me try to explain something," Emma said, sliding in next to him. "One night I did a dance for this guy—"

Jack put his hands over his ears. "I do not want to know about this. I do not want to know!"

"Just listen," Emma said, pulling his hands down.

"Fine. But don't give me details for the sake of details."

"Alright. One night I met this man at the bar and ended up doing a dance for him. His name was Jason. He was young, well-dressed, kind of cocky, but in an attractive way. He'd only just arrived and wanted to get settled so we didn't speak for very long. Jack? Are you listening?"

Jack nodded grimly and began to rip up a Platinum Club matchbook into tiny pieces.

"Later I went into one of the VIP rooms and started talking to a guy named Damien. He was drinking a lot, spending a lot of money—he paid for several dances. He really bought into the whole experience and felt that there was something special between us; he really liked me."

"There'd better be a point to this."

"He wanted me to stay with him in the VIP, but he was on a boy's night out and his friends were winding him up, interrupting, wanting to go to the bar, that kind of stuff, so we parted ways. He was adamant that I find him in the club later. To be fair, he was a little green and—"

"Green?" Jack sniggered and swept the mountain of silver cardboard morsels onto the carpet. "I didn't just hear *you* call a guy green."

"Inexperienced, then."

"So Damien thinks you've had a magic moment, I get that bit."

"Toward the end of the night, I saw Damien upstairs at the bar with his friends. One of them was Jason, the guy I danced for at the beginning of the night. Damien starts to introduce me to Jason saying, 'This is the girl I told you about. This is her, this is the one!' Instantly, the atmosphere changed. It completely changed from being lighthearted and fun to something else. They both knew that the other had been for a dance with me and that Damien really liked me—he had put that out there, admitted it, spoken about me earlier. I suddenly became more valuable; Jason physically stood much closer to me, put his hands around my waist—he was almost aggressively in my personal space and said, 'I *knew* this was the girl you were talking about.' He then said he was taking me downstairs for another dance straight away. This upset Damien, you could see it in his face, because he felt a personal connection to me—he liked me in a real sense, for my personality, as a person."

Jack made a show of swallowing to stop himself commenting.

"Two minutes before, everything was friendly and easy-going, then it turned into the two of them competing. I became something else to them, it was about who could win."

"One, I don't understand that story. Two, I don't like stories about you being a successful stripper, especially when you can't tell the story properly. Three, how on earth does that relate to me?"

"It relates to you because it's how you live. You only want things that other people want."

"Emma, that is in no way the same. You could have chosen a better story to illustrate that point. You're purposely trying to give me the willies. And I am not as easily led like a fucking sheep, regardless."

"I'm not saying you're easily led, I'm saying that in your world, it's all about market value. Whatever the market is willing to pay for something is what denotes its value. Thus your belief that your job makes you a powerful man, because it's based on how much control you have of a marketplace. You don't like hearing me use myself as the example. In here, the more a woman takes off her clothes the more power she has."

Jack considered this and dismissed it. "That's not empowering! Listen to me, Emma. Being so detached from reality that you can rob men without a conscience is not a feminist act. Acting like you're having an orgasm while you think about what groceries to buy the next day is not a feminist act. It's fucked up. The girls that work here have nothing going for them. I guarantee you they have volatile, messed-up backgrounds or no family. I promise you they have no kind of confidence about themselves and need constant reassurance about how good they look or if their ass is still perky. And they *only* care about money. It's not a recipe for a healthy individual. You're a clever girl and there's a remote chance you are still using your brain at this stage in your illustrious career, but the others in here? They're abusing the situation, they're about one thing and one thing only, and they'll say or do anything to get it."

"You don't do that when you tell some guy about a company merger that might never happen? We're only doing our jobs, Jack. No one is forcing men to walk in here."

"Women talk about not wanting to be objectified, and not getting the same rights as men, but if men were working like the con artists in here there would be a national uproar. Life is not about a constant transaction of funds into the T&A account, no human emotion required, sign here. It royally fucks me off!"

"Sounds like you know a lot about strippers," Emma said.

Jack raised his eyebrows.

Perhaps Jack was right about being unemotional. No, she knew he was right. Most of the girls at the club kept their real lives as far away from their Platinum lives as possible.

Phoenix hated weakness in people, but whether Emma was dancing for a CEO or a plumber, it was their vulnerability that she felt so attracted to. Phoenix only cared about the surface of things, what was false was fine, but to Emma, she was less exposed than her customers were; their nakedness was reflected in their eyes, in that moment of want and need; it was the most perfect, real thing she had ever experienced. She wasn't so sure about the power all the girls got that came from controlling a situation and having a man at your mercy. Didn't the man love you for how you made him feel about himself? Not because you were someone incredible, but for how he felt around you? It could be anyone saying the right words in his ear.

"We've gone off topic," Jack said. "You never finished your story of girl power in the champagne room. What happened when you went for a dance with the guy that 'won' you over his lovesick friend?"

"Well, I felt differently about him."

"Why?"

"I don't know, but I really did. It was very different the second time I danced for him. It was more intense because he was like the alpha male staking his territory."

"You can't use some lonely, spotty kid who falls in love over the first pair of tits he sees as an example of my lifestyle and priorities."

"What makes you think these were lonely, spotty kids?"

"Who else is going to get caught up in one-upping their mate in a strip club? Or believing that you were really interested in them?"

"These were Premier League football players. They didn't seem lonely to me, and they had fairly decent complexions."

Jack nearly spit out his drink. "These guys fighting over you were footballers?" he said after stifling his coughing. "Over you? Which ones? What team did they play for?"

"I'm not sure what team." Emma knew the team. It was Jack's favourite.

"What were their names again?"

"Jason somebody, I don't know...Middlesex, I think."

"You danced for Jason goddamn Middlesex and Damien Lafayette?" Jack sat up like Emma had just announced she found a winning lottery ticket in the bin.

"Correction, I *robbed* Jason Middlesex," Emma said, grinning.

Jack shook his head. "I don't believe this..."

"Further proves my point. The more important the person, the more likely they are to want to play the game. He felt powerful having me, I felt powerful having him; I played into it, too."

Jack wasn't listening. He was staring into his drink, unable to rein in the smirk on his face. "Jason Middlesex..." he said. "He was the leading goal scorer for Chelsea last year, did you know that?"

Emma's value with her father had just increased, and she wasn't sure if it was for the right reasons. That Jack was impressed with her felt good, even if it was with misguided motivation. Emma left it there, didn't mention that Jason had invited her, insistently and provocatively, back to the hotel with him *and* Damien, to continue where they left off. Didn't mention how pissed off Phoenix had been when Emma didn't go.

Suddenly she was full of stories, and eager to share them with someone who didn't work at the club and couldn't counter with a better experience. She liked having dozens of remarkable, and more often, contentious things she could talk about. "See that girl over there?"

"Who? The one with the big head?"

"She doesn't have a big head!" She did have a big head.

"Emma, that's an abnormal-size head for a human being. For a Great Dane, perhaps that's of average circumference, but not for a person. How the hell did she get hired here?"

"Her name is Eve, and she used to work in Las Vegas."

"Why?"

"That doesn't matter."

"Of course it does."

"Why does it matter?"

"Because I'm trying to get a feel for her as a person."

"It's not important that you get a feel for her as a person, Jack. Now you're trying to wind me up, aren't you?"

Jack shrugged. "Maybe, maybe not. I might want to know."

"Forget it."

"Oh come on, tell the story. I won't ask why she moved to London. I won't ask any questions. I'll sit and listen to the scandal about the mastiff with the boob job."

Emma wished she could sit closer to Jack. She wanted to climb into his lap, curl up and fall asleep. She wanted him to carry her home like an oversized rag doll, grunting as he took the stairs slowly so not to wake her. She wanted him to tuck her into bed and then stay for a moment, like parents do, to watch their children breathing, to listen to them dream.

She continued, "Eve's had plastic surgery."

"You're joking with this, right? Who hasn't in here?"

"She's had plastic surgery...down *there*."

Jack laughed. "You know the correct words for women's parts, right?"

"Very funny."

"Why did she do it?"

"Apparently, the before version was unsightly and she wanted to make it...prettier. Here's the thing: when she dances, it...makes this weird squeaking noise."

They both cackled at this.

"This is fun," Emma said, and then wished she hadn't made that admission.

"How fucked up are we, that we are hanging out here?"

"And liking it!" Emma added.

They started laughing again. When they had caught their breath, Emma said: "Jack, I have to ask, since you are a familiar—and generous—visitor to the prestigious Platinum Club, does your wife know you're here?"

Jack raised his glass. "Let me answer that question for you openly and honestly. She does *not* know I'm here. Because that would make us—and by us, I mean you and I—beyond fucked up, and my wife would definitely leave, taking my money and probably your money, too."

"Over my dead body," said Emma buoyantly. She lifted her glass. "Here's to dancers, lies and alcohol."

Jack ordered another round of drinks. Emma supposed it helped that they were both drunk. And possibly both high. For once, they were both misbehaving; they were both acting irresponsibly at the same time, a rare planetary alignment was taking place.

"Did you...do you think Imogene is dead?" she asked.

If Jack had a reaction to this question, it didn't show. He loosened his tie and spoke in a tone Emma had never heard when talking about her mother—without a warning. "That would have been too easy," he said. "But I'll tell you what, she's dead to me. You need to leave all that alone, you've got to let all that go. I mean it."

"I don't want to."

"Where do you think she is?"

"Living in South America, writing scripts and running a tiny theatre group out of the mountains," Emma said, without hesitation.

"Then that's where she is," Jack said. "And you have to move on. Because she has. And baby, we can't do this anymore."

"Help me leave it alone," she told Jack. "You have to give me something more of Imogene, it's not fair."

"Don't get me started on what constitutes fair."

"I mean it."

"Okay, here's something. Your mother was an incredibly smart, beautiful woman who wasn't afraid to go for what she wanted. She was strong-willed, independent and creative. She also was the most selfish, self-centred, damaged beyond repair, inconsiderate individual I have ever known. How's that for a little something? Does that do it for you?"

"You're lying."

"She didn't leave because of me or you, Ems. Honestly. There was nothing we could have done to stop it. I thought I could change her. I thought she would come around."

"I think if you had let certain things happen, then maybe I'd have more of her to remember. I would have a better sense of her and then maybe I would be able to leave it alone."

"Certain things, like what? Letting you smoke dope with her when you were in diapers? There wasn't anything *to* let happen."

"What about Portugal?"

"What about it?"

"Would it have been so bad if I'd gone for my birthday? I know I was young, but I would have had that in my development, somewhere, you know? I would have—"

"Emma..."

"Wait, let me say this," Emma said. "I would have had a chance at keeping something in my nature that was a direct result of my mother's character. A tie to the language maybe... or the food—culturally, a link to Brazil through that, I dunno.

But I would be able to take that special trip with me, plus the knowledge I had parents who thought I should experience that."

"You did go to Portugal," Jack said.

"No I didn't."

Jack's eyes softened. "Emma we took you there. We stayed for three days and you cried the whole time. You hated the airplane, you hated the rat-arsed hotel we ended up staying in because Imogene left it to the last minute to book something, and you hated all the food."

"When...when did we go?" As she spoke, the pity in Jack's face and the pathetic croak of her voice caused a chain-reaction of heat to spread across Emma's chest and neck. She shouldn't have brought this up, she was a fool to think Jack was the only one who found this hard to talk about.

"We went for your birthday, just like it was planned. Flew into Lisbon, weather was hotter than hell."

Emma focussed hard on the weave of the carpet.

"I told Imogene you would be too young to remember it." Jack struck a match to light his cigarette, the brief blaze illuminating his face. "Looks like I was right."

Journalism was so much harder than fiction because you had to tell the truthful story. Emma hated having to describe things as they really were. Real life always needed that little extra, or it could end with unsatisfying open endings. Emma had a sixth sense about this—by the time she was just a few chapters into a book, she could tell whether or not she would be left hanging in the breeze without sufficient answers. She wasn't so simplistic that she wanted happy endings all around; she only wanted an ending that made sense. There was no excuse for it either. The writer controlled what was told. If the writer promised something in their story, it was their responsibility—under punishment of death—to pay it off by the end. And now, Emma had an awful, awful feeling about Imogene. She was nearing the last page of that story and she wasn't going to get her deserved answers—the answers she was owed for enduring three hundred pages of promises. What was worse, what could possibly be worse than her mother being dead? That she was alive and chose for Emma to be dead to her.

She knew it was true. Hers was an unsatisfying ending. Neither of them was going to see Imogene again. And it would never not hurt to think of her.

"She was very talented," Jack was saying. "Imogene was a really gifted actress. She studied method. You know what that is?"

Emma nodded. "You become the character?"

"She used to say the secret to being a good actor was being able to believe in something that's just a figment of your imagination. She said I had no idea what it took, the strength you needed to go down to the places you had to go, to become another person—" Jack stopped. "Was she right? Is that what it's like?" he asked, gently.

"That's exactly what it's like, Jack." Emma said.

. . . Now I remembered that the real world was wide, and that a varied field of hopes and fears, of sensations and excitements, awaited those who had courage to go forth into its expanse, to seek real knowledge of life amidst its perils.

JANE EYRE

emma
+365

Epilogue

"You sure you're OK with this?" Stephen asked in her ear.

"I'm fine," Emma said. "It's going to be fun."

He didn't look convinced, but he gave her knee a squeeze and followed his friend Marcus out of the taxi.

Blue was a new club in Covent Garden making its name by promising a couple-friendly, sophisticated exotic dancing experience. It was sleek and futuristic, with pod-style bar stools, polished metal doors and a glowing electric blue bar.

Within minutes of ordering drinks, their booth was full of women.

Emma smiled and made small talk, but she was overcome with the feeling she used to get before she went onstage at Platinum—like her stomach had lost its bottom, shaking as if her quivering bones had turned to ice.

It still felt like it was yesterday.

Stephen came back from his private dance flushed, and grinning from ear to ear. "Long live capitalism," he announced.

"You look like you had a nice time."

"Ems, I know intellectually that the entire thing was completely calculated and money motivated... I know that."

"But you loved it, nonetheless?" Emma smiled. "Don't say I didn't warn you."

He shook his head. "I thought I was different than the typical bloke. I mean, look at Marcus—he's history."

Marcus had scuttled to the bank machine twice and was now having his credit cards worked over by a girl named Mahogany. She was whispering in his ear, holding his hand and stroking his leg with two-inch-long fingernails. Marcus nodded attentively at everything Mahogany said, his eyes resting permanently on the centre of her cleavage.

"Why don't you have a dance?" Stephen reached for his wallet. "It'll make me feel less like a pervert."

"Yeah, go on." Mahogany untangled Marcus's hand from hers. "Don't be shy. You'll love it." She waved over to a dancer standing by the bar. "Have a dance with my friend Honey— she's good."

A woman with bloodshot eyes, a surgically enhanced chest and pouty mouth strolled over. She had a large tattoo of a rose on her wrist, a cigarette in one hand and a drink in the other. It was Kat.

Imperceptibly, Emma shook her head, tilting it faintly in Stephen's direction. Kat read the message and returned her open mouth to a closed position. She extended her hand to Emma and Stephen. "Hi, I'm Honey. Nice to meet you both."

Stephen handed her a twenty. "Would you please take my girlfriend for a private dance?"

"Of course I will." Kat folded Stephen's money over her garter and pulled Emma to her feet. "Now, if we're not back in thirty minutes, call the police!"

"Have fun!" said Mahogany, before returning her attention to Marcus. "See? She's going for a dance. Let's go have one more, huh?"

As soon as they got around the corner, Kat squealed and wrapped her arms around Emma. "How the hell are you? What are you doing now? What club are you at? You look freakin' great, Phoenix. Very classy."

"I'm good. Call me Emma though, I don't use that name anymore."

"I get you. I'm Honey now."

They sat down behind a curtained off area. "You're looking well," Emma said. "When did you cut your hair?"

"You like? And how about these?" Kat pulled open her dress. "I finally saved enough of a wedge to get them done—36DDs!"

Blue's private rooms weren't so private. Emma could hear Marcus on the other side of the curtain saying, "Mahogany... you're so beautiful... I really, really mean it..."

"What's it like working here?" Emma asked, lowering her voice.

"Good, but not great." Kat screwed up her face.

"Why are you here, then? Platinum's got to be better than this."

"I'm barred." Kat reached for Emma's drink. "I'm pretty much barred from everywhere that's ace."

"Why?"

"I don't know... partying too much, drinking, whatever. I was just messing up all the time, missing my stage call, I couldn't be bothered. I was so done with it all, you know? The same old hustle, the same old lines. I was on the burn out, big time. So I quit—for a while."

"That's great..." Emma smiled. She didn't know what to say. They sat for a moment, listening to the music.

It had been a year before she finally left Platinum, and once Emma was gone, she simply had to stay gone. There wasn't a way she could see to bridge real life with club life. Emma stayed true to Phoenix as best as she could; she had proven she could be loyal. But Phoenix believed that fortune played its cards face up, that if you learned some tricks you could get one over on fate, and that just wasn't true for Emma.

It took months and months of baby steps with Jack while Susanna fluttered around catering to their indelicately re-born relationship. It helped that Emma eventually sold her work to one of the big broadsheet newspapers—the success and critical acclaim of her stories gave her a small piece of Jack's respect.

"I'm sorry I didn't call you after the story came out," she said.

Kat broke eye contact. "No biggie."

"No, honestly, I should have."

"Jade said she always knew you were different than the rest of us," Kat grinned. "Trey was pissed! That was the best bit— the stuff you wrote about him being such a jerk-off. None of us were mad about it, really. It's not like people don't sell their stories, happens all the time."

"When I stopped dancing," Emma said, "I was pretty burnt out too. I needed to get my head clear and own up to some things that needed sorting. Then by the time I'd done that..."

Kat raised her eyebrows. "Can't believe Phoenix has retired..."

Emma nodded. "Can hardly believe it myself. I've got a job working in book publishing now—"

"Ohmygawd!" interrupted Kat with a shriek. "I just remembered the time we scored a private room with those two male models from Belgium—remember? And they missed their flight because they came back in the next night? We completely rinsed them!" She laughed.

"That wasn't me," Emma said. "I think it was Jade."

"Are you sure?" Kat furrowed her brow. "I could have sworn it was you. Well—they missed their flights, anyway."

They listened to the DJ call Britney to the bar stage.

"You look good," Kat said. "I like the glasses. Are they the same ones you used to wear on fantasy night?"

Emma smiled. "I don't even know where those are anymore." They were in her top drawer of her dresser, in the little sequin bag that also held a black satin and lace garter. Stephen wouldn't let her throw them away.

"I remember the first time you came out and did that librarian thing on stage with your hair up and your glasses and your little skirt. You totally killed it that night!"

Emma sighed. "That was my most successful persona, wasn't it?" Still was.

"Yeah, but then you did it every themed night after that for a million years!"

"That's one thing I learned from Chanel," Emma said. "If it works, don't change it." And the bookish girl with a heart of brass worked so very well for her. Phoenix loved that moment when she would pull the pencil out of her hair and rip the buttons open on her prim white shirt. All the attention, all of whatever that was—just for her. "How is everyone?" she asked. "Bambi? Do you ever speak to her?"

Kat puffed cigarette smoke out of her nose. "Why do you care?"

"I don't know. I just do..."

"Still sleeping with Adolfo, still paying her lazy, cheating boyfriend's bills. Had to have her stomach pumped a couple of months ago."

Emma was horrified. "Why? Drugs?"

Kat shrugged. "OD. What else? Oh, and Chanel's still a jammy cow—I'm sure you've heard. She's retired. Bought a villa in Spain outright."

Stephen stuck his head through the curtain. "Everybody decent?" he said.

"Never decent," said Kat. "Not in this place."

Emma stood up. "Sorry, we were just chatting."

"Take care," said Kat, giving Emma a hug. She whispered, "Is that really your boyfriend? He's cute, but he seems so... regular."

Emma hugged her back. "He is."

"Give me a ring," Kat said. "We can go out for a drink or something."

"Sure," Emma said. "I'm just going to the loo," she told Stephen.

She walked out past a group of men at the bar doing shots and went down the hall to the bathrooms. Two dancers came out of a stall, giggling and slamming the door behind them. Emma stood in front of the well-polished mirror, listening to the muffled, bass vibrations of the DJ bubbling in. She took her glasses off and put them in her purse and took a deep breath, tasting the musky perfume lingering in the air. She opened her handbag and pulled out a shimmery gloss, which she ran over her lips until they looked like wet glass. She ran some cold water on her wrists and dried her hands slowly and surely. She said her goodbyes. And then she opened the bathroom door and followed the dark hallway and icy air-conditioning that would lead her back to the club.

Acknowledgements

Thank you to those in my life both past and present, who gave their support professionally and personally to my writing career: Cynthia Craft, Lisa Griffiths, Stephanie Epiro, Wendy Okoi-Obuli, Mica Romelus, Casey Gillespie, Veena Verdi, Kelly Maddren, Alison Hudd, Natasha John-Lewis, Glen Yearwood, Schuyler Coppedge, Susan Gordon, Christine Page, Tiffanie Darke and Howard Norman.

To Ivan Mulcahy, my agent, and Charlie Viney of Mulcahy & Viney, and the Key Porter Books dream team of Rob Howard, Daniel Rondeau, Kendra Michael and especially my editor Janie Yoon, whom I hope to work with again many times over, and Jordan Fenn for "getting it" from day one. Thanks also to Sherry Naylor from Meisner Publicity.

To all the dancers, in all the clubs.

And, of course, to the grizz and her father.

For the reader's interest, the quotes on pages 40, 67, 77 and 154 are from *Macbeth* by William Shakespeare, The Falcon Shakespeare Edition, 1965.

Emma's outburst on page 45, ("I will not do as you ask!") is from *Jane Eyre* by Charlotte Brontë, Penguin Popular Classics, 1994; as are the quotes on pages 47, 49, 50, 206, 214, 268 and 284.

Emma's mutterings ("Curiouser and curiouser") on page 65 and the "Drink Me" reference on page 140 are from *Alice's Adventures in Wonderland* by Lewis Carroll, SeaStar New Ed edition.

The quotes on pages 252 and 269 are from Tennessee Williams' *The Glass Menagerie*, Penguin Classics, published in *A Streetcar Named Desire and Other Plays*, 2000.

The *Tell-Tale Heart*, mentioned on page 234 is by Edgar Allan Poe.

The song played when Emma makes her stage debut on page 69, "The Thong Song," is from Sisqo's album, *Unleash the Dragon*, Def Jam Records; the song "In the Air Tonight," mentioned on pages 115, 248 and 249 is by Phil Collins and is from his *No Jacket Required* album, Atlantic/WEA Records; "Crazy," the song Emma and Jason sing in the VIP on page 175 is by Aerosmith on their album *Get A Grip* from Geffen Records; Phoenix's onstage song mentioned on page 159 is "Dirty Diana," by Michael Jackson from the *Bad* album, Epic Records; in the dressing room, Kat sings the song "V.I.P." by R. Kelly from his *R* album on Jive; Jade's stage show song, "Hey Big Spender," is by Shirley Bassey, on her *I Am What I Am* album from Aardvark Records.

About the Author

VANESSA CRAFT is a freelance journalist who has written for the *Toronto Star,* the *Globe and Mail* and *FASHION* magazine. While living in London, England, she wrote for the *Sunday Times*, Channel 4, *Zink* magazine, and was a regular guest on BBC Radio 5's *Book Panel*. She is currently working on her second novel.